SEVEN THREADLY SINS

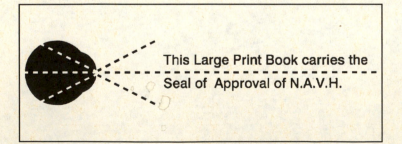

This Large Print Book carries the
Seal of Approval of N.A.V.H.

A THREADVILLE MYSTERY

SEVEN THREADLY SINS

JANET BOLIN

WHEELER PUBLISHING
A part of Gale, Cengage Learning

GALE
CENGAGE Learning®

Farmington Hills, Mich • San Francisco • New York • Waterville, Maine
Meriden, Conn • Mason, Ohio • Chicago

GALE
CENGAGE Learning®

LIBRARY OF CONGRESS CATALOGING-IN-PUBLICATION DATA

Bolin, Janet.
    Seven threadly sins / by Janet Bolin. — Large print edition.
        pages ; cm. — (A Threadville mystery) (Wheeler Publishing large print cozy mystery)
    ISBN 978-1-4104-8430-7 (softcover) — ISBN 1-4104-8430-0 (softcover)
    1. Embroidery—Fiction. 2. Murder—Investigation—Fiction. 3. Large type books. I. Title.
    PS3602.O6534S49 2015
    813'.6—dc23   2015026519

Published in 2015 by arrangement with The Berkley Publishing Group, an imprint of Penguin Publishing Group, a division of Penguin Random House LLC

Printed in the United States of America
1 2 3 4 5 6 7 19 18 17 16 15

To people who warm others
with threadly creations and laughter

ACKNOWLEDGMENTS

Welcome to our fifth excursion to Threadville.

Many thanks to my editors, first Faith Black and then Jackie Cantor, who gave me wonderful suggestions and have been my guides. Anonymous copyeditors toil over my manuscripts. Thank you to Annette Fiore Defex for the cover design, and Tiffany Estreicher for the design of the interior text. Danielle Dill at Berkley Prime Crime and Jessica Cooney at Penguin Random House Canada help send books and publicity wherever they need to go. Thank you!

Robin Moline — many people tell me they love the paintings you create for the covers.

Thank you, Berkley Prime Crime, for discovering Robin.

My special thanks to my agent, Jessica Faust of Book-Ends, LLC, for coming along on this writing adventure.

I can always turn to friends for support,

including Krista Davis; Daryl Wood Gerber, who also writes as Avery Aames; Laurie Cass, who also writes as Laura Alden; Janet Cantrell, who also writes as Kaye George; Marilyn Levinson; Mary Jane Maffini, who is also half of Victoria Abbott; Erika Chase; Vicki Delany, who also writes as Eva Gates; and all of the gang at the Killer Characters blog. Many thanks to all of you.

Sergeant Michael Boothby, Toronto Police (Retired), carefully reads my manuscripts and tells me, "Police officers wouldn't do that." Thanks, Mike, for making me rewrite and work harder. But as I've said before, my characters have a will of their own, and they don't always follow Mike's suggestions.

I also thank Constable Ed Sanchuk and the Norfolk County detachment of the Ontario Provincial Police who taught the Citizen's Police Academy. What a learning experience!

Many thanks to Joyce of Joyce's Sewing Shop in Wortley Village, Ontario, for your ongoing support, help, and that wonderful day that we all laughed really, really hard. And thanks for inviting me back so we could laugh some more!

And my special thanks to Kelley Richardson from Joyce's Sewing Shop for her comments and suggestions about faking crewel work with embroidery machines.

Jackie Green of Green Bee Designs gave me a suggestion (embroidering appliqués in the hoop) that improved the project at the end of the book. Thank you, Jackie!

Also, thank you to Laurann of My Sewing Nook in Caledonia, Ontario, for an afternoon of Threadville-like laughter and friendship.

And thank you to the Oxford Quilters' Guild in Ingersoll, Ontario, for your warm welcome, laughter, and the delicious potlucks.

Many volunteers put in long hours to plan and organize conferences and conventions where we can learn together. Thanks to the organizers of Malice Domestic, GenreCon Sarnia, and especially to the Bloody Gang at Bloody Words, who put on a wonderful if bittersweet last Bloody Words. We will miss you.

And to my friends, family, and readers . . . thank you all for joining me in Threadville.

1

Years ago, during the gawkiest of my teen years, well-meaning women gushed, "Willow, you're so tall, you could be a model!" I knew they meant it as a compliment, but I'd had no interest in becoming a model. And now I was thirty-four, and I still didn't want to be one.

So why was I stripping down to my undies and about to wear a series of peculiar outfits on a fashion show runway?

It was for a good cause, I reminded myself. The proceeds from the fashion show were going toward a scholarship fund for the Threadville Academy of Design and Modeling, TADAM for short, rhyming with madam. Scholarships at the school, which had opened only weeks before after amazingly speedy renovations during the summer, would mean that additional fashion design and modeling students would live in and visit Elderberry Bay, also known as

Threadville. Our textile arts shops were thriving, but more customers were always welcome.

Besides, Ashley, the part-time assistant in my embroidery boutique, In Stitches, was a senior in high school. She wanted to learn fashion design here in Threadville where she could continue to live at home and work in my shop. Ashley's talent should guarantee her a TADAM scholarship.

The shiny red polyester curtains surrounding our temporary dressing cubicles did not seem to belong in the luxurious conservatory where we were holding the fashion show, but at least we had some privacy.

Or did we?

A resounding *slap* came from the cubicle next to mine.

A man chuckled low in his throat. "If you think you're going to be a model, you can't be prudish about letting other people adjust your clothing."

Curtains rustled. Shoes thwacked against the wood floor as someone strode away from the next cubicle.

I peeked out, but the man had disappeared. He must have walked down the narrow corridor between red-curtained cubicles and, from there, out onto the stage.

The conservatory, a Victorian glass confection, was warm and humid, and smelled of damp earth and rich, green vegetation. High above, panes of glass glowed orange, tinted by one of mid-September's spectacular sunsets.

To my right, in the direction the man had gone, a woman yelled, "Places, everyone!" She sounded angry.

It was going to be a long night.

And this was only the dress rehearsal.

I pulled on slinky purple cropped pants and a matching peplum top that I'd made and trimmed with gold machine embroidery. I felt like a misplaced toreador in the outfit, which was gaudier than the clothes I usually designed and created for myself. Maybe, before I'd agreed to sew and model four outfits, I should have asked to see the sketches that Antonio, TADAM's director, had said he'd provide. By the time I saw the sketches, I'd already committed myself and couldn't back out.

A good cause, I reminded myself. The outlandish garments were to be auctioned off for the scholarship fund.

I slid my feet into fuchsia and gold sandals that Feet Accomplished, Threadville's shoe store, had lent to the fashion show. Bravely, I joined the lineup of models in the walkway

13

between cubicles.

And there was Madam TADAM herself, Antonio's wife, Paula, who was also the academy's administrative assistant. She was wearing a sagging straw-colored dress, wielding a clipboard, and glaring at the person immediately behind me.

I turned around. One of the modeling students, a tall blonde, appeared to be having difficulty walking in her flip-flops. Her face was red and her mouth was pinched. Was she the aspiring model who had slapped the man? Maybe she was merely grumpy about the flip-flops or the rest of her outfit. If I hadn't been told that the clothes in the fashion show had been designed at TADAM, I'd have guessed that her skimpy shorts and halter top had been bought off the rack, and not in an exclusive boutique, either.

TADAM had begun classes less than a month ago, and none of the students could have had much time to prepare, which probably explained why most of the clothes on the student models didn't seem very imaginative, especially compared to the outfits that my Threadville friends and I had made.

However, we were only in the Weekend Wear segment of the show. By the time we worked our way up to Glitzy Garb, the

TADAM students' work would probably shine.

Music played and the line began moving as models started down the runway.

Antonio's voice boomed through the sound system. He used the words "lovely" and "beautiful" over and over again.

We shuffled forward.

The blonde behind me, who didn't look old enough to vote, but was my height, about six feet, even in her flip-flops, whispered to me, "Stand still, and I'll get your hair out of your zipper."

My hair was shoulder length, light brown, and naturally straight. It was also flighty, and I'd managed to zip some of it into the back of my top.

The girl worked quickly, and I could turn my head without ripping out a hank of my hair. She no longer looked grouchy. Her smile was friendly, and her face had returned to pale pink with no splotches.

I whispered my thanks.

Paula clapped her hand on her clipboard and shushed us.

At the front of the line ahead of me, my best friend, Haylee, the owner of Threadville's huge fabric store, disappeared onto the stage. Over the music, Antonio announced that the "lovely Haylee" had tailored her linen and silk golf shorts and shirt. A strange crunching noise — static? — interrupted his spiel.

A student went out between the blue velvet stage curtains, and then Haylee returned. As she passed, she gave me a high five along with a waggle of eyebrows showing that she was amused and maybe annoyed as well. She rushed off to change into her next outfit.

The girl in front of me wiggled out onto the runway, was described as "lovely" and wearing a "beautiful" outfit, and then it was my turn.

2

I slithered out between heavy blue plush curtains onto the lip of the stage. Carpeted in black, a runway stretched from the stage almost to the other end of the conservatory's oval main room. In a polo shirt, khakis, and loafers, Antonio stood to my right, behind a podium perched precariously close to the edge of the stage. A light on the podium illuminated his notes and a line of what looked like fat, white beads.

Bending toward the microphone, Antonio announced to the nonexistent audience that the "lovely Willow" was wearing a purple outfit trimmed in gold stitching. I strolled down the runway. The sunset now bathed the conservatory in warm, almost magical pink tones.

Near the foot of the runway, one of TADAM's male teachers leaned against the trunk of a palm tree, but his pose was far from casual. His arms were folded over his tight black muscle shirt as if he were attempting to contain an explosion. Glowering, he uncoiled, sprang forward to a camera on a tripod, and took a rapid sequence of flash photos.

What was I doing here?

Self-conscious and dazzled by the flashes, I pirouetted. As I traipsed clumsily back toward the curtains, the girl who had released my hair from the zipper passed me. Although I had stumbled, she seemed to float down the runway.

Antonio described her as the lovely Macey, popped one of the white "beads" into his mouth, and crunched down on it. His chomping, the noise I'd mistaken for static earlier, was amplified throughout the conservatory.

I batted the blue velvet curtains out of my way, glanced toward Antonio's frowning wife, scooted into my dressing cubicle, and unzipped my top.

As I pulled it over my head, Antonio's voice boomed out, "No, Macey! As lovely as you are, you're not here to seduce anyone. Walk naturally, the way the lovely Haylee and the lovely Willow did."

What a rude and discouraging thing for him to say to one of his students. My first impulse was to put on the comfy cutoffs and T-shirt that I'd worn to the dress rehearsal, walk out, and refuse to perform in the next night's fashion show.

Publicly criticizing one of his students was bad enough, but comparing her unfavorably to Haylee and me, who had no interest in becoming models, was unconscionable. Besides, that photographer in the shadows had unnerved me, and my performance had been anything *but* natural.

Why was Antonio being so hostile to Macey? Would he treat Ashley the same way? Maybe I didn't want her to attend TADAM, after all.

Breathing heavily, someone tiptoed into the cubicle beside mine. Hangers clinked, and one of Macey's flip-flops sailed underneath the curtain into my cubicle.

A perfectly manicured hand with long, delicate fingers reached for it. "Sorry. I kicked too hard."

"No problem." Quickly, I stepped out of my sandals and pulled off the purple pants. Maybe Antonio was having a bad day. Ashley deserved a scholarship. Selfishly, I wanted her to go to school in Threadville so she could live at home and continue working part-time at In Stitches.

People padded past, going to and from the stage.

"Macey?" I recognized the voice. It was Naomi, one of the three women who had raised Haylee. Naomi owned Threadville's quilt shop. "You did very well."

"Thanks." Macey's dull reply lacked expression.

I poked my head out. All three of Haylee's mothers were in the aisle between the dressing cubicles.

Edna murmured, "Macey, do you want us to tell Antonio that you were very good and will make a great model?"

"No, thanks." The girl still sounded like she was trying to mask her emotions.

I turned my head toward her cubicle. "Would you like us to quit the fashion show in protest?" My stage whisper came out more harshly than I meant it to.

Naomi winced. "That could do more harm than good, Willow, don't you think? To Macey."

"I guess you're right." After Haylee's mothers scurried away, I pulled my head back into my cubicle and muttered, "But I didn't walk at all well. I have no idea what I'm doing out there."

A shaky laugh came from Macey's cubicle. "Thanks. Neither do I, but I'm learning."

I contradicted her. "You were great!"

The second segment was Ambitious Attire. Antonio liked alliteration.

When he'd handed me the sketch of a dress and jacket, he'd said it was supposed to be a dress-for-success outfit for a businesswoman. He'd told me to make it light brown to match my hair. Although I'd fitted the dress and jacket carefully and had kept the shiny cocoa-toned machine embroidery to a tasteful minimum, I felt dowdy in so much brown. The pumps that Feet Accomplished had provided for me to wear with the outfit were the color of a churned-up mud puddle. Charming. And I couldn't count on the sunset to enliven the outfit, either. The sky above the glass-roofed conservatory had faded from pink to sallow gray.

Antonio had told me not to carry a briefcase or handbag. "TADAM will supply a surprise," he'd promised with a wink.

The shoes were too big. I clomped to the end of the lineup.

Macey crept up behind me. "You look fab."

We'd passed all of the red-curtained changing cubicles, but a section of the stage behind the podium had also been curtained off in red polyester. A thirtyish woman with an enviable mass of shoulder-length auburn curly hair emerged from that larger cubicle.

21

I'd never met her, but I guessed she was TADAM's assistant director, Loretta. She carried several identical homemade cardboard briefcases covered in glossy white paint. Apparently, Antonio's "surprise" was a fake briefcase for each of us to carry.

However, Loretta ran out of briefcases before she got to me. Her outfit was what I'd expect to see at a fashion design school — a stylish skirt and flowing jacket, both in delicious plum silk, worn over a carefully crafted mint green tank top. She frowned at my head and thrust a handful of hair clips at Macey. "Pin her hair up before she goes onstage," she ordered. "And both of you, grab briefcases from the next two people who exit the stage."

Macey's hair was neatly pinned back, and she wore a blazing red dress underneath an unbecomingly bulky sweater in a shade of royal blue that clashed with the red so much that both garments seemed to jitter and twitch when I tried to focus on them. In one hand, she carried navy pumps like my brown ones. She set the shoes down, eased her feet into them, and whipped my hair into shape.

By the time that Haylee, in one of her expertly tailored pantsuits, came off the

runway, Macey and I had each nabbed briefcases.

Using her clipboard to move one of the
blue velvet curtains out of my way, Paula
nearly sheared the covered, machine-
embroidered buttons from my jacket sleeve.
"You're on."

I couldn't pick up my feet without stepping out of those extra-large pumps. Unlike
any successful businesswoman that I'd ever
seen, I trundled past the modeling student
returning up the runway.

Antonio brayed, "With the simple removal
of her jacket and the addition of a necklace,
the lovely Willow transforms her beautiful
outfit into one appropriate for a romantic
dinner and evening on the town." He
popped a candy into his mouth but did not
turn off the microphone. *Crunch, crunch.*

I was supposed to gracefully drop a
chunky faux gold chain over my head and
shrug out of the jacket to reveal the sleeve-
less dress. I hadn't anticipated wrestling
with the necklace, the jacket, and a cardboard briefcase at the same time, and my
dropping and shrugging were anything but
graceful. Finally, I unsnagged the chain
from my hairdo and subdued the jacket.

The man in the black muscle shirt
snapped dozens of pictures, and again ap-

peared to find my performance lacking, which wasn't surprising. With any luck, he and the next night's audience would see very little besides that dazzling white briefcase. With it in one hand and my jacket in the other, I slid my oversized shoes around in a circle. Maybe the move passed as a slow twirl. I had to sort of skate back up the runway, which seemed longer than ever.

Backstage, Paula hissed at me, "Carry your shoes when you're backstage. They make too much noise. And give that briefcase to the next person in line who doesn't have one." She scowled at Macey. "What's keeping you? You're supposed to be out there while the girl in front of you is still on the runway."

Did Antonio and his wife treat all of their students this way, or only Macey? I wished I could stick around and encourage Macey when she came offstage, but I needed to change into my Distinguished Dressing outfit.

This was not to be formal — that was the last part of the show. This was supposed to be a cocktail dress.

It was, to say the least, a very unusual cocktail dress.

Following the sketch and instructions that Antonio had given me, I had concocted a tiered, ruffled, balloon-like mini-dress from white and baby blue organza, with tiny flowers machine-embroidered at the edges of the ruffles. He'd ordered white gladiator sandals for me to wear with the dress. Fortunately, they zipped up the back and I didn't have to buckle twenty tiny straps. If Loretta gave me a shepherd's crook with a bow, I'd pass for Little Bo Peep on stilt-like legs.

Fortunately, she didn't, but she raced down the line, unpinned what was left of my glamorous hairdo after the "gold" chain had pulled tendrils from it, and arranged my hair in two ponytails, one above each ear. Glancing into the full-length mirror near the stage curtains, I mistook myself for a two-year-old in a fun house mirror, the kind that stretched one to a ridiculous height. With a wide and phony smile on my face, I paraded down the runway.

Antonio praised "the lovely Willow." If I heard that description one more time, I'd throw a tantrum. He munched another candy loudly and *then* turned off the microphone.

Because the dress was short and I'd expected the runway to be high, but maybe not quite this high, I'd made a pair of ruffled organza bloomers to wear underneath the dress. At the end of the runway, I turned slowly, hoping the dress wouldn't flare out and display the bloomers to that man in the muscle shirt and his camera. Trying not to channel Bo Peep, I strolled past Macey, who was in a sleek black dress hardly bigger than a bathing suit. Antonio turned on the mike, described the dress as sexy, and then boomed out that Macey should sway her hips more when she walked. The poor girl couldn't win.

I rushed to my cubicle to put on my evening gown.

Antonio had sketched a tight velvet gown that was backless, came down in a V just below the waist in front, and featured a slit almost to the wearer's left hip bone.

I had made the back and the V neck less plunging, or I'd have needed to glue the bodice on, and I had ended the slit mid-thigh.

Antonio hadn't specified where I should add machine embroidery to this outfit. To emphasize the gown's long lines, I'd edged both sides of the slit with a narrow geometric design. I had strayed from Antonio's design another way, as well. I'd used reddish bronze velvet instead of the drab and unflattering olive brown that he had suggested.

I could no longer see the sky or focus on the glass panels forming the roof. Bright overhead lights illuminated the backstage.

I brushed out the girlish ponytails and let my hair hang to my shoulders. Along with the embroidered satin evening bag I'd made, I carried metallic gold stiletto sandals.

While I waited in line, Loretta teamed up with Macey to pin my hair into the world's fastest French braid. I caught a glimpse of myself after I put on the heels and right before I went onstage. The dress fit well and looked, I thought, very good. Fortunately, the shoes were the right size. Imitating 1930s movie stars, I undulated down the runway. Reflections of fairy lights on trees inside the building sparkled from the conservatory's glass panes.

Muscle Shirt again took scads of pictures. Ignoring him, I turned around and passed Macey in a dress that Cinderella might have worn — before the fairy godmother fitted her out with princess gowns.

Antonio gave me an approving smile, let his gaze drift over my curves, and murmured, "Nicely done, Willow!" He hadn't turned off the mike, which meant that everyone else in the conservatory would have heard his too-intimate tone. Nause-

27

ated, I slipped behind the curtains and ran to my dressing cubicle to finally change into my usual evening attire — cutoffs, T-shirt, and sneakers.

Antonio called to us, telling everyone to come onstage. Standing in the spotlight on the runway, he said that we'd done marvelously, and that he'd make certain that, by the next night, his modeling students were as good as Willow and Haylee and "the other Threadville ladies."

Edna muttered, "I wasn't good. Whoever heard of a five-foot-two-inch model who wasn't under the age of ten?"

Loretta said we should leave our outfits and shoes in our dressing cubicles for the next night. "And tell me if anything needs dry-cleaning, polishing, or freshening. The fashion design students will fix everything before tomorrow's show."

I decided that asking for replacements for the gigantic shoes would be too much bother for everyone. I would have to wear them for only a few minutes.

Antonio gave us instructions for the end of the next night's show. As we came offstage after the Glitzy Garb segment, we would be handed a slip of paper stating which of our four outfits we were to wear to the awards ceremony.

Awards ceremony?

"If the paper says nothing, that doesn't mean you're to come onstage stark naked." He smiled to show it was a joke. "It means you don't have to attend the awards ceremony."

Maybe the awards were only for TADAM students. Giving Threadville proprietors awards for our creations would be silly. We'd been sewing for years, and Antonio had designed all of our outfits. The students were only beginning.

The paper, Antonio said, would also have a number on it. We were to file out in numerical order, with the first person going to the farthest reaches of stage left. He pointed. "Stage left is on your left when you're on the stage and facing the audience. The second person will stay to her right, and so on down the line. And stand naturally, remembering that your outfit is of the utmost importance. But do smile." He flickered a sample smile at all of us. "And after the awards ceremony, change back into your Glitzy Garb outfits, go around the corner to the TADAM mansion, and strut your stuff during the reception and the auction."

I was beginning to feel like one of Little Bo Peep's sheep. But I wouldn't look much like a sheep in the revealing gown that Antonio had designed, and if the next evening was cool, I'd be strutting goose bumps and wishing I had a woolly sheep's coat.

Antonio added, "You're probably wondering how to return your Glitzy Garb outfit to us after the reception. You can change in the TADAM mansion if you like." His leer warned me not to choose that option. "Or you can bring the outfit back here Sunday morning and leave it in your cubicle with your other outfits, along with a note about anything that needs repairs. Loretta will open the conservatory at nine on Sunday morning."

Finally, Ashley, Haylee, her three mothers, and I escaped into the warm September evening. Above us, the sky was deep indigo velvet, sprinkled with diamonds.

I walked beside Ashley. Usually, she was exuberant, but tonight, the seventeen-year-old lagged as if something were bothering her.

3

Had Antonio's behavior upset Ashley? I asked her, "Do you still want to attend TADAM?"

"It would be perfect."

So that wasn't what was bothering her. Still, I hadn't appreciated the way Antonio and Paula had treated Macey, and the picture-taking teacher in the muscle shirt had freaked me out. "Going away to school could be good, too," I suggested. "Though I'd hate to lose the best assistant I've ever had."

Ashley stopped walking. "I don't think I'll be able to go away." She gulped.

Hoping the women ahead of us wouldn't hear, I asked quietly, "What's wrong?"

She toed at grass sprouting between the concrete slabs on the sidewalk. "I haven't told you this because, well, just because. My dad . . ." Her voice dwindled. She took a deep breath and started over. "My dad lost his job. My mom's gone back to work and my dad is throwing himself into finding a new job. That means I need to spend more time looking after my little sisters and brothers. I don't know how long it will take him to find a job. If I don't get a good scholarship to TADAM, I may not be able to go to school anywhere."

I offered, "You always have a job at In Stitches. Or a reference if something better comes along."

She started walking again and looked away from me as if studying the pretty Victorian homes on her street. "Thanks, Willow. It would be hard to think of a better place to work than In Stitches."

The same was true for me. I had tried another career, investment management, before moving to Threadville and opening In Stitches. Ashley had more design talent than most of the Threadville tourists who came every day for workshops and classes. She was smart, helpful, and eager to learn. I imagined someday attending her college graduation, along with her parents and all of her little sisters and brothers.

Would TADAM be good enough for Ashley? In addition to Antonio's and Paula's strangely hostile treatment of Macey, the school had seemed to come out of nowhere and had opened in a rush in mid-August. I supposed we should give it a chance to prove itself.

At Ashley's front walk, I impulsively gave her a raise. She thanked me. Head down, she moseyed toward her front porch.

I caught up with the others.

"What's wrong with Ashley?" Naomi asked.

I told them the girl's news. We all agreed that we would do our best in the next night's fashion show. We would help TADAM raise scholarship funds in the hope that maybe Ashley would benefit.

"And there's that Macey, also," Edna said. "Why did Antonio and Paula pick on her?"

"Did they pick on other students?" Haylee asked.

Haylee's birth mother, Opal, answered, "Only Macey, that I noticed."

"And she seemed like such a sweet child," Naomi said.

"She was." I told them that she'd been helpful to me, and I also described the slap and a man's amused response.

"Who was the man?" Haylee demanded. "That creepy guy taking pictures of us?"

I admitted that I wasn't sure. "I've never heard that photographer speak, and this guy was lowering his voice artificially, probably trying to sound sexy."

"And probably not succeeding." Still walking, Edna held up her left hand, flashing her sparkly engagement and wedding rings under the streetlight. "Men who think they're sexy often aren't."

Haylee and I grinned at each other. Edna might think of her new husband as the sexiest guy in Threadville, but Haylee and I each had our own ideas about that.

Unfortunately, however, Haylee's heartthrob was still mourning his late wife. I hoped he would eventually notice Haylee.

And my nominee for the sexiest guy in Threadville? Clay Fraser, owner of Fraser Construction. We both worked long hours, and except for our usual Tuesday evening volunteer firefighting practices, I hardly ever saw him. With any luck, he'd been too busy to hear about the fashion show the next night and wouldn't attend it.

Haylee and her three mothers and I said good-bye on Lake Street. They headed toward their apartments, which were above their shops in a Victorian building. My machine embroidery boutique, In Stitches, was across the street in an Arts and Crafts bungalow with deep eaves and a large front porch. I could have reached the apartment underneath my shop by going through In

Stitches, but this time, I unlatched the gate and walked down the hill through one of my two side yards to the patio, where I opened the sliding glass door and let my pets outside.

Sally-Forth and Tally-Ho, both part border collie, were littermates. Sally always made it her duty to herd the two tuxedo cats, Mustache and Bow-Tie, during their short visits to the great outdoors. She did a surprisingly good job of it, and soon the young cats were safely inside again, and Sally and her brother were racing around my hillside backyard.

In Blueberry Cottage, lights were on and windows were open. Clay and his company had renovated the quaint wooden structure after moving it up the hill from its original position, too close to the river and occasional floods. Edna's mother's spinning wheel whirred. Edna's mother had helped plan the renovations to Blueberry Cottage. Since she'd insisted there should be space for her loom and spinning wheel beside the hearth, I hadn't been surprised when she'd asked to be my tenant.

She was a good one, though I had the feeling she was aware of everything I did, day and night, and I had finally installed drapes in my apartment's wall of floor-to-ceiling windows facing Blueberry Cottage.

Edna's mother living in my backyard was almost like having a mother nearby. Or a grandmother. However, as Dora Battersby liked to point out, Opal and her best friends, Edna and Naomi, had only been seventeen when Haylee was born, and Dora was in her early seventies, rather young to be the grandmother of a thirty-four-year-old. She did like to supervise both Haylee and me, however.

Sally and Tally ended their playtime and came in. The dogs and I went to bed. Mustache and Bow-Tie spent a good part of the night doing their best to remind us that cats were nocturnal creatures.

In my shop the next day, Ashley and I gave two machine embroidery workshops, one in the morning and another in the afternoon. One of my favorite hobbies, the one I'd built into an online business and this retail shop, was using sophisticated software to create original embroidery designs. Each year, the machines and software improved, and no fabric that sat still for longer than a few seconds was safe from the avid embroiderers of In Stitches. Many of our students lived in and around Threadville, while others came almost daily on buses from northwestern Pennsylvania and northeastern Ohio.

In machine embroidery, we used a stiff backing known as stabilizer to keep the fabrics in our hoops from moving around or bunching up. Ashley and I demonstrated a new super-sticky stabilizer. We used sticky stabilizer so we wouldn't have to insert thick fabrics like fleece, corduroy, and terry in our hoops. Instead, we clamped the stabilizer in the hoop, removed the non-sticky backing, and stuck the cloth onto the gummiest part of the stabilizer. With this new stabilizer and its fiercer-than-ever grip, there was no question of accidentally pulling the fabric loose. We placed water-soluble stabilizer on top of the fabrics to prevent our stitches from disappearing in the wales, nap, and soft cotton loops.

While we worked and experimented, some of our students teased us to model the outfits we would be wearing in the fashion show that night.

"You'll have to come to the show," I said.

"We are coming," they insisted, "but we can't wait. Describe them."

Smiling, I shook my head. Ashley made a zipping motion across her mouth.

After we closed the shop and Ashley went home, I fed the animals and took them out, ate a quick supper, trotted to the Elderberry Bay Conservatory, found my cubicle, and put on the lurid purple and gold pants set.

The sun again reddened the sky above the glass roof as I joined the line of models waiting to march out onto the runway. Beyond the heavy blue curtains spanning the front of the stage, chairs scraped against the ornate tile floor, and people chatted and called to each other.

Her clipboard in one hand and a man's suit jacket in the other, Paula, who was again wearing a dress resembling a stretched and shapeless burlap bag, burst between the closed blue stage curtains.

In navy suit pants, white dress shirt, and gold silk tie, Antonio surged through the curtains behind her, grabbed her shoulder, and demanded, "Give it back." His pants were held up with the same belt he'd worn the night before, one with a large, shiny square belt buckle.

Antonio's wife whirled and came close to bopping her husband with that clipboard. "No way. You're not gobbling candy and who knows what else during the show."

Loretta joined Paula and stood almost nose to nose with Antonio. Loretta's outfit was similar to the flowing silk of the night before, but instead of plum and lime green, tonight's was a richer silk, in ivory. "If you must eat candy during the next hour, Antonio, stay backstage to wrangle the models and *I'll* narrate the show."

Like Antonio and Paula, she looked about to sprout a smokestack from her head.

If anyone was going to "wrangle" me, I preferred Loretta to Antonio with the roving eye. Roving hands, too? Was he the man that Macey had slapped the night before?

Paula must not have liked the idea of her husband wandering backstage among the models, either. She turned on Loretta. "You? You couldn't —"

Antonio interrupted her. "Who's the boss here?" He glared at Loretta. "*I* am, and if *I* say I'm going to describe the fashions for our audience, then *I'm* the one who's going to do it."

He lunged for the jacket that Paula held.

She dodged him. "I'll hang your jacket backstage. If you must feed your addiction, come grab a candy between segments. I took them off the podium and put them back in your jacket pocket."

Addiction?

Antonio must have become aware of the silent line of models watching the argument. He smiled at us. "Giving up smoking is harder than you think." He glanced at his watch. "Showtime!" Jacketless, he strode out between the curtains. The crowd hushed. He welcomed everyone, then the music began and the first model tripped out to the runway.

Antonio's descriptions were no more specific than they'd been the evening before. Everyone was "lovely" and wore a "beautiful" outfit. When it was my turn, I was glad that the lights in the conservatory were limited to the spotlights on the runway and the teensy lights tucked among the conservatory's greenery. I didn't see anyone I recognized. A video camera was on a tripod near the tallest of the palm trees, but no one was shooting flash pictures. Where was the sullen man in the muscle shirt?

Back in my cubicle, I changed into the brown dress-for-success outfit and carried the shoes to the line. Macey handed me tissues and pointed to the humongous brown shoes. "Stuff those into the toes of your shoes so you can keep them on."

Shushing Macey, but speaking every bit as loudly, Loretta told Macey to pin my hair up again. She did, and then I headed for the spot where the stage curtains overlapped each other.

The tissues in my shoes cramped my toes. Stumbling, I brushed Antonio's jacket off the chair, but when I stooped to hang it up, Paula nudged my backside with the clipboard. "Don't worry about that. Just get out there!" Her whisper was urgent, as if we were in the midst of an emergency.

Out on the runway, I managed to smile despite fumbling with the necklace and the bright white briefcase, but this time, I looped the faux gold chain over my neck without tangling it in my hair.

When I came back between the curtains, Antonio's jacket was hanging on the back of the chair again, but the chair was still in the way of models going to and from the runway. I silently moved it about a foot from the opening between the curtains, but not too far, I hoped, from Antonio if he developed a sudden desire for candy.

In my cubicle, I threw on the Bo Peep cocktail dress and gladiator sandals. I hoped that Loretta would leave my hair alone, but she again tied it up in ponytails high on the sides of my head.

Telling myself that my childish hairdo didn't matter, I sashayed out onto the runway with an exaggerated sway of hips, turned, started back, and looked saucily over my shoulder. Who cared if everyone saw the ruffled bloomers I wore under the short dress? The outfit was ludicrous, and I saw no reason to pretend I took it seriously.

Applause, probably from our loyal Thread-ville tourists, broke out from the audience. I was afraid that Antonio might disapprove of my dramatics, but he winked.

Maybe I should have been more sedate.

I was more of a performer than I realized. During the Glitzy Garb segment of the show, I didn't exactly ham it up in the slinky, slit-up-to-here-and-back-down-to-there velvet gown, but I didn't walk like a prim schoolgirl, either, and I couldn't resist a second pirouette on my way back up the runway.

Whistles came from the audience. My customers and machine embroidery work-shop students were obviously having fun.

As I pushed my way between curtains, I again bumped into the chair holding Anto-nio's jacket. Someone had put it back after I'd moved it.

Antonio's wife handed me an envelope with my name scribbled on it. "Change quickly," she demanded.

I slipped off my heels and zoomed to my cubicle.

Inside the envelope were three pieces of paper. The full page was a typed letter, signed by Antonio, thanking me for participating in the TADAM scholarship fund-raiser.

The half page was a printed voucher for a discount on evening classes at TADAM. Fashion design courses? They could be fun, and I might learn new skills.

On a torn quarter page, someone — probably Antonio, judging by his signature on the letter — had scrawled my name along with the words *Distinguished Dressing*.

Great. I had to go onstage during the awards ceremony, and I was supposed to wear that Little Bo Peep dress, the worst of all the outfits that I'd made and modeled.

Maybe I was winning a prize for the silliest cocktail dress? Or the most flirtatious look over my shoulder?

I put on the goofy dress, zipped up the gladiator sandals, and joined the line. TADAM students were in the front, while my Threadville friends and I were at the back. I was at the end, and would be the last model to file onto the stage. Good. I'd have less time out there to make a fool of myself.

Loretta glanced at my hair, shook her head, muttered something about not having time to fix it, and left my nice, though hasty, French braid in place. Phew. I did not have to go onstage in those silly ponytails again.

In front of me, Ashley wore the beautiful suit she'd made for the Ambitious Attire segment of the show. It was emerald green and featured one of her original freehand embroidery designs across the back, a true example of wearable art. If it were my size, I'd be planning to bid on it at the silent auction, but I towered over the seventeen-year-old.

Cheers erupted when the first model, Macey, stepped out onto the strip of stage in front of the blue velvet curtains. Encouraged by the support, we all gave our best performances as we brushed past the curtains, walked carefully into the spotlight along the edge of the stage, and smiled into the dark conservatory, lit only by twinkly lights.

We hardly deserved a standing ovation, but that's what we got. Maybe it wasn't an awards ceremony but merely a curtain call. Unsure of what to do next, some of us bowed and some of us curtseyed. The irrepressible Edna, in a bling-encrusted evening gown, put one hand above her head and twirled. All she needed was a set of castanets.

Antonio was at the podium, still not wearing his jacket. He'd managed to endure the show without noticeably crunching candy.

He smiled and repeated "thank you" until the audience settled back into chairs and silence.

Antonio asked everyone to hold their applause and comments until all of the awards had been announced. When our names were called, we were to take two steps forward from the line — small steps, he cautioned us with a smirk, or we'd fall off the stage. Then we were to pirouette, carefully, to show off our outfits, and return to our places. We would pick up our certificates as we left the stage at the end of the show.

Macey won the award for the most improved modeling student. Another student was the most improved design student. There were awards for creativity, attention to detail, and appropriateness for the occasion.

Then he waved toward the Threadville ladies — in addition to Naomi, Edna, Haylee, Opal, Ashley, and me, there was Mona, who owned a home décor boutique. Antonio announced, "These seven women, who are not students at TADAM, have donated their time and talent to the fashion show, and for that we are forever in their debt." He chuckled into the microphone. "However, between them, they've managed to commit what I like to call . . ." He chuckled again, a

laugh that sounded both intimate and horrid. " 'The seven threadly sins.' "

4

A woman called out in a shocked voice, *"What?"*

Edna gasped and stared toward the back rows of chairs.

Was her mother in the audience? The voice had sounded like Dora's.

Antonio held up a hand. "Hold your applause, please, until the end."

I had not heard any applause, but people in the audience laughed, as if Antonio had been joking about the seven threadly sins that we had supposedly committed. Maybe he had been, but why did I suspect that his joke concealed at least seven deadly barbs?

Antonio turned his head toward the lineup of models. "Naomi, please step forward and show us the outfit you made for Weekend Wear."

Antonio rested his forearm on the podium and purred into the microphone as Naomi modeled her ensemble. "Now, as you may be able to see, Naomi sewed together hundreds of little scraps to make her shorts and top. Hundreds! What threadly sin did that cause her to commit, do you think?"

No one answered.

"C'mon," he cajoled, "can't someone remember all of the deadly sins? Or are you all too busy committing them?"

A smattering of laughter greeted his little joke.

Antonio urged, "What would sewing a bunch of scraps together create?"

"Quilts!" Again, the woman near the back of the audience sounded like Edna's mother.

Ignoring her, Antonio stabbed a forefinger into the air above his jet-black hair. "Stitching tiny scraps together would frustrate and anger anyone and would *have* to make that person commit the threadly sin of wrath!"

The audience laughed and clapped.

Next, Antonio called Edna's name. Edna stepped forward and twirled, smiling. Her gown reflected lights in millions of tiny rainbows. "Edna has certainly followed my directions for creating Glitzy Garb," Antonio proclaimed. "Just look at all the shiny things she's attached to her dress!"

People murmured appreciatively.

"But here's the thing." Antonio flashed another of his conspiratorial smiles. "Has

48

Edna left any sort of bling or bauble for anyone else in all of Threadville?"

Edna nodded her head vigorously. Her shop was full of every sparkly trim and notion that any seamstress or crafty person could desire.

"Impossible," Antonio boomed. "She's taken them all for herself! She's committed the threadly sin of greed!"

Again, amusement rippled through the audience.

I tried to remember the other five deadly sins after wrath and greed. I was the seventh in line for this unusual honor. I doubted that wearing a ridiculous dress was a deadly — or threadly — sin.

Antonio called out, "Haylee!"

Obviously game for whatever fun Antonio was about to poke at her, Haylee waved and stepped forward.

Antonio leaned even farther forward. "Now, you'd think that all of the Threadville ladies would be accomplished at making clothes." Each of his breaths thumped into the microphone and was amplified throughout the glass-domed room. "Haylee owns a huge fabric store. I examined the outfits she made, including this business suit. Every detail is perfect. Now, we know that Haylee *hails* . . ." He smiled to show he

49

was repeating the sound for maximum effect. "From New York City. So she obviously brought the outfits she wore this evening with her when she fled to this Lake Erie shoreline. Since she could not have made the clothes herself —"

A woman in the back of the audience shrieked, "Yes, she did!" Edna's mother, Dora Battersby, was definitely in the audience. Not only that, she was in full battle mode.

Again holding a hand in the "halt" position, Antonio went on smoothly, "I award Haylee the prize for committing the threadly sin of sloth!"

Antonio's allegations were unkind and untrue.

What were the other deadly sins? I couldn't think of even one. Opal's turn was next, then Mona, and then Ashley.

Ashley was only seventeen. Whatever Antonio was going to claim about Ashley's creation, I would do all I could to remove the sting.

I considered bolting from the stage and taking Ashley with me. Instead, I muttered to her, "Unless he says something nice to you, don't believe him."

Ashley whispered, "Don't worry."

Meanwhile, what would Antonio say to

Opal? She stepped forward.

Antonio made a show of staring at her, drawing it out until audience members snickered. Finally, he spoke. "Now, I don't know *how* Opal made her outfits, but she made every single one of them out of yarn or string. Macramé? Cat's cradle? I don't know how she did it, but the end result is *dreadful!*"

This time, Dora Battersby wasn't the only heckler.

Antonio quelled them with a look. "And her Ambitious Attire ensemble, which she stitched together, she tells me, from granny squares, whatever those are, is the worst outfit of them all. No one will want to buy any of Opal's creations. So by showing off her talents with a knitting needle or crochet hook — does that make her a hooker?" He smiled at his own joke, but no one laughed. "Whatever she used, Opal has committed the threadly sin of pride."

Opal turned toward us. Bright red spots burned on her cheeks. She stepped into her place again, though.

Mona didn't wait to be called. She leaped forward — not off the stage, fortunately — and gyrated in a circle while waving and smiling at the audience.

"Ahhhhh." Antonio drew the syllable out.

"The lovely Mona." He licked his lips. "Her Distinguished Dressing cocktail dress is skimpy and very, very tight." He fanned his face. "Don't get me wrong. I'm a red-blooded male, so of course *I* like it. But because she makes my blood run faster, Mona has committed the threadly sin of lust."

I was afraid that Mona might take offense, but wiggling her hips, she blew about a thousand kisses to the audience. This time, they didn't try to contain their laughter.

"Play it for laughs," I whispered to Ashley. "No matter *what* he says."

She nodded and turned her head to give me an exaggerated wink. "I'm fine."

But how could I help being concerned about her? She already had too much stress in her life. I had to protect her.

"Ashley," Antonio called, "turn around and show us the back of your jacket."

Smiling, Ashley spun and gave me another wink.

"Now, see there?" Antonio pointed at Ashley. "I told Ashley to create something that a successful fashion designer might wear to a business meeting. And she embroidered pictures of different items of clothing all over the back of her jacket. She's obviously copying designs created by actual designers.

So what threadly sin did she commit?"

No one answered.

"Don't all speak at once," he joked.

Dora Battersby yelled, "None!" I couldn't see her in the darkness, but I smiled toward the back of the crowd.

"Envy!" Antonio crowed. "At her young age, Ashley has not yet found her own creative feet, and *envy* made her copy the work of others."

Fortunately, Ashley's back was still toward the audience. The corners of her mouth trembled.

I raised my chin and winked at her.

She tossed me a watery smile. Then, disobeying Antonio's earlier instructions, she crossed in front of me and disappeared behind the curtains.

"Shame!" Dora hollered, echoing my thoughts. I wanted to run after Ashley and undo the damage that Antonio had tried to inflict on the girl, but I was the last person onstage to have committed one of Antonio's seven threadly sins, and I wasn't going to wimp out now. I'd rush to Ashley in a minute.

Behind me, Naomi whispered, "I'll go." She followed Ashley out of view.

What *was* the seventh deadly sin, anyway? My mind went blank. Behind the curtains, chair legs scraped against the stage floor.

"Willow!" Antonio called.

Play it for laughs. Stepping forward in the poufy dress and bloomers, I waved at the audience, even though I couldn't see them.

"Willow," Antonio repeated, "by now you must have figured out by the process of elimination which threadly sin you've committed."

I shook my head. Dramatically, I waved my arms out to my sides, drawing attention to the cutesy, ruffled dress.

"C'mon," Antonio urged. "You know what it is. Tell us."

The audience was silent, waiting for my response.

Without thinking, I blurted out, "Adultery?"

The audience roared.

Antonio let out a wolf whistle. "Is that it, Willow?"

"It can't be." I hollered to make myself heard. "I'm not married."

More laughter. Antonio murmured into the mike, "*You* don't have to be. Talk to me after the show, Willow. Maybe we can arrange something." He added a nasty chuckle.

Everyone could have heard him, but no one laughed, and I made a very rude face of distaste that he couldn't completely see, but the audience could. I shouted, "In this dress, it's more like *child*ery!"

Dora called out, "Bravo!"

After the laughter died down, Antonio spoke into the mike again. "No. Look carefully at the dress that Willow has made. Doesn't it make her look fat?"

Dora shouted, "No!"

Again, Antonio acted like no one had spoken. He went on, "By making a dress that will allow her to eat most of the food we'll be serving at the reception after the show, which, by the way, you're all invited to, Willow has committed the seventh threadly sin, which is . . ." He paused dramatically, then proclaimed, "Gluttony!"

I pranced in a circle, billowing the monster dress out and showing off my long, slender legs. To make certain everyone appreciated my ruffled bloomers, I raised the hem of the dress and dipped in an exaggerated curtsey.

The audience howled.

With a gesture a kid might use to encourage her playground gang to follow her, I skipped toward the gap between the curtains.

I'd succeeded. I'd played it for laughs, and I hadn't let Antonio's jibes get to me. I'd also, perhaps, stolen the show.

Antonio tried to regain the audience's attention by growling into the mike, "I'll *definitely* speak to you later, Willow."

But people were still laughing and clapping.

I pulled the blue velvet curtain back, turned toward the audience, widened my eyes in fake amazement, and made a show of patting my heart.

Loretta flew at me, nearly knocked me down, continued past me between the curtains, and elbowed Antonio aside. She made a shooing motion at him.

He didn't shoo. A superior grin playing across his face, he took two steps away from her, then faced the audience.

5

Loretta bent toward the mike. "Antonio was joking about the sins." Anger threaded through her words. "Here at TADAM, we admire the ladies who invented Threadville and keep it going, and we're grateful to them for all they've done for us tonight and during the weeks leading up to the show. None of them have committed *any* sins."

Antonio budged past her and leaned over the podium. "Rats," he complained. "I was hoping for a little adult —"

Before he could complete the word, Loretta turned off the microphone, then gave an abrupt hand signal to someone near the main doors of the conservatory.

Overhead lights came on. Laughing and calling greetings to each other, people stood.

I searched the back of the audience for Dora.

She waved wildly at me. She was flanked by two tall and handsome men.

Oh no. Not only Haylee's heartthrob, but mine, too.

And I was wearing the world's most ridiculous dress. I needed to disappear.

Arms folded and feet braced, Antonio and Loretta glared at each other.

I dove between the dark blue plush curtains and nearly plowed into Paula.

She glowered at me as if I'd planned the entire fracas and executed it on my own.

Although I looked about two years old, I managed to restrain myself from sticking out my tongue. If she wanted to blame someone for the way the show had ended, she should have a good look at her husband.

Antonio had set us up. He had designed outfits that he could describe as seven threadly sins. He'd done it on purpose. We'd spent hours creating clothes for his fundraiser, and then we'd ended up taking the brunt of his unkind jokes. Loretta had attempted to spin his remarks, but she hadn't erased his cruelty.

Someone had again moved the chair that his jacket was on, and I saw it only after I crashed into it and knocked the jacket onto the floor. Did he really have to keep his candies that close? He may have slipped through the curtains between the show's segments for more candies when I was in my dressing cubicle, but he'd definitely been onstage during the entire awards ceremony.

Maybe, before Loretta stormed out to the podium, she had taken pity on him and moved the chair in case what she was going to say would cause him to duck backstage for a distracting piece of candy.

I picked the jacket up. My toe must have nudged something — I couldn't see what — that had been underneath the chair. Clattering, the thing rolled away and disappeared beneath the red polyester curtains hiding the briefcases and other props. I wasn't about to get down on my hands and knees and show off my bloomers to search for a piece of candy that Antonio probably wouldn't want after it had spent time on the floor.

Hurrying toward the cubicles, Mona brushed past me. We had very little time to change before the reception.

Opal came backstage and patted my arm. "It was bad enough that he made fun of my granny squares, but you don't look fat and never will."

I grinned at her. "Don't worry. I had fun out there."

She eyed me skeptically. "Well, that's a plus."

Behind Opal, Edna held out her hand.

"I'll hang that jacket up. I'm already in my Glitzy Garb outfit. You two go change."

I handed her the jacket and hurried toward my cubicle.

Clay had been at the show.

Maybe he would also attend the reception. I was glad I was supposed to ditch the ballooning confection that Antonio had said made me look fat and would allow me to indulge in gluttony.

Shifting her weight from foot to foot outside her cubicle, Macey asked me to guard the gap between her curtains while she changed into her evening gown. It would make me have to rush into my own gown, but I agreed. Was she afraid that Antonio would join her in her cubicle to "adjust" her clothing?

Brushing against cubicles and causing some of the gleaming red curtains to part company with each other, Antonio sauntered toward me. Women in cubicles gasped and pulled their curtains shut.

Antonio was wearing his suit jacket again. Crunching on candies, he stopped next to me. "The lovely Willow!" His breath was minty. "Need help getting out of that dress?"

"No."

He leered. "Need help committing adultery?"

"No." I tried to smile.

"You do realize that you can commit adultery even if *you're* not married. You just need a married man." He puffed out his chest.

Behind him, near the stage, his wife squinted toward us. She wouldn't be able to hear his murmuring, but I was certain she could guess that he was flirting — if that was the word — with me.

I tossed my head. "No, thanks. Gluttony is my thing."

He laughed, then looked at the dressing cubicle I was guarding. "Macey, are you in there? Do you need help? You did a great job out there."

"I'll help her if she needs it," I said quickly.

With an appraising look at my lips, he pulled a round, white candy from his jacket pocket. "Need something for your gluttony?"

I backed into the curtains around Macey's cubicle. "No, thanks."

"You'll be well fed at the reception. See you there." Finally, with a mocking salute and a crunch of molars against candy, he strolled toward the curving ramp that would take him to the conservatory's main doors.

I would go to the reception, but I would stay only long enough to be polite, then I would leave TADAM to its own devices. And vices, too. I wanted nothing more to do with Antonio.

Eyes smoldering and without saying a word to anyone, Muscle Shirt barged out of the doorway near the ramp, side-stepped Antonio, strode past me and the dressing cubicles, and disappeared through the gap in the stage curtains next to Paula and Loretta, who appeared to be arguing.

What a fun group.

Antonio was no longer in sight. He must have headed down the ramp toward the main doors.

"He's gone," I whispered to Macey.

She asked in a small voice, "Who?"

"Antonio."

She came out of her cubicle and had me zip up the back of her gown, then she insisted on standing outside my cubicle while I changed. "I don't want to walk into the reception by myself," she explained. I remembered being insecure when I was her age, but I had a feeling that this was more than insecurity. She was frightened, probably for a good reason. Antonio might be lurking in the conservatory or on the way to the TADAM mansion, and the man was a little too persistent about giving attention where it wasn't wanted.

As it turned out, Macey didn't have to go to the reception with only me. By the time I was wearing the russet velvet gown again, Mona, Ashley, Haylee, and all three of Haylee's mothers were waiting with Macey outside my temporary dressing room.

The area behind the stage curtains was now illuminated only by light coming over the top of the curtains from the part of the conservatory's main room where the audience had been. Loretta and Paula were gone. Maybe they'd followed Muscle Shirt out between the stage curtains.

We started down the ramp. Walled shoulder height in stone with lush and fragrant greenery rising beyond the walls, the ramp wound downward in a curve toward the main doors.

Edna walked with determination, nearly stomping on the ornate, hand-painted floor tiles. "I'm not going to help that man with any more fund-raisers."

I agreed. "He did that deliberately."

Naomi was never fond of conflict. "He probably thought he was being funny. But teasing often isn't anywhere near funny."

Haylee was less tolerant. "I thought he meant to hurt people's feelings."

"C'mon, girls," Mona said. "He was just being a *man.*" The way she pronounced the last word was almost a caress.

"Well, *I* thought he was flirting with you, Willow, and Macey," Opal said. "That's how some men try to get attention."

I pressed on the wood and glass door to the outside. "He was despic—"

Loretta spoke from right behind me. "Don't take what Antonio says seriously. He means well."

Where had she come from, and how much of our conversation had she heard? The look I gave her wasn't very friendly or accommodating.

After we all filed outside, Loretta locked the conservatory's double doors. "He was trying to make the fashion show into something everyone would remember," she said. "He just got carried away. He appreciates all you've done."

How odd. When she'd said basically the same things to the audience about ten minutes ago, she'd seemed angry at Antonio, but now she was apologizing for him, and she showed no sign of her previous rage. Maybe I'd misread her earlier.

I glanced over my shoulder at the conservatory. Although I was still annoyed by Antonio and his mean stunt, the magic of that glass confection calmed me. All the lights inside it were out, and the sparkling pinpricks on its bubbled antique glass were the reflections of stars.

We teetered in our heels along the sidewalk leading out of the park and turned right. At the next intersection, which was fortunately close, we turned right again and went halfway down the block to the Victorian mansion that was now the home of the Threadville Academy of Design and Modeling.

Loretta said, "I hope you'll all make use of the vouchers we gave you toward night school classes. The vouchers are worth a lot, and although you're all experts in your fields, you might learn something at TADAM."

Mona turned to Loretta. "Paula doesn't look happy." Mona occasionally lacked subtlety.

Loretta's response was breezy. "I'm sure she was just overwhelmed, trying to make the show a success. We've all been working hard at that."

Wriggling, Mona tugged at her tight, stretchy dress. "Would you say Paula's good for Antonio? Does she make *him* happy?"

I succeeded in not laughing. Mona had been through at least two husbands and was always on the lookout for an available man, even if the availability was mostly in her mind.

Loretta retorted, "I don't know. It's none of my business."

"It doesn't matter," Edna told Mona. "He's *married.*"

"Married, schmarried," Mona scoffed. "As if I'd let a little detail like *that* bother me. I could have had Gord if I'd wanted."

Opal, Haylee, Naomi, and I all chimed in, "No, you couldn't have!" Gord had become smitten with Edna when he'd first encountered her, and I could never imagine him giving Mona more than an amused glance. But maybe Mona would interpret an amused glance as a declaration of true love.

Mona stared straight ahead. "Ooooh, now *there's* someone who can park his lasso on my bedstead anytime."

Gord, Clay, and Haylee's heartthrob, Ben, were waiting with Dora on the front porch of the TADAM mansion.

"Who," I asked innocently, "Edna's mother?"

Mona slapped at my arm. "I'd take either Clay or Ben, but Clay never seems to see anyone besides you."

I wasn't sure about that. Maybe he just didn't notice Mona.

She wiggled her hips again. "That Ben

who owns the Elderberry Bay Lodge, though — he makes my toes curl."

And that was good? My high-heeled sandals were making *my* toes curl, and I wasn't exactly fond of the feeling.

"They're both too young for you," Edna stated with finality, if not with tact.

Mona smoothed her long, platinum hair over one tanned shoulder. "Maybe Ben needs an older woman to help him get over the death of his wife. Older women can be so nurturing." She frowned at Edna. "And it's not like I'm as old as you are."

Edna was slightly over fifty, Mona was in her mid-forties, and Ben and Clay were in their late thirties.

And, of course, most of us had different plans for Ben.

Maybe he did, too. As we climbed the stairs to the porch, he greeted all of us, but his warmest smile was for Haylee.

Yes!

Gord grabbed Edna and gave her a big smooch. "You're lovely," he said.

"Not too greedy for sparkles?" she teased.

"Never." He put an arm around her and led her into the mansion. "You sparkle all by yourself."

Loretta followed them into the vestibule, with Mona right behind her, pestering her about where Antonio would be. The front door closed behind them.

Dora Battersby held out her hands and stopped the rest of us from going inside. "We need to plan our strategy."

6

Dora scowled at the closed door of the TADAM mansion. "I don't trust that Antonio." She turned to Ashley. "You and this other young lady, Macey, is it?"

Macey nodded.

Dora ordered, "You two stay together. Don't let that man be alone with either of you." Dora grabbed Clay's arm. "Do not let Willow out of your sight."

I sputtered, "I can look after myself!"

Clay slid an arm around my waist. "Glad to." He murmured into my hair, "Gluttony, as *if.* Mm."

"That was a ridiculous dress."

"You rocked it."

Smiling up into those dark brown eyes, I thanked him.

Dora took Ben's hand. "Ben, you stay with Haylee and protect her from *that man.*"

Ben smiled. "My pleasure."

I could tell that Haylee was trying hard

not to break into a huge grin.

Dora wasn't done choreographing the group on the porch. "Opal and Naomi, you two stay together."

Opal laughed. "We're older than Antonio."

"Not enough." Dora frowned. "Those so-called complaints about your outfits were his attempt to get all of you to fawn over him and prove that you aren't as bad as he said."

"I thought so, too," Opal said.

"Maybe he's only trying to be liked," Naomi suggested.

Dora raised herself to her full height, bringing her head up past Clay's and Ben's elbows. "Then he's going about it all wrong."

Ashley asked her, "Who's going to protect you?"

"I am definitely too old for that man, so I'll watch over the rest of you. If any of you need my help, ask. I've encountered that type of man before. Often, it's all hot air, but let's not test it, okay?"

We all agreed.

"Let's go in, then," she said.

Apparently struggling with a grin of his own, Ben opened the door. Dora preceded the rest of us into the mansion.

Inside, gleaming dark oak paneled the

walls of a grand foyer. Paula was halfway up a sweeping, red-carpeted staircase. She didn't turn to see who had entered. Muscle Shirt and Loretta disappeared from the broad hallway into a room to our right.

I asked Clay, "Did you restore this mansion?"

"No. Elderberry Bay took it for back taxes years ago. They kept the conservatory and some of the land surrounding it as a public park but couldn't make up their minds what to do with the mansion itself. Finally, they sold it and its grounds — there's still a big yard and a carriage house — to TADAM for a dollar with hopes for future tax revenue and in the understanding that TADAM would restore, preserve, and maintain the building and property." He studied the floor, stained dark to match the walls. "They did a good job." He was being polite, I could tell, as if he didn't want to point out flaws.

I knew from the restorations he'd made to the Threadville shops and the Elderberry Bay Lodge that he was a perfectionist. Raising one eyebrow in exaggerated bewilderment, I looked up at him.

He tightened his arm around my waist. "Tell you later." We went through the doorway where Loretta and Muscle Shirt had gone. Pocket doors that could be closed

71

to separate the front parlor from the back one were tucked away, combining the two rooms into a large one, perfect for the crowded reception. We went to a table underneath a side window. TADAM students poured wine and told us to help ourselves to sandwiches, cookies, tarts, and bars from heaped-up platters. They all looked very tempting.

Gluttony.

Behind me, someone breathed, "Aha!" I smelled mint. How had Antonio crept this close? "The lovely Willow!"

Clay was still beside me, but with a glass in one hand and a cookie in the other, he no longer had his arm around me.

With difficulty, I turned around without bumping into Antonio or knocking cookies or wineglasses off the table. I made my voice as formal as my posture. "Antonio, this is my friend, Clay Fraser."

Antonio wrinkled his forehead and repeated Clay's name in drawn-out syllables. "You're the local builder?"

Clay nodded.

"You were our second choice for our restorations. Like it?" He waved his hand around to indicate the double parlor but didn't wait for Clay's answer. "We decided to go with a lower bidder, a big firm out of

Erie. They did a superb job. We're keeping the mansion as much like a home as possible, so although the former bedrooms on the second floor are now classrooms, they still have their original details, including closets. And we've turned the third floor into the director's suite. I designed the kitchen on this floor, and it's the crown jewel of the place. Come see it. Tell me if you could have done anywhere near as well." He clasped Clay's elbow and led him toward the back of the house.

Maybe I should have gone with them. But Clay didn't need protecting, not even from Antonio's obvious plans to rub it in that Clay's company had not won the job of restoring the mansion.

Clay wouldn't care, and was probably trying to disguise his amusement. For one thing, although Clay kept hiring more employees, he could hardly keep up with the jobs people were begging him to do. For another, Clay would not have enjoyed working for someone who made suggestive remarks to nearly every female around, and was aggressively competitive with men.

Standing with their backs to the front windows, Loretta and Muscle Shirt stared into the crowded room. As if unimpressed by Muscle Shirt's impersonation of a boulder, Loretta darted away. Seconds later, she passed the parlor door nearest me. She was heading in the direction that Antonio and Clay had gone.

Antonio had been carrying neither a glass nor a plate, probably to keep both hands free so he could touch people who didn't want to be touched. Scolding myself for being snarky, I joined Dora near the partial wall between the two parlors.

"I told you to stay with Clay," she muttered.

"He went to see the kitchen with Antonio, so I figured I was safe from unwanted mauling."

"Is Antonio that bad?" She looked about to charge into the kitchen to confront him.

"He didn't touch me, but . . ." I leaned down and whispered to her, "I think Macey had to slap him yesterday before the dress rehearsal."

Dora looked about to explode. *"What?"*

A student passed us with a platter of cookies.

When he was out of earshot, I murmured to Dora, "I'm not positive. Want to check out the silent auction?"

"You're just changing the subject, but okay, let's. Have you tried the wine?" With a grimace of distaste, she set her glass on the nearest table. "Plonk," she said.

I took a sip of my wine. It was sugary and bland. I put my nearly full glass beside hers, and we fled to the vast entry hall. Ben and Haylee had their backs to us and were heading toward the rear of the mansion, where, judging by where Antonio had taken Clay, the kitchen must be.

Beyond the foot of the stairs, Dora and I entered a large and beautifully paneled room that had probably once been a dining room but could now be used as a classroom.

Tables lined the walls, leaving the center of the room free so we could view the auction sign-up sheets. To make it clear which outfit was for sale on which sheet, a photo of that particular outfit, with one of us modeling it, was printed at the top of the sheet.

Macey and Ashley were giggling at a picture of me twirling in my Bo Peep dress.

I had tried not to show off my ruffled bloomers during the dress rehearsal when Muscle Shirt was taking those pictures. I hadn't succeeded.

"Cute," Ashley teased. Her grin was mischievous. She and Macey started around the room one way to look at the pictures. Dora and I went the other way.

Dora tapped the shot of Macey in cutoffs

and halter top. "She bought that at a mall."

She moved to a photo of Mona. "And that woman can't sew a stitch. Why is she pretending she can?"

Mona wasn't nearby, but I heard her laughing in the kitchen. I said quietly, "She likes to pretend she does all the upholstery and makes all the window coverings and sofa cushions in her shop, too, and we haven't told her we know she doesn't."

Dora demanded, "Why not?"

"We've pretended to believe her ever since she opened that shop. How could we change now?"

She folded her arms. "*I* could. Want me to?"

I pulled her to the next table. "No way. You'd spoil our fun."

"You and Haylee have some very odd notions of fun."

Near the door to the kitchen, Antonio said in a husky voice, "The lovely Ashley *and* the lovely Macey!"

Ashley squealed, "Don't!"

I whipped around. Ashley was pushing Antonio's hand away from Macey's backside, and Macey looked about to lash out.

I never would have guessed that Dora Battersby could move that fast. Like a steamroller in chunky heels, she motored across the room toward Antonio.

His face reddening, he clutched at his neck. Pretending he was only desperate for a candy when he'd obviously been too close to one of his students — and to my seventeen-year-old assistant?

I was right behind Dora, who was yelling, "How dare you!"

Antonio patted a pocket bulging with candy. "Where's my —" Watching Dora barrel toward him, he squeaked out a wheezy, "Help!"

In those heels, Dora barely topped five feet. Antonio was a good ten inches taller, but Dora made a fist and reared her arm back. "*I'll* help you."

I caught Dora's hand and held it. "No!"

Dora struggled but didn't manage to hit Antonio.

He staggered dramatically away from us.

His wife burst out of the kitchen. Screaming, she reached toward her husband and missed.

Antonio tipped backward, banged his head on a table, slumped to the floor, and lay there, not moving.

7

Paula's scream and Antonio's crash on the hard maple floor brought Mona, Ben, and Haylee from the kitchen. Others crowded in from the parlors and foyer.

Paula knelt beside her prone husband and patted his face. "Antonio!"

He didn't respond.

Tears streaming down her cheeks, Paula jumped up and pointed at Dora and me. "Call the police and have them arrest those two women! They killed my husband."

Even when she wasn't swinging a clipboard around, Paula was unpredictable. I backed away.

She stabbed a finger toward me. "Don't you go anywhere. Someone, stop those two women from escaping."

I was about to pull my phone out of the little evening bag I'd made for the fashion show, but Ashley was already talking breathlessly to the emergency dispatcher.

Dora yelled, "Gord!"

Her son-in-law, the popular doctor who had ushered many of Elderberry Bay's citizens, including Ashley, into the world, rushed into the former dining room and started CPR on Antonio.

Haylee and Ben, who were volunteer firefighters, knelt beside Gord. Clay was a firefighter, too. Where was he?

I was on the force, but if Paula thought I'd tried to kill Antonio, she probably wouldn't want me attempting to revive him.

Within minutes, police chief Vicki Smallwood rushed into the mansion.

Paula shrieked that Dora and I had killed her husband.

Vicki sent me an astonished look, but all she said was, "Clear out, everyone, except Haylee, Ben, and Gord. The rest of you, go wait in that big room across the hall and stay there near those tables of food until I let you go."

Paula aimed her forefinger, trembling and curling into a witch's claw, at Dora and me. "I don't want those two murderers going out of my sight."

Vicki Smallwood showed her tough, practical side. "Then go *with* them into the next room."

Paula tugged at her lank brown hair. "I'm

staying with my husband. They beat him up and killed him."

Seeing the question in Vicki's clear blue eyes, I shook my head.

Vicki relented. "Okay, Willow and Mrs. Battersby, stay here with us, please." She looked down at Antonio. "He doesn't *look* like anyone beat him up."

Gord lifted his head from giving Antonio mouth-to-mouth. "And he's not dead." He signaled for someone to take over the resuscitation effort. Haylee blanched. I edged farther from Antonio. Clay was still nowhere around.

Ben knelt beside Antonio and took over. Apparently, Antonio still needed both mouth-to-mouth breathing aid and chest compressions.

Gord stood and frowned at Vicki.

She said tersely, "An ambulance is on its way."

Gord asked Paula, "Does your husband have heart trouble?"

Paula took a long time to answer, as if she couldn't quite force words past her lips, which were twisted in what appeared to be anger. "I'm not sure." She glared at Dora and me. "But maybe he got heart trouble from those two women knocking him out and *attempting* to kill him."

Gord persisted, "Does he have medication for a heart condition?"

Paula shrugged, opened her mouth, closed it again, and finally managed, "He takes a lot of pills. I don't know what they're all for. He was already taking them when we got married." She twisted her watch on her wrist. The bracelet was loose. "Six months ago," she added.

"Does he keep any medication with him?" Gord's tone was sharp.

Paula wrung her hands. "He might."

Wouldn't married couples know important facts like that about each other? And if Paula truly didn't know, wouldn't she make an attempt to find out, even in these stressful circumstances? But she only stared down at her husband as if she lacked bones, muscles, or the will to do anything. Shock, I guessed.

Gord and Vicki dropped to their knees and thrust their hands into Antonio's jacket pockets.

If I were married, would my husband and I keep life-or-death secrets from each other?

Where was Clay?

Holding some of Antonio's candies on the flat of her palm, Vicki tilted her face up toward Paula. "Could these be some of his pills?" Vicki looked skeptical but for once didn't sound sarcastic. As I'd noticed the night before, those candies resembled fat, white beads. They certainly didn't look like pills.

Paula shot Vicki a scorn-filled look. "That's candy. He eats them to help him give up smoking."

Vicki asked Gord, "Did you find any pills?"

He shook his head. "Only more candies."

Vicki poured Antonio's candies into an evidence bag, then offered the bag to Gord. He dumped the candies he'd found into the bag, also. Apparently, the director of a fashion design school had not minded that handfuls of candy were distorting his jacket pockets, which was not exactly a typical runway look.

Vicki pulled a comb and wallet out of the jacket's inner chest pocket, and then two large batches of keys from his pants pockets. Hanging on to the wallet, she put the keys and comb into another evidence bag.

Paula growled, "What do you think you're doing?"

Vicki was noncommittal. "He's going to the hospital. I'll look after his property for him until he can do it himself."

Paula held out a hand. "Give it to me."

"You can come in the ambulance with us."

Vicki didn't hand any of it to Paula.

Paula squinted at Vicki as if suspecting that Vicki was about to help herself to Antonio's cash or credit cards. "Give me his wallet." The once-black leather wallet was thin and worn, like a favorite possession that Antonio hadn't been able to bring himself to replace.

"Fair enough," Vicki agreed. "Mind if I have a look at his ID first?"

Paula gave a begrudging consent.

Vicki studied Antonio's driver's license and wrote in her notebook, then gave the license and wallet to Paula. "You'd better collect everything else you'll want at the hospital so you'll be ready to go with the ambulance."

Gord added, "And bring his medications, too. All of them. Whatever you can find."

Paula dashed away, into the kitchen. I heard her pound up what was apparently a set of back stairs. Ben continued working on Antonio, for what seemed like a long time without any noticeable improvement in the man's color.

Breathing heavily and carrying a large tote bag, Paula returned. She handed Gord a plastic bag filled with bottles.

He examined the bag. "These all look like vitamins and supplements."

"That's all I could find," Paula told him.

Gord was the sweetest man imaginable, but if he studied me the way he was studying Paula, I'd be worried. Or confessing all of my sins, both threadly *and* deadly.

Emergency medical technicians strode in, checked Antonio, attached him to an oxygen unit, and bundled him onto a stretcher. Paula complained that Vicki didn't need to ride with her and Antonio in the ambulance.

"Okay," Vicki said. "Gord, mind going in my place? I'd like to talk to the people here. I'll drive to the hospital and pick you up later."

Gord examined Vicki's face. She raised one eyebrow and gave him a tiny nod.

"Sure," he said, "I'll go in your place, Chief Smallwood."

If I read that little exchange correctly, Vicki was asking Gord to keep an eye on Paula, as well as on the invalid, and he was agreeing.

Did Vicki suspect that Paula had already harmed Antonio?

Paula snapped, "I can look after my own husband. And ambulance attendants are going along, right?"

Vicki leveled a stern look at Paula. "Gord's a doctor. I'll give you a ride home from Erie, too, if you need it." She turned away from Paula. "Willow, I need to talk to you."

"Me, too?" Dora asked.

"After I talk to Willow," Vicki told her.

Walking behind the stretcher, Paula called over her shoulder, "Arrest them both for attempted murder!"

Why did the woman keep harping on the word "murder"? If we had punched Antonio, she might have had a case for accusing us of assault, but we hadn't touched him.

Murder?

Ignoring Paula's outburst, Vicki asked everyone except me to clear the room. "But anyone who heard or saw Antonio fall, don't leave the building. I'll want your statements, too."

Ashley and Macey looked at each other, then Ashley braced her shoulders. "Willow and Mrs. Battersby did not touch Antonio." She wagged an index finger between herself and Macey. "We were there. We saw."

Vicki nodded. "Fine, thank you. Please go with the others, and I'll talk to you two later."

I asked Haylee where Clay was.

Haylee looked uncomfortable. "He left."

I made a vague gesture toward the floor. "Before Antonio collapsed?"

She nodded. "He went out the back door." She scooted toward Ben, who was waiting for her in the foyer.

How strange. Still, it wasn't as if Clay and I had a date. I hadn't expected him to attend the fashion show, but leaving without saying good-bye wasn't exactly his style.

And I don't usually look this glamorous.

Dora must have noticed the disappointment I was trying to conceal. She patted my arm.

Vicki told her gently, "I do want to speak to you, Mrs. Battersby, but after I talk to Willow, okay?"

Dora saluted. "Don't call me Mrs. Battersby like I'm some ancient old grandmother. Even Haylee and Willow call me Dora. But I get it. You have to question us separately to see if our stories match."

Vicki made a pretend scowl. "I know you Threadville women. You've been passing each other messages that I can't understand ever since I arrived, and probably before, also."

Dora rose to the bait. "No, we haven't!" Head high, she marched out of the room.

One corner of Vicki's mouth quirked up. "She's so easy to rile. Okay, Willow, what happened?"

I told her that I suspected that Antonio had pinched Macey's rear end, and maybe Ashley's, also, and that I'd been afraid that

Dora had been about to take a swing at him. "I grabbed her hand and stopped her. But he fell, anyway. It was the strangest thing. Neither of us touched him."

"How did he look?"

"Surprised."

"Mrs. Battersby — Dora — can have that effect on people," Vicki deadpanned.

I couldn't help smiling at her description of Dora. "His face became red and puffy, like he was angry. Or embarrassed at being caught possibly touching girls."

"Did he say anything? Apologize, for instance?"

"He did this pretend thing like he was choking, you know, clutching at his throat. And he said, 'Help me.'"

Writing in her notebook, she didn't look up. "Think he was choking? I mean, actually choking?"

"I didn't think so at the time. I thought he was only trying to distract us from his behavior. But he could have been choking. He started feeling around in his pockets as if he were hunting for his candy, and he said, 'Where's my —' but he didn't finish the question. He gasped, 'Help,' and then fell."

She sent me one of her piercing glances. "Did he take anything out of his pockets?"

"Not that I noticed. I'm sure he didn't put anything into his mouth."

"And he was clutching his throat? Not his chest?"

I tried to picture the moment. "I think so. Maybe he had a candy in his mouth and it went down the wrong way."

"Hmmm." Another of Vicki's indecipherable comments. She pointed her pen toward the foyer. "Tell Dora Battersby that I want to talk to her. Then you can go."

I didn't have to tell Dora. As soon as she spotted me coming into the double parlor from the foyer, she marched off, head high, to the mansion's former dining room and her interview with Chief Vicki Smallwood.

The only other people in the large room were Ashley and Macey. They left, though, carrying platters of goodies to the kitchen where, I guessed from the noises, people were putting away food and washing dishes.

Although Vicki had told me I could leave, I decided to wait for Dora so we could walk Ashley home. The dogs and I had always walked with Ashley when she left In Stitches after dark, and even though Ashley was seventeen, I would find it difficult to send her off alone. Besides, her home was only a short detour for Dora and me. Macey was safe from unwanted attention from Antonio

88

at the moment, but if she lived in the village and wanted to join us, that would be fine, too.

I felt a little guilty about my relief that Antonio couldn't bother Macey and Ashley while he was on his way to the hospital.

Maybe he wasn't suffering. After those first few moments of clutching his throat, he hadn't seemed to be. I hoped he'd stay in the hospital for a very long time, and when they released him, he would move on to a career that didn't involve being around students.

Although I couldn't hear Dora's words, her tone was indignant and assertive. I couldn't help smiling. Later, she and my other Threadville friends would help me remind Ashley and Macey that they should not put up with harassment — from anyone.

But Dora hadn't needed to clobber anyone about it. If I hadn't stopped her, would she have hit Antonio? I suspected she'd merely wanted to startle him into behaving himself.

She returned to the reception room as Macey and Ashley came back from the kitchen. Dora sent Macey into the dining room to talk to Vicki, then turned to Ashley. "I told our police chief to charge that horrible man with assault for pinching you and Macey."

Ashley's mouth was a grim line. "Only Macey. I told him off. I mean I started to, but he went all funny. Don't worry. I'd never let him or anyone else get away with anything like that. But it must be hard for Macey. She's dependent on him for grades."

Dora and I chimed in, "That doesn't matter."

I continued, "He should not get away with that."

Dora added, "Maybe he won't. Maybe he'll lose his job."

"He owns the Threadville Academy of Design and Modeling," I told her.

Dora pinned Ashley with a glare. "Don't you be thinking of attending TADAM, young lady."

Ashley's face closed. "I can look after myself."

Dora scowled at her for what must have felt to Ashley like interminable seconds. "See that you do."

Macey returned, and Ashley went to talk to Vicki.

Dora and I gave Macey basically the same lecture we'd given Ashley.

I said gently, "That wasn't the first time he'd touched you, was it, Macey?"

Macey looked scared, backed away, and lowered her eyes. The slight shake of her head was barely discernible, and so was her soft reply. "No."

I pressed harder. "Last night when we were in our changing cubicles before the dress rehearsal, I heard you slap him, and I also heard his comment about models having to let people help adjust their outfits."

Macey shivered and rubbed her bare arms. "It was nothing."

Dora demanded, "Had he done things like that to you before?"

Macey looked up at us again and shook her head decisively. "No."

Macey's denial had been firm, but Dora gave her a stern look verging on disbelief. "If you ever need help, you can count on Willow and me."

I rested my forearm on Dora's shoulder. "But we won't beat anyone up, right, Dora?" I teased.

"I'll do whatever it takes." Dora's voice carried.

Vicki peered into the parlor and stared at Dora with something like horrified fascination.

I opened my mouth to tell Vicki that Dora would never harm anyone, but hadn't I already said that Dora had raised her hand as if about to hit Antonio, and that I grabbed her arm before she'd had a chance to draw back?

I got along reasonably well with our police chief, but she never lost an opportunity to remind me what would happen if I broke the law. She and I both wanted to see justice prevail, but our methods of reaching that goal sometimes differed, and she had an unfortunate tendency to conclude that I was interfering with her investigations when I was merely trying to help.

Vicki asked Macey, "Can you join Ashley and me, please? I need to tell you both something."

Macey tossed me a humorless grin, then followed Vicki into the dining room.

We couldn't tell what Vicki was saying, but she was probably reiterating what Dora and I had already told the girls. Maybe Vicki was going to charge Antonio for pinching Macey.

Dora may have thought the same thing. Her dark eyes brightened. She raised her eyebrows and took one stealthy step toward the foyer.

Then there was a loud crash in the kitchen. Glass shattered. A woman screamed.

8

Dora sprinted to the kitchen. In my higher heels, I wobbled right behind her.

Vicki was already there. Macey and Ashley gawked from the dining room doorway.

The TADAM student who had poured my wine sobbed, "I dropped a tray of glasses."

Bits of glass were all over the floor.

"It's nothing to cry about," Dora said, although she could have sounded more sympathetic.

Macey must have thought so, too. Ignoring fragments of glass, she dashed into the kitchen and gave the girl a quick hug. "It's okay, Samantha."

Vicki turned to Dora and me. "I'll call you two at home if I need you."

Dora folded her arms. "We'll help Samantha clean up before we go. And we'll wait for Ashley so we can walk her home."

Vicki said drily, "I think she'll be okay now." Apparently giving up on dismissing us, she ushered Ashley and Macey back into the dining room.

I asked Samantha where I could find a broom. She didn't know, but Dora had no qualms about searching until she found one.

Out in the backyard, a light shined as a door opened. Was this the carriage house that Clay had mentioned?

For a second, I saw Loretta and Clay silhouetted in the doorway, and then the light went out, the yard was dark again, and I doubted that I'd really seen Loretta and Clay.

Especially not in each other's arms. And then separating, and Loretta taking Clay's hand and pulling him out of the carriage house as she switched off the light . . .

No, I could not have seen any of that.

But I had. All of it.

I grabbed the broom from Dora and wielded it with speed and power that made her exclaim, "What's gotten into you, Willow?"

Samantha smiled, sort of.

"You're all dressed up," Dora scolded me. "Let me do that. What if your young man comes in and sees you playing Cinderella?"

The back door slammed open. Loretta burst in. "What's wrong?"

I straightened and stared at her. Where to

begin? With the broken glasses, or the news that Loretta's boss had collapsed and been taken to the hospital?

What I really wanted to do was shout at her to leave Clay alone.

Her hair was messy and her lipstick was smeared.

Clay came in behind her and shut the back door. Something like embarrassment crept across his face. He straightened his tie, but it was too late.

I'd seen the red smudge near one of the buttons on his white shirt.

My heart felt like it was down there on the floor, shattered with all that glass.

Loretta prompted, "Someone screamed just now?"

Samantha gulped between hiccups. "I'm sorry. I dropped some glasses and they broke."

Dora scowled at Clay as if she'd also seen the red lipstick on his shirt. Uncharacteristically restrained, she stooped and held the dustpan while I brushed fragments of glass into it, then she dumped the contents of the dustpan into the wastebasket. Finally, she stood and turned to Samantha, who was staring apologetically at Loretta. "There," Dora said in a surprisingly soothing voice. "All cleaned up. No harm done."

"Except to the glasses —" Loretta began.

Dora interrupted her. "Glasses can be replaced. They weren't good ones, anyway."

Loretta argued, "Yes, they were. Antonio buys only the best."

Dora shook her head. "Trust me."

I did. Dora had been an interior designer before her retirement, and she had an encyclopedic knowledge of nearly everything that could go into a home.

Dora added, "Arguing about fifty-cent glasses is not important. If you heard other screams earlier, it's because your boss fainted and his wife screamed, and they're both on the way to the hospital."

Loretta faltered backward. And landed conveniently against Clay. "Screams?" she whimpered. "Earlier? Antonio and Paula? What's wrong with them?"

Vicki spoke from behind me. "You didn't hear a scream about forty-five minutes ago?"

Loretta shook her head. "No, I was busy." She turned her head and smiled up at Clay. "Getting reacquainted with my first love."

Clay's voice was as flinty as his face. "We were discussing renovating the carriage house so it could be used as an apartment, either for TADAM staff or as a source of income for TADAM."

For over forty-five minutes? If the mansion

had a sub-basement, my heart was some-where in it, and sinking fast.

Dora looked out the back window. "Let's do it!"

That seemed like a rather enthusiastic re-action, considering that all I could see through the back window were shadows of shadows. But then, Dora was always eager to design. I felt a pang. What if she liked the mansion's carriage house better than Blue-berry Cottage and decided to rent it? I'd need to find a new tenant, and although she could be a little too snoopy about what might be going on in my apartment, I liked her, and we looked out for each other.

Besides, my hopes of anything interesting *ever* going on inside my apartment were in smithereens. Was Clay as excited about find-ing Loretta again as she was about finding him?

He had never acted like he was having trouble getting over a first love.

Then again, I was never sure where I stood with him.

At least I knew that he and I were friends, and I'd hoped we were becoming more than friends. I should have been less dedicated to my career. I should have put more time and effort into romance. Making that decision now could be a little late, though.

While I was debating with myself and carefully not looking at Loretta and Clay, Vicki was explaining that Antonio had become ill and that Paula had gone to the hospital in the ambulance with him.

"And so did my son-in-law, Gord," Dora proclaimed. "He's a doctor."

Loretta sagged farther into Clay. "This is very upsetting. I should go, too, but I'm not in any shape to drive."

Of course not, if she insisted on pasting herself so closely to Clay that she'd have to sit on his lap in her driver's seat.

Vicki waved the notion away with one hand. "You'd just be in the way. I'll give you the hospital number. Do you have a pencil and paper?"

Samantha grabbed a magnetized notepad and pen from the fridge and thrust them at Loretta. "Here."

Ashley's phone jingled. She read a text, then asked, "Can we go home now? My dad's getting worried."

Vicki nodded. "You're all free to go." She recited a number to Loretta, who wrote it down.

I touched Dora's shoulder and told Ashley, "We'll walk you home."

Clay eased around Loretta. "Mind if I join you?"

I didn't mind, but my mouth refused to open.

Dora answered for all of us. "Of course not!"

"Clay," Loretta wheedled, "you can't go. I'm sorry, but I got lipstick on your shirt. Because of my extensive education in textiles, I can wash the stains out. Piece of cake."

"I can do it." Clay's voice was still surprisingly stony.

Loretta pouted. "I don't know how to lock up the mansion and carriage house."

Vicki stared at Loretta like she was a particularly repulsive insect that had just scurried out from behind a baseboard. "I'll give you a hand. It's part of my job description, and I have Antonio's keys. Besides, I don't mind looking around a little more before I go."

"I guess I can do it myself," Loretta began.

Vicki snapped, "No need."

I almost smiled at Vicki's stern police officer act, but Loretta stopped arguing with her. And with Clay.

Dora asked, "Macey, are you going our way?"

Macey told us an address that was just around the corner, between TADAM and Ashley's house. "You'll come with us, too,

99

Samantha, won't you?" Macey explained that Samantha was one of her roommates.

Samantha nodded. "Yes, please." It came out barely above a whisper.

Dora shepherded the three girls and me out the front door ahead of her and Clay, then draped her hand over Clay's arm.

Macey and Samantha led the way, with Ashley and me behind them, and Dora and Clay following us.

All I wanted to do was put distance between myself and Clay and his lipstick-stained shirt. I didn't want to examine my unexpectedly strong feelings of desolation. I didn't want to think about Clay until I was home alone.

And I definitely didn't want to talk to him and possibly betray feelings that he couldn't return.

I didn't own him, I reminded myself. We weren't a couple — except in some of my more unrealistic dreams, I guessed — and never had been. Maybe I'd been like Mona, reading too much into a smile, a glance, or a swift embrace.

As I hurried the three girls along, Dora clunked behind us in her thick heels, keeping Clay farther and farther from us. Dora had been able to race toward Antonio and, later, from the reception room to the kitchen in those heels, so I was certain she was walking slowly on purpose, maybe to give me a chance to lecture the girls about not allowing a teacher to take advantage of their desire for good grades.

Dutifully, I launched into my spiel. "You know, you don't have to —"

Ashley interrupted me. "Chief Smallwood told us the same thing."

"What?" Samantha asked. "Told you what?"

Macey and Ashley filled her in, allowing me to merely walk along, trying not to think about the man a block behind us. Despite the revealing velvet dress and the stiletto heels, I felt like a dowdy chaperone.

We dropped Macey and Samantha off at their apartment, then headed toward Ashley's house.

Ashley asked me, "Don't those shoes hurt to walk in?"

"Yes, but . . ."

"We can slow down. It's like you're trying to get away from Clay. You don't have to worry about Edna's mother stealing him from you. She's old."

I stifled a laugh. Apparently, Ashley hadn't recognized the real threat, despite Loretta's coy reference to lipstick.

It was all my imagination, I told myself.

No, it wasn't.

Ashley stopped at the walk leading to her front porch. "Are you going to wait for Clay and Dora?"

"They're probably having a conversation about design. They don't need my input."

In the darkness, illuminated only by streetlights, Ashley cocked her head and gazed up at me. "You're acting weird tonight."

I summoned up a smile. "What a thing to say to your boss."

Ashley clapped a hand over her mouth and squeaked between her fingers, "I'm sorry. I didn't mean —"

I interrupted her. "Only joking. See you tomorrow."

Speed-walking the rest of the way home, I tried not to hobble too obviously or precariously.

However, in those shoes, I wasn't about to negotiate the downhill slope through my side yard to my apartment. Instead, I went into my shop.

I locked the door, unplugged the nightlight, and hid in the darkness. I was sure that Clay would accompany Dora all the way through my yard to the door of Blueberry Cottage, and I wasn't ready to talk to him.

Sure enough, I heard their voices out on the sidewalk, and then the gate to my side yard clanged.

Seconds later, from downstairs in my apartment, Sally-Forth and Tally-Ho began the excited barking that signaled they'd heard or seen someone they liked outside. They raced up the stairs to the door of In Stitches, which I kept closed, and down again. They knew I was in the shop, and they were trying to get me to let them out to greet their friends.

I didn't move.

After a few minutes, the dogs settled down. Listening, I stayed out of sight of the front door and windows.

I knew I was being silly. I was stressed from staying up late every night for weeks to complete the garments I wore in the fashion show. I'd have enjoyed all that pattern-making, sewing, and machine embroidery if I had designed the clothes, or if I had liked them. And then last night, the dress rehearsal hadn't been a lot of fun.

Tonight had been even worse.

If Antonio hadn't possibly damaged Ashley's ego, I could have laughed off his joking insults about our seven threadly sins, but the undercurrents of nastiness surrounding TADAM had been too much, especially capped by Paula's accusations of assault and murder.

No, the worst part of the evening, of the past weeks and months, had been seeing Clay's arms around Loretta.

I heard footsteps on the shop's front porch. I crouched behind sewing cabinets. Someone tapped on the glass door. I held my breath and didn't move. What if Clay wanted to tell me how happy he was to find Loretta again after all these years?

The dogs barked, galumphed upstairs, snuffled at the door at the top of the stairs, barked again, and thudded downstairs.

After a few minutes, I decided that whoever had been on my porch was gone. I tiptoed to the door at the top of the stairs.

Four furry bodies greeted me the second I opened it.

I decided that if Clay was persistent enough to return to my backyard and apartment door, I would talk to him after all.

Bravely, I turned on lights, tromped downstairs, slipped into the moccasins I kept by the patio door, and let the animals outside.

"There you are," Dora called out.

The dogs romped to her back porch. They loved Dora, but they also loved Clay. My carefully suppressed hopes returned. Was

Clay, by any chance, sitting with Dora on her back porch?

I waited for the cats to finish their careful digging, then shooed them inside and closed the patio door before I wandered down to talk to Dora and whoever might be with her.

Dora was in one of her Adirondack chairs. "Clay was looking for you," she said. Except for my two dogs, she was alone.

"I must have been upstairs in my shop."

The dogs had arranged themselves on each side of her, conveniently close to her hands. She scratched their ears. "He said he would check there. Didn't he find you?"

"I guess I was downstairs by then. Too bad I missed him."

"You don't sound very convinced."

I merely shrugged and crossed my arms over the low-cut dress. I should have thrown on a sweater before I came out into the rapidly cooling evening.

Dora prodded, "Don't you want to hang on to Clay?"

"You can't hang on to something that's beyond your grasp."

"He's not. He likes you. I can tell. I couldn't get him to say even *one* word about that redhead. She probably threw herself at him."

Easy for Dora to say. "I'll let him make his

own decisions."

"If you hide from him," she countered, "what's he going to think?"

"That I'm giving him time and space to sort things out."

"And playing hard to get?"

"I hope he doesn't think I'm 'playing' anything. I need to sort my feelings out, too." Oops. I'd told Dora too much.

"I didn't like that so-called first love, anyway."

"She's pretty, and that auburn hair is fabulous."

Dora harrumphed. "A big tangle."

Especially after her long rendezvous with Clay in the carriage house . . . But I only said, "And she's the only staff member at TADAM who seems to have much fashion sense."

"That won't matter to Clay. If he's after beauty and fashion sense, he only needs to look at you."

I laughed and squeezed her shoulder. "You're sweet. But it's been a long day. I'd better say good night."

"I'm always here if you need me."

It was strange to think that less than a year ago, I'd believed that I would never get along with her. Then I'd learned that her occasionally caustic personality hid a kind heart. Life had a way of changing one's mind.

Like about Clay. No, I wasn't going to dwell on him and my squandered chances.

The dogs and I went to bed. Now that they were grown, the cats made a pretense of being ready to spend the night quietly, but I knew them. They'd get up around three and prowl around.

Dead tired, I hoped to fall asleep immediately, but I kept seeing that carriage house door opening, and light surrounding Clay and Loretta, locked together like a pair of lovers.

And then Loretta taking his hand, pulling him toward the door, and turning out the light . . .

I gave up, eased out of bed, and dressed again, this time in dark jeans, a black hoodie, and black sneakers. I paused beside Sally's and Tally's beds. Sally was snoring. Tally opened one eye, looked at me, and closed it again. They were no longer puppies, eager for every adventure.

Even the cats only watched from my great room as I tiptoed upstairs to my shop and shut the door to the stairway.

9

Outside, streetlights cast puddles of brightness, but my friends' shops and apartments were dark. Tiptoeing onto my front porch and locking the door of In Stitches, I wished I could talk to Haylee, but she was probably asleep. Besides, what would I tell her? That I was about to walk around town, definitely not *really* checking up on Clay or looking for his truck?

It was more like I wanted to prove to myself that his truck wasn't parked near Loretta's home.

Wherever that was.

Antonio had mentioned a director's suite on the third floor of the TADAM mansion. Did Loretta also have a suite up there? Probably not, or she wouldn't have asked Clay to help her lock the mansion.

Not knowing where else to go, though, I pulled my hood up to cover my hair, jammed my hands into the front pockets of my jeans, and headed toward the TADAM mansion. The night was quiet, and bright stars almost filled the black sky. I missed the comforting presence of Sally and Tally, but they tended to be noticeable, and I didn't want to be recognized, especially if I saw Clay's truck. Clay lived several miles outside the village, so his truck shouldn't be anywhere near.

Shouldn't be . . .

But I wasn't really looking for him, I reminded myself. I was walking around to calm myself so I could eventually go home and sleep.

A light burned in the third floor of Ashley's family's gingerbread-trimmed Victorian house. Was Ashley doing homework? Or was her father fretting and revising his résumé?

My footsteps deliberately quiet, I eased around the block and kept going until I was across the street from the two-story apartment building where Macey and Samantha lived. I hadn't seen Clay's truck. Maybe I should wander to the village's wide beach on the shore of Lake Erie, sit on the sand, hug my knees, watch the waves and the stars, and risk becoming so lulled that I would barely make it home before I dozed off.

An unoiled hinge squeaked, the sound drawn out as if someone were trying to keep anyone else from hearing.

I froze beside the thick, lumpy trunk of a beech tree.

Across the street, someone came down the porch steps of Macey's apartment building.

I edged behind the tree trunk.

For a second, the girl was underneath a streetlight. It was Macey, wearing black tights, running shorts, and a matching long-sleeved T-shirt. Her long blond hair was bundled into a black scarf. She turned as if checking to cross the street. No vehicles were coming, but she stayed on her side. Tall and limber, she loped almost silently down the sidewalk toward the lake.

I supposed that a modeling student would jog whenever her schedule allowed it, even after midnight, but the all-black outfit, her furtive movements, and the quiet way she had disappeared into the night were almost eerie. Maybe I was assuming that other people would be as nervous as I was about being seen. Maybe she had not been checking to see if anyone was following her or watching her.

And then I did hear a vehicle, a block or so southeast of me. Its engine was smooth and quiet.

I looked south, the direction that Macey had checked before jogging north. No vehicle or lights, but a pedestrian on the sidewalk across the street from me was hurrying in my direction.

Only one person had been wearing flowing ivory silk that evening. Loretta.

Hoping she wouldn't spot me, I stayed in the shelter of the beech tree.

Loretta trotted up the steps to the porch of the apartment building where Macey lived, pulled the door open, and went inside. Moments later, a glow lit trees behind the building, as if someone in a rear apartment had turned on lights.

The two-story building housed, I guessed, four apartments per floor. Did many of the TADAM staff and students live there?

Had Loretta just left the vehicle I'd heard?

And had that vehicle been Clay's truck?

Even a block or two away, his powerful engine and big tires would have sounded noisier, wouldn't they? Almost confident that Loretta had not been in the vehicle I'd heard, I eased out from behind the tree and strolled south, where I might catch sight of the vehicle, and it would not be Clay's truck. Would *not* be.

I did not question my logic.

But where had Loretta been? She would

have locked the TADAM mansion, with Vicki's help, more than an hour ago, and Vicki's squad car had not been near the totally dark mansion during my almost-purposeless meandering of the past thirty or so minutes.

At the first corner, I turned east and again walked toward the TADAM mansion, looming behind its wrought iron fence and overgrown gardens.

It looked so Gothic and menacing that I couldn't help crossing the street, which took me closer to other Victorian houses. They were a few years newer, but almost as gloomy.

There was no sign of Clay's truck, and I again told myself that the quiet vehicle I'd heard could not have been his pickup with its heavy-duty tires.

I was almost famous for denying what I didn't want to believe.

Cars were parked in driveways, but none were on the street near the Elderberry Bay Conservatory where we'd modeled our "threadly" sinful outfits. I could almost smile about the entire mess now.

And I could go home. Maybe I would be able to sleep. I hadn't brought my phone along. What if I'd missed a call from Clay?

A dim beam of light moved inside the

conservatory.

I stopped as if I'd collided with one of its antique glass panes.

One of the beautiful Gothic wooden doors, the one that Loretta had locked behind us when we left the conservatory, was ajar. The person inside the conservatory could not be Loretta unless she had run through the park while I skulked past the TADAM mansion. So who was in the conservatory at this hour?

I should have brought my phone.

Vicki was Elderberry Bay's police chief, and its only police officer. She patrolled the village and many square miles of country-side around it. Whenever she wasn't on active duty, troopers from the Pennsylvania State Police took over. Maybe Vicki had driven to Erie to fetch Gord and Paula from the hospital, if Paula could leave her husband's side. If so, the state police would be on call.

I told myself not to be suspicious of everyone and everything. The village could have hired a security guard to check on its buildings and parks during the night.

Still, no vehicles were parked nearby.

Maybe the security guard lived within walking distance of the conservatory. It made perfect sense.

And I was getting cold. I started north, toward home again. I'd walked a half block when the hairs on the back of my neck prickled. Although it seemed impossible to actually *feel* someone watching me, I turned around.

Muscle Shirt was on the sidewalk near the conservatory. Standing with his feet apart and his arms folded over his chest, he was facing me. Watching me?

Glad that my hood hid my long, light brown hair, I forced myself to stride normally, away from him, toward home.

When I looked again, he was gone.

I really, really wanted to know if he'd been the person inside the conservatory, and if the door was now closed. But there was no way I was going anywhere near that man's vicinity in the dark by myself.

Maybe Loretta had been with Muscle Shirt a few minutes ago, and not with Clay.

And earlier in the evening, maybe Clay had not *wanted* to hug her. I would give him the benefit of the doubt. He would explain it all to me, and we'd end up in a satisfying clinch.

I nearly floated up the steps to the porch of In Stitches. Finally, I would be able to sleep.

Maybe not right away, however — the

dogs greeted me at the top of the stairs. Sally cast longing looks toward the leashes hanging near the door.

Why not? They hadn't been with me a few minutes ago, and if Muscle Shirt saw me with them now and recognized me, he might not guess I'd been the woman in the black hoodie. I snapped leashes on the dogs, pushed the hood off my head, and shook my head to make my hair cascade over my shoulders. To add to the disguise, well, really not a disguise since I was now trying to be recognizable as myself, I grabbed an embroidered white fleece jacket that I'd hung as a sample in the shop and put it on over the sweatshirt. My hair should mostly cover the lump of sweatshirt hood under the back of the jacket.

In the past, Vicki had occasionally come upon me when I was dressed all in black and snooping, with or without a dog or two, where she didn't think I should be. If she saw me sauntering around in a white jacket with the dogs at this hour, she might think I was on the completely innocent mission of walking my dogs at night. It wasn't like I was snooping into one of her cases, either. Originally, I'd come out to see if I could find Clay with Loretta, which was none of my business, but wasn't Vicki's, either. Vicki might even agree with me about that.

Now, though, I admitted to myself, I was checking on the mysteriously open conservatory door. Maybe that was really Vicki's job.

And maybe Muscle Shirt worked nights as a security guard.

I let the dogs set the pace as I guided them to the conservatory.

I didn't see anyone around. Sniffing the ground, the dogs happened — with only a little guidance from me — to lead me to the door that had been ajar. It was now closed. A wedge of wood that probably often served as a doorstop was in the grass nearby. I tried the knob.

Locked.

After we were safely out of the park and back on the sidewalk, the dogs wanted to continue toward the TADAM mansion. I'd seen enough of that place, and now it was nearly one thirty, but I let them lead me there, anyway. What if they were tracking Clay?

If they were, they didn't find him. We went on and turned the corner in time to see Macey run lightly up the front steps of her apartment building. She must have gone inside, because by the time we passed the front porch, no one was there and the door was shut.

We passed Ashley's house. The light in the third floor was off. Apparently, most of the village had gone to bed for the night, and the dogs and I should, too.

We went home. I checked my phone.

No messages. I hadn't expected any, especially from Clay saying that Loretta had rushed at him and buried her face in his shirt.

So why was I disappointed?

Settling the dogs for the night again was easy. Unfortunately, the cats were ready to play.

I slept through their shenanigans, but I wasn't terribly rested when my alarm went off earlier than usual to give me time to return my Glitzy Garb outfit to my backstage cubicle at the conservatory. I took the animals out, fed us all, showered, and dressed for work in black slacks, a matching blazer, and a hot pink T-shirt that I had embroidered with fetchingly cartoonlike little zombies.

I put the high-heeled sandals I'd worn to the reception into a bag and folded the velvet gown, still on its hanger, over my arm.

As promised, the door to the conservatory was again unlocked when I arrived only minutes after nine. I didn't see or hear anyone.

Inside the conservatory, radiators hissed and clanked, and the building itself creaked. A fanciful glass dome sheltering tropical plants shouldn't seem creepy, but it did. Maybe I should have waited and come with Haylee and her mothers. Or Ashley. Even listening to Mona's chatter about her conquests, real and imaginary, might have been better than walking up the half-walled ramp and going backstage by myself.

Strange breezes and whisperings seemed to sway the red curtains surrounding the cubicles. Finding mine had been easy enough when the area had been crowded with people, but now the cubicles all looked alike. I went to approximately the right place and parted the curtains.

Not my clothes. I recognized the red dress and bulky blue sweater that Macey had worn, so I was close.

I pushed my way into the next cubicle, and there were my outfits, with the shoes lined up along the side curtains. I hung up the gown, set the high heels beside the gladiator sandals that went with the hideous Little Bo Peep dress, and turned to go.

Why was one of those bright white brief-cases in my cubicle?

10

I had carried a white cardboard briefcase only while I was on the runway, and then I'd passed it to another model. I had never brought one into my cubicle.

Maybe TADAM students had paired the briefcases with some of the Ambitious Attire outfits. They wouldn't have had enough to go around.

I peeked into Macey's cubicle. One of those shiny white briefcases was on a chair underneath that royal blue sweater. There was no briefcase in the cubicle next to Macey's, but one was in the cubicle on the other side of mine, and I spotted them in cubicles across the narrow aisle from Macey's and mine.

I returned to my cubicle. During the rehearsal and show, the cardboard briefcases had been slim and sleek, but this one bulged as if it had indulged in a little gluttony of its own.

I peeked inside. Food? Had I guessed right about the gluttony?

I gripped the crackly plastic package by one corner and pulled it out. The top had been sliced off neatly, and fat pastel candies that resembled beads threatened to spill out and bounce all over the floor — exactly what I did not need in this freakily almost-silent backstage.

Antonio must have had more candies than the stash he kept in his pocket. But the mints I'd seen on the podium and that Vicki and Gord had taken from Antonio's pockets had been white, almost perfect orbs. Most of the candies in this package were more elongated, and the candies near the top of the bag were mostly pale green, pink, and yellow. Maybe Antonio had sorted through the package and chosen only the most perfectly spherical white mints to eat first.

The label said *Jordan Almonds.* These were the traditional wedding almonds in sugary coatings. Antonio's breath had smelled minty. Mint-flavored wedding almonds?

Maybe these candies had belonged to someone else and they'd ended up in a briefcase that had somehow gotten into my cubicle. I shoved the package into the briefcase again.

Turning again to leave, I noticed that one of the tissues that I'd stuffed into the toes of the mud brown pumps was partway out, as if I'd dislodged it when I'd removed the shoe. I squatted and pulled it the rest of the way, then scrabbled in the toe of the other shoe and got that one, also.

I straightened the shoes. Something rattled in the one that had contained the loose tissue. I picked up the shoe and turned it over.

A vial fell out. I grabbed it before it rolled underneath the curtain into Macey's cubicle.

The prescription label had torn off the outside of the little vial, but the name of the medicine was clear.

It was one that people with severe allergies carried to prevent themselves from going into shock and dying from an allergic reaction.

Suddenly, it all fell into place. Antonio, popping candies from his jacket pocket into his mouth without looking. Antonio, turning red, clutching his throat, not his chest, and asking, "Where's my —" If Antonio had a severe almond allergy, and had accidentally eaten a candy-coated almond instead of a mint, he could have collapsed from shock, not from a heart attack.

But when Gord had asked Antonio's wife

about heart medication, wouldn't that have been the time to mention that he had allergies and maybe should be treated for a reaction?

Why hadn't she?

What if Antonio had been checking his pockets for his medication, and hadn't found it there, and neither had Vicki and Gord?

I bit the back of my hand. Last night when I'd left the stage after the awards ceremony, I had kicked something that had been under the chair where Antonio's jacket had been hanging. It had rolled beneath the red curtains of the curtained-off cubicle where the briefcases had been stored. I had assumed it was one of Antonio's mints.

And it may have been. But it had sounded very much like this little vial had when it rolled away from me just now.

By not seeking out what I'd kicked last night and asking who had lost it, I may have contributed to the seriousness of Antonio's collapse.

The ambulance had taken him to the hospital in time, hadn't it? And he'd be fine, wouldn't he?

And then, wouldn't he ask if someone had hidden his medication? Maybe it had fallen out of his jacket one of the many times his jacket was knocked off the chair. Still, he might wonder how he had, if he'd known better, eaten an almond. Had someone slipped a Jordan almond or two into his pocket and hidden his medication underneath the chair in hopes he'd suffer a severe reaction? Nearly everyone in the fashion show had touched that jacket, partly because we'd all bumbled into the chair, knocked the jacket off, and hung it up again.

Had someone tried to kill Antonio? They couldn't have known when he would eat the almond, but they may have been sure he would eat it, eventually.

And they didn't plan to be near him when he did.

I felt the blood drain from my head. After they set him up for a possibly deadly allergic reaction, had they returned to the conservatory and placed the incriminating objects among my things?

I could phone Vicki and ask her to come see the almonds and the medicine. I could tell her my theories.

I shook myself out of my wild imagining. I was tired and cranky, not only from lack of sleep but because of the annoyances of the rehearsal, the show, the reception, and its aftermath.

Vicki would undoubtedly tell me I was

making up scenarios that didn't exist. No one had tried to kill Antonio. He would live. No one had tried to implicate me in an attack on him, either.

Maybe I should throw out the package of Jordan almonds and the vial I still clutched. Maybe the vial was empty. I couldn't tell from its weight and couldn't hear liquid slosh when I shook it next to my ear. I should probably forget all about it.

Voices and footsteps clattered in the part of the conservatory where the runway was. Chairs banged together. A male voice called, "I'll go see if I can figure out how to take down the cubicles." I heard someone leap up onto the stage.

Maybe the man was coming to retrieve the candies and medicine vial, empty or not.

With quick, jerky motions, I tucked the vial where I'd found it and stuffed the tissues back into the shoes.

I rose and stuck my head out between the curtains. No one was near. As if I were an escaping criminal, I tiptoed out of the backstage and down the ramp leading toward the outer doors.

I didn't see anyone inside the conservatory, but in the main room, chairs were being slammed around by laughing, shouting people. TADAM students? I glanced over my shoulder as I pressed the door open. I didn't see anyone.

No one was outside the conservatory, either.

But I again felt like I was being watched, which wasn't surprising near a glass building.

I hurried to In Stitches and went inside in time to open the shop for Ashley, who worked with me on weekends and usually arrived early.

White-faced, she opened the shop door and stopped, trembling, on the threshold.

11

I rushed to the door, pulled Ashley into the shop, and asked, "Is something wrong?"

Ashley brushed hair from her face. "I just heard on the radio that the director of TADAM died on the way to the hospital last night. Do the police think that Macey or I had anything to do with his death? We didn't, you know."

I grabbed at the top of a sewing machine to steady myself. "Of course you didn't. And Edna's mother and I didn't slug him, either, as much as we might have wanted to. Gord guessed that Antonio had a heart attack." And maybe Gord had been right.

And those almonds . . . ?

"Do you think Chief Smallwood believed Macey and me when we said we didn't do anything except push his hand away?"

"Yes. And you had every right to push his hand away." I didn't tell her my possibly wild conjectures about the almonds and the allergy medication. "Did they say what caused his death?"

"Only that he'd collapsed at the fashion academy he'd recently opened and had succumbed on the way to the hospital."

Maybe my guesses weren't that far off. I would have to tell Vicki about the candy and medicine vial I'd seen in my cubicle, and about how they could be connected to Antonio's death.

But Vicki had been out late last night and probably wasn't on duty this morning. As usual when she was off duty, a state police trooper would be available. I could call the state police.

Explaining it all to Vicki, who had seen Antonio and the rest of us last night, would be easier. I decided to wait until afternoon or early evening, when Vicki should be on duty.

Ashley looked at me with hope in her eyes. "So do you think it's okay if we take that course?"

Busily arguing with myself, I hadn't a clue what she was talking about. "What course?"

"A night school course at TADAM. Remember, they gave us vouchers for a discount? And it's a big discount. My dad says I can take the course if you do. But I don't know if the school is going to continue now that Antonio's . . ." She gulped. "Gone. Who will run TADAM?"

His wife? Or Loretta, the assistant director?

Maybe no one. TADAM would close its doors, and Loretta would move very far away. That would be perfect.

Well, almost. I had to consider Ashley and her need to go to school here in Threadville. "It wouldn't hurt to find out if they're still planning to give that course." I wasn't very enthusiastic.

Ashley fished an envelope from her backpack and took her voucher out. "There's to be a free introductory session on Monday night — that's tomorrow — and if we like it, we can sign up for classes that will be held every Monday night for six weeks! Wouldn't that be awesome? To help me decide if I really want to go there next fall?"

"Won't you have homework Monday nights?"

"I'll get it done."

She would, too. And I didn't want to tell Ashley my other reason for attending the introductory course the next night — I would welcome a chance to learn more about Antonio, his wife, and the staff and students at TADAM. Had one of them hated him enough to kill him? If so, whoever it was had gone to great lengths to make Antonio's death look accidental, and then in case that didn't work, the killer — the *alleged* killer — had planted clues that would point to someone else.

Me.

There was a problem with the alleged killer's strategy, though. I hadn't met Antonio until a few weeks ago, and I had not known of any allergies he might have had.

But how would I prove that? I'd been alone in my shop with him when he gave me the drawings and instructions for the outfits he'd wanted me to make. And I often served cookies with nuts in them, including almonds, to visitors to In Stitches. Anyone could say that I'd offered him one, and that he'd turned it down and had told me why.

Who would have known what his allergies were?

His widow.

Had Paula returned from the hospital in time to rearrange evidence backstage before I arrived there this morning?

Although I wanted nothing more to do with the Threadville Academy of Design and Modeling, I told Ashley, "I'll go with you to the introductory class tomorrow night."

Ashley's eyes shined. "Thanks, Willow! I was just reading the fine print. They say the class will be canceled if not enough people sign up for it, so let's make sure that they do!"

She designed and printed posters about the course and the sample class, then went off to deliver them to the other Threadville shops.

On Sundays, we didn't give workshops. The people who rode the tour buses wouldn't be in Threadville until Tuesday, so they wouldn't see Ashley's posters until after Monday's free class, but after Ashley returned, the store filled with customers, and we had many opportunities to demonstrate our sewing machines, their embroidery attachments, and some of the amazing things we could do with them.

Ashley was not only a talented embroiderer; her enthusiasm was contagious. People often came to In Stitches to buy a simple sewing machine and left later, quite happily, with a model that would do much more than they'd dreamed.

Although I waited until I thought Vicki would be on duty, my call was forwarded to the state police. I explained that I'd seen evidence that someone may have tried to harm Antonio. The dispatcher said an officer would drop by.

A half hour later, a state police cruiser

parked in front of In Stitches. I asked Ashley to look after the shop and teased her about her worried expression at the sight of the cruiser. "You'll get wrinkles before you're twenty."

She smiled.

I went on, "I need to show him something I saw at the conservatory this morning, if it's still there. It may have something to do with Antonio's death."

A dimple showed as her smile widened. "Stop frowning," she warned me, "or *you'll* be the one getting the wrinkles."

"Not before I'm twenty!" But I did stop frowning and went out to the porch to meet the trooper, a young guy I'd never seen before. I asked him, "Shall I meet you at the Elderberry Bay Conservatory?"

"How about telling me what you want me to see?"

Since I was taller than he was and didn't want to loom over him, I suggested we sit in the comfy rockers on my porch. He perched on the edge of the seat, rocked forward, and planted his police boots firmly on the plank floor.

I told him what I'd found backstage at the conservatory and why I thought it might be important. "The things I saw may have been removed since this morning. And besides, they may have nothing to do with the death of the man who was eating mints most of the evening."

The trooper closed the notebook and shot me a half-friendly smile. "Probably not, but I'll check it out."

"Want me to come along? My assistant can look after the store."

"No need. You've told me where to find the things. That conservatory should be open right now, but if it isn't, I'll call someone to let me in." He thanked me and returned to his cruiser.

I was disappointed. For one thing, I'd have liked a ride in the shiny and powerful car, if he'd offered one. Mostly, though, I wanted to point him exactly to what I'd seen that morning. If the cubicles were still set up, he might go into the wrong one and decide there was no evidence.

Also, I'd have liked to do a little more surreptitious sleuthing myself.

Maybe Vicki wouldn't have taken me with her, either, but I'd have had a better chance of learning what happened from her than from a state trooper.

Inside In Stitches, Ashley was bagging purchases and telling three more customers about the next evening's introductory class at TADAM.

By the time we closed In Stitches for the evening, Ashley had sold three sewing machines, two embroidery attachments, and some very sophisticated software. I'd already increased her hourly rate. Now I increased her commission percentage, too.

On her way out the door, she interrupted her thanks to say, "Don't forget about the course tomorrow night."

"I'll walk you there. And home afterward, too."

"Thanks! My folks will let me go, then, at least to the free class."

I locked the shop and went downstairs, where my pets did their best to distract me.

I hadn't heard from Clay.

That wasn't unusual, but Dora had told me he'd been looking for me after he walked her home. Later, he hadn't called to ask where I'd been and whether I'd made it safely to my apartment.

That wasn't like him.

Even more unusual, I hadn't heard from Haylee since last night, right after she'd been evasive about where Clay had been when Antonio collapsed.

12

Haylee had appeared uncomfortable when she told me that Clay had left the mansion. Maybe she'd noticed him with Loretta, and she hadn't wanted to tell me.

Later, I'd seen Loretta and Clay together in the carriage house. Not only together, I reminded myself. Hugging each other.

Usually, Haylee and I talked to each other at least once a day.

I took all four pets out, then ushered the cats inside. Sitting on my picnic table with my feet on the bench, I watched Sally and Tally play and explore. In many ways, I envied those two dogs for their happy, uncomplicated lives.

Half surprised that Dora didn't come out of Blueberry Cottage to chat, I called my dogs and we went inside. I fed my pets and told them, "When the going gets tough, the tough go shopping."

No response from the dining animals.

"For fabric," I prompted them.

Still no response. Obviously, fabric stores excited me more than they excited my funny little animals. I phoned Haylee and asked if I could visit her shop.

Of course she said yes.

I went upstairs, let myself out of In Stitches, and ran across the street to The Stash.

It was only mid-September, and lots of people must not have decided yet what costumes to make for Halloween. Haylee had filled tables near the front of her store with Halloween fabrics.

Mutely, I stared at them. Colors and patterns jumbled together.

Haylee asked, "Do you need anything in particular?"

Haylee was my best friend, but suddenly, I didn't know how to tell her about Loretta and Clay.

"Willow?"

Running my hand down glossy black fabric embellished with metallic gold spiders and their webs, I blurted, "Clay has found someone else."

I didn't look at Haylee, but her silence said everything.

I stroked the golden filaments on the cloth in front of me. "You knew, didn't you?"

She cleared her throat. "I don't *know* anything like that. Besides, I doubt that you're right."

"You could sound more convinced."

"Clay likes you, Willow. He wouldn't suddenly change his mind."

Still without looking at Haylee, I moved down the row to dancing skeletons embossed on velvet, soft underneath my fingers. "You saw him with her, didn't you?"

"Who?"

"Loretta from TADAM. When Ben was trying to revive Antonio, I asked you where Clay was and you avoided answering."

"I did see them together, but I didn't think it meant anything. She barged into the kitchen when Antonio was telling Clay how much better his contractor had done than Clay could have — as if! Loretta stared at Clay for a few seconds, and then she very dramatically asked him if he was Clay Fraser. When he said he was, she threw herself at him and claimed she recognized him from fourth grade. You know Clay. He never wants to hurt anyone. I didn't think he remembered her, but he disentangled himself and they talked for a while, then they went out the back door together, and I didn't see either of them again. What makes you think he's fallen for her? He seemed to be politely attempting to ditch her so he could return to you."

"But he didn't." Finally, I raised my head.

Her mouth was a small o. "He didn't? What happened after Ben and I left?"

"I . . . I saw them. Together. They were in the carriage house, and they were hugging each other. Then she took him by the hand and pulled him back to the mansion. Dora and I were in the kitchen when they came in. Loretta explained that Clay had been her first love, and he said that they'd been discussing ways of turning the carriage house into an apartment. Probably a love nest for the two of them." I meant it as a joke. Clay had built himself a large home on acres in the country.

Haylee laughed at my rather flat attempt at humor, but it wasn't exactly a hearty laugh. "What did Clay have to say about that?"

"Not much. They must have been out there together at least forty-five minutes."

"Huh . . ." It was more like a sigh than a word, almost a resigned belief that Clay had fallen for Loretta.

I immediately leaped into denial mode and tried to give Clay the benefit of the doubt. "He did seem to want to get away from her. He said he'd walk the rest of us home, but Loretta wanted him to stay behind and help her lock the mansion."

"And he did?"

"No. Vicki had Antonio's keys. She said she'd help Loretta, instead." I grinned at the memory of Vicki's adept treatment of Loretta. "So Loretta had to stay with Vicki, who sent the rest of us, including Clay, away."

"Good for Vicki! What did Clay say after that?"

"I don't know. I went ahead with Ashley, Macey, and Macey's roommate, Samantha. Dora made Clay walk with her. Then Dora must have dragged her feet on purpose. Clay couldn't catch up with us."

"So, knowing Clay, he escorted Dora all the way to Blueberry Cottage, and by then you were outside with your pets, and you had a chance to talk to him."

I looked down at my feet. "I stayed out of sight until he was gone."

"Willow!" Haylee wasn't easily scandalized.

"Loretta's lipstick was smeared, and Clay had a red smudge of it on his shirt."

Haylee's face froze for a second before she pointed out, "She was all over him! He didn't reciprocate."

Not when anyone else was watching. "She

made certain that everyone noticed the lipstick, too. She apologized for getting lipstick on his shirt. She offered to remove the stains."

"Nothing like putting a man on the spot for the spots on his shirt."

I gave her a weak smile. "I guess it is a little funny."

"What did he do, tear off his shirt right then and there and hand it to her?"

"No. He went all stony and said *he* could take out the stains."

"Aha. He obviously wasn't falling for it. Or for her."

I balled embossed velvet into one fist. "I suppose there's hope."

"There is. Talk to him."

"Don't they say that if you want something, you have to let it go?" I didn't sound very sure of myself.

"That doesn't seem to be Loretta's method."

"Meow!" I let go of the velvet. Fortunately, I hadn't creased it, much. Something like excitement shining from Haylee's eyes caught my attention. I asked, "What happened between you and Ben?"

"Nothing. He walked me home."

I clapped my hands. "Great."

She shrugged. "He's a gentleman. He

didn't even touch me. But get this. He said he'd see me at firefighting practice Tuesday evening and when we reconvene at the pub like we always do. It's a start, I guess, for him, actually mentioning that we'd all go out together afterward."

"It's almost a date!"

"Oh puh-leeze. Clay will also be there on Tuesday for practice and at the pub. The four of us always have fun together. You and Clay will be back where you were before that woman intervened."

Maybe the best thing would be to pretend, at least around Clay, that I hadn't seen him with his arms around Loretta. I changed the subject. "Meanwhile, want to go to the free introductory fashion design class at TADAM tomorrow evening? Ashley and I are going."

"I heard about Antonio's death. Too bad. He wasn't old. But I didn't think much of TADAM. Do we have to return there, even for a class?"

"After Antonio collapsed, his wife accused Dora and me of murdering him. But he wasn't dead. And she was cagey about whether or not he had heart trouble." I told Haylee about the candy and allergy medicine that someone may have planted in my cubicle that morning. "But the state trooper didn't seem impressed by my deductions."

"Vicki probably wouldn't have been, either. She thinks we make things up so we can investigate."

"Still, I wonder if Paula, who would have known if Antonio was allergic to almonds, slipped him some, and also hid his allergy medication."

"Loretta did it!"

I wanted to believe that and wanted to hope that Loretta would be jailed for murder. But if Antonio had been intentionally harmed, we needed to look at every suspect, not only at people we wished would vanish from Threadville. "Maybe that dissatisfied-looking man in the muscle shirt arranged things so that Antonio would go into shock and maybe die."

"Dissatisfied?" Haylee repeated. "He looked just plain mean."

"Who wouldn't, around the rest of that crew?" I told her about seeing him outside the conservatory shortly after I'd seen a light moving inside it and had noticed an open door that, last we'd known, had been locked. "I'd seen Loretta go into what I think is her apartment building a few minutes earlier. Then, when I went back with the dogs later, the conservatory was locked again."

Haylee suggested, "Maybe Paula, Loretta, or Muscle Shirt hid the evidence right after the fashion show, and before the reception."

"Muscle Shirt and Paula were already at the reception when we got there." I frowned. "And Loretta beat us there, too, even though she locked the conservatory behind us. I'd only just left my cubicle when she caught up to us at the main door. To have hidden things in my cubicle before she joined us, she'd have had to have been quick."

Haylee raised an eyebrow. "She's a fast worker, all right."

I laughed. "Who wouldn't be, around Clay?"

"You."

I raised my shoulders in a helpless shrug. "I'll work faster, if I get another chance."

"You will. Wasn't Loretta supposed to open the conservatory this morning at nine? She could have gone early and moved the evidence around."

I stroked orange fleece printed with smiling yellow pumpkins. "Could be. I didn't arrive at nine on the dot, and the door was already open. At first, I didn't see or hear anyone. Then people — TADAM students, probably — started moving chairs in the main room."

"Maybe Paula was the one with the flashlight in the unlocked conservatory. Vicki offered to drive both Gord and Paula home from the hospital last night, if Paula was ready to go when Gord was. Let's find out what Edna may have learned from Gord about if and when Paula returned."

We left The Stash. I'd be back soon, no doubt, to touch all the wools, corduroys, and flannels that Haylee had stocked for winter sewing.

Beyond Opal's yarn store, Edna's shop, Buttons and Bows, had closed for the evening, but it was still unlocked, and we let ourselves in. Edna sold almost every type of button and trim imaginable. The front room of Buttons and Bows was narrow, with buttons lining the wall, floor to ceiling, on the left side of the aisle, and ribbons, lace, fringe, and trims lining the right side of the shop. Edna kept things in almost rainbow order, but many of her notions were gold, silver, or sparkled like diamonds, and had to be displayed outside the spectrum.

It was a beautiful sight.

Edna must have heard her door chimes jingle their "Buttons and Beaux" tune. She called to us from her back room. It was wider than the front room, with tables holding shallow bins of beads, sequins, crystals, and notions like bias tape and various types of fasteners. Edna held up a deep red zipper with crystal teeth like rubies. "Isn't this lovely?"

We agreed that it was. After admiring the latest in wooden beads shaped like baby animals, I asked her, "Did Vicki bring Gord home last night?"

Edna blushed. "Yes, he arrived around one thirty this morning, the poor dear, and told me what had happened to Antonio."

Oops. One thirty was about the time I'd been wandering around the village with the dogs. I hoped that Vicki hadn't spotted us prowling around. I hadn't seen her, but Vicki often noticed more than I wanted her to and may have seen us.

I asked Edna, "Do you know if Vicki also drove Antonio's wife, I mean widow, home at the same time?"

Edna bobbed her head up and down. "She did. Gord had to sit in the backseat, which, he said, is cramped. The widow sobbed all the way back from Erie, and Vicki actually asked Gord if he carried sedatives with him. Gord told me that he thought the sobbing really irritated our calm and collected police chief."

Haylee asked, "And did Gord have sedatives, Edna?"

"He's not a walking pharmacy. Besides, as far as he knew, he was only going to a fashion show and a reception." Edna picked up a handful of tiny white pearl beads and let them flow like water between her fingers and back into their bin. Slowly, as if words were hard to find, she said, "I shouldn't pass along gossip, but . . . being a doctor and assisting the coroner, Gord has seen his share of grief and crying over the years. He thought Paula was faking it."

I asked, "Did Gord tell Vicki that?"

Edna raised her chin. "He couldn't, with the grieving widow right there. Vicki brought Gord home first, and I don't think he's talked to Vicki since."

However, after I told Edna about the candy-coated almonds and the medication vial missing its prescription label, she came up with the same idea I'd had. "Someone could have tucked an almond into Antonio's pocket and hidden his allergy medicine to try to kill him, and then planted those things in your cubicle. I'll ask Gord to talk to Vicki about the *grieving* of the new widow."

We told Edna we were going to the next night's free introductory class and asked if she planned to attend.

"I do now, after what you've told me. We

should all go."

I walked with Haylee back to The Stash. As we parted, Haylee said, "Stop fretting about Clay and Loretta. She won't get her claws into him."

"There's no point in worrying." I was proud of what I thought was a nonchalant tone.

"But you will, anyway."

She was probably right.

13

Mondays, the Threadville shops weren't open. I took my animals outside, fed them, baked cookies to serve in the shop during the week, fulfilled orders for embroidery designs, planned the week's classes, and worked on a jacket I was making for myself. Red, with petite ruffles and touches of embroidery around the hem and cuffs, the jacket would look great with jeans or a skirt during cool autumn days.

After supper, the phone rang.

Clay calling, finally?

It was Ashley. "Are you still going to the class at TADAM?"

"Wouldn't miss it."

"We should go early in case it gets crowded."

I had to smile. Last I knew she was afraid that the course would be canceled due to lack of interest.

But now she had another concern. "I hope

the class won't go on too long. If it does, I'll have to leave early to pick up my sister from band practice. They're rehearsing at the conservatory. They're having a concert there next week."

"The conservatory is open today?"

"It's not usually open on Mondays, but the band teacher told the kids he'd have the key."

Maybe yesterday's state trooper hadn't been excited enough about my "evidence" to close the conservatory as a potential crime scene. If I helped pick up Ashley's sister, I would have another chance to snoop backstage. I told Ashley, "I'll come, too, even if we have to leave the class early."

"They'll call *that* a threadly sin, too!"

Apparently, she'd recovered from the insult that Antonio had thrown at her.

After my pets were safely inside following another outing, I put on a deep green blazer that I'd made and embellished with tiny embroidered fall leaves, went out to my patio, and locked the sliding glass doors.

Purse in hand, Dora stood on the back porch of Blueberry Cottage.

"Yoo-hoo!" she called. "Are you going to that fashion design course tonight? I'll walk with you!" She marched to my patio. "Did you confront Clay about That Woman yet?"

Escorting her up the hill to my front yard, I suggested, "I'm not sure that confronting a man about another woman is a great ploy, unless one wants to alienate the man."

"As long as you're *happy.*"

"There's not much I can do if he's fallen for her."

"Encourage him to fall for you, instead. You could have tried harder."

I tried to sound indifferent. "It may be too late."

"You give up too easily."

Haylee hadn't thought that Clay seemed interested in Loretta, but Haylee hadn't seen the embrace and the lipstick. Maybe an upbeat approach would get Dora off my case. "Who knows? Next time I see him, Clay and I may be back to normal."

"He's special. Look at the job he did on Blueberry Cottage before I moved in."

Laughing, I opened the gate. "It's no wonder you like it, since most of the ideas were yours."

She pointed to the front porch of In Stitches, then across the street to the other Threadville shops. "And he did all of these renovations, too, and don't forget the Elderberry Bay Lodge. Clay helped Ben restore it to its Victorian glory." She barely took a breath before adding, "I wonder where

Edna and the others are. What if the class fills up? They'll miss it."

"I left early to pick up Ashley. Mind going the long way around, or do you want to wait for Edna and the others?"

"I'll come with you."

Looking happier than she had recently, Ashley joined us near her front walk. "My dad's lined up a couple of good job interviews," she told us. She chattered about the potential jobs, neither of which would require moving away, until we turned the corner to the TADAM mansion.

The Threadville tour bus from Erie was parked outside it.

I stopped walking. "I wonder how they found out about the introductory course."

A dimple showed in Ashley's cheek. "I may have made a few phone calls."

"I hope Haylee, Edna, Naomi, and Opal arrive in time to get in." Dora's voice was dark with foreboding.

Inside the mansion, the room where Antonio had collapsed was set up as a classroom, with rows of chairs facing a long table, an easel, and a voluptuous dressmaker's dummy with an impossibly small waistline.

Someone had written *Welcome to TADAM* in fancy, curlicued script on the newsprint

150

pad on the easel.

Dora needn't have worried about Edna, Haylee, Opal, and Naomi. They were sitting near the back of the crowded room.

I muttered to Ashley, "I think you drummed up enough business."

Laughing at the dummy's unreal proportions, she threw me a smile. "We know just about everyone here, don't we?"

It seemed that all of Threadville plus a busload of our usual tourists had come to the introductory fashion design class. Greeting those nearest us, we sat down.

Loud footsteps sounded from the foyer, and then Loretta came swooping into the room in a stylish but impractical purple cloak. She wore it over tight black suede short shorts, turquoise tights, high yellow suede boots with an allover pattern of cutouts showing off the tights, a formfitting black tank top, and possibly the world's widest belt, in purple leather with cutouts matching the pattern on the boots. She stopped and posed, her face and body both expressing extreme, fake-looking amazement. "Wow! I didn't expect such a turnout." Her cloak swishing and her heels hammering the rock maple floor, she marched to the front of the classroom.

Beside me, Dora muttered, "I didn't

expect her *turnout,* either. What superhero does she think she is, Super-Designer?"

I had to suppress a fit of giggles, and the people around us laughed, too. The woman in front of Dora turned around and gave her a high five.

"Tough crowd," Ashley whispered. But she was still smiling, obviously eager to begin her education in fashion design. She'd been doodling in her notebook and had copied the *Welcome to TADAM* page perfectly, every curlicue in place.

Dora murmured to me, "I hope your young man sees her in *that* getup."

I grinned and shook my head. In my opinion, Loretta looked better than I had last night in my Little Bo Peep dress. And after he saw me wearing that, Clay had come inside with a smudge of Loretta's lipstick on his shirt. I hoped he wouldn't see her in those snug shorts and tank top. He might appreciate them more than this all-female crowd seemed to.

I was sure she had designed the dramatic outfit herself. I wasn't being catty, of course, but I thought the combination made her resemble a superhero wearing a wrestler's trophy belt.

Someone slipped into the chair behind me and touched my shoulder in greeting. I glanced back. Our police chief, Vicki Small-wood, who always professed to know nothing about sewing, was attending a fashion design course? Instead of her uniform, she wore jeans, a white shirt, and a camel blazer. For once, her blond hair wasn't tied back in a ponytail but fell in a neat bob to her shoulders. I gave her a thumbs-up and faced the front again.

Loretta had been staring toward us with an unreadable but not very friendly look on her face. However, she welcomed us all. Wiping her eyes and swallowing hard, she made a speech about how much everyone at TADAM would miss Antonio. She offered her condolences to his family.

Paula did not seem to be in the mansion's former dining room.

Bravely straightening her shoulders and raising her chin, Loretta announced, "Tonight, Kent Quarrop and I, who are teachers here at the Threadville Academy of Design and Modeling, will give you a preview of the night school course we'll be offering the public this semester, Design 101. Kent and I have very different approaches to design, both highly successful. I'll let him tell you about his after I finish my demonstration." She flashed a smile at us. "But first, let me explain a little about

Saturday night's fashion show."

Her face took on a mask of tragedy. "I'll let you in on a little secret about Antonio, TADAM's late director."

Everyone in the room seemed to stop breathing. I leaned forward.

Loretta lowered her voice. "Antonio did his best to foster creativity, and one of the many ways he did it was by tricking his students into digging deep and coming up with ideas that were so original that his students often surprised themselves. He would give an assignment that sounded straightforward, and then award the highest marks to people who had *not* followed his instructions." Her mouth twitched in another smile. "The students tended to catch on quickly."

Dora cleared her throat, quietly for her.

I grumbled silently to myself about Loretta's latest defense of Antonio's actions. The Threadville store owners had *not* been his students when he gave us sketches and instructions about the outfits he wanted us to model in his fashion show. We'd been trying to help him by doing exactly what he'd asked, even when, as in my case, we didn't like the designs he had proposed.

It had been a trick, all right, but I doubted that he'd been trying to foster creativity. All

154

of us were good at coming up with original designs.

Unless I was mistaken, Antonio had wanted attention. Maybe he thought of himself as a budding stand-up comic and had used us as the butt of his questionable jokes. I remembered Loretta's anger at him on Saturday night, and how, only a few minutes later, she had tried to spin what he'd done into something commendable. Now she'd come up with a possibly more praiseworthy reason for Antonio's behavior. Was she trying to make us forget her original display of anger?

I didn't buy Loretta's explanation. Worse, I suspected that honesty was not high on the list of traits she valued in herself. Maybe she lied frequently, like maybe about knowing Clay in fourth grade. She could have merely recognized him as the area's most well-known contractor and then made up that first-love story to quickly get close to him.

I didn't need to ask myself why she, or any woman, would want to do that. All she had to do was look into his warm, brown eyes. I stifled a sigh.

But what if she had placed those candies in Antonio's pocket and wanted to be with someone else when they took effect, and

Clay was her chosen, handy, and very tempting alibi?

Loretta grabbed a marker, turned with a theatrical swirl of her cloak, and ripped the top page of newsprint from the easel. "My design technique begins with sketches." On the next page, she quickly drew the lines of a simple, slinky dress with a cowl neckline. "Based on my sketches and the size I want the finished dress to be, I draft a pattern. I know the measurements that go along with the size I'm creating, and with the complicated techniques that I've developed, I create a pattern. In Design 101, we'll keep things simple, and we'll all work on drafting a pattern for a dress similar to the one I've sketched."

Dora harrumphed again. "How *original.*"

Behind me, Vicki muttered, "I'll be original, too, and design cargo pants and a bulletproof vest."

I turned and wagged my finger at her and her oh-so-angelic smile.

Bent over her notebook, Ashley scribbled a sketch identical to Loretta's, and then she drew several similar dresses, with sleeve, pocket, and neckline variations. Ashley could go far with design, but would TADAM offer her enough good, solid training?

Carrying a bolt of satiny silver fabric, Muscle Shirt swaggered in from the kitchen. He plunked the bolt on the long table.

Loretta smiled at him. "This will be the first time Kent sees the sketch I made, and I haven't told him what I was going to sketch. He will show you the technique *he* uses to construct the garment I've sketched."

She maneuvered one shapely, pale arm from inside the cloak and gestured toward her sketch. "Ta-da!"

Kent, aka Muscle Shirt, stared at the sketch for a moment. Did the man never smile? Or speak? Without saying a word, he unrolled a length of fabric from the bolt and pinned part of one end of it to the overly curvaceous dummy. Then he took the longest dressmaker's shears I'd ever seen and slashed at the fabric. A few minutes of pinning, a few more of slashing, and he tossed four pieces of fabric, two for the front and two for the back, into the lap of a woman in the front row.

"Here," he said. Apparently, he *could* speak. "Sew the front and back seams, insert a zipper, narrow-hem the sleeve and neck edges, sew the sides up, and hem the bottom. Shouldn't take you much longer to stitch it together than it took me to cut it out."

We all applauded. People chattered.

Ashley giggled. "I don't think that any real person is built like that dummy."

"Mannequin," Dora corrected her with a glint of mischief in her brown eyes. "And I was watching him. He left lots of extra fabric at the waist."

The woman in front of me turned around. "If he'd thrown those pieces to me, Willow, I would add some machine embroidery."

I smiled and nodded. "Me, too."

A woman's voice rang out over all the others. "What is going on here?"

14

Her limp brown hair uncombed and her eyes puffy and red, Paula stood in the doorway leading to the kitchen. "This is a house of mourning! Get out!" The old maroon bathrobe she'd thrown over threadbare pajamas was many sizes too big for her. I guessed it had belonged to Antonio.

Feeling terrible for invading her privacy and grief, I stood up, as did most of the people around me.

"Whoa, whoa, whoa!" Loretta shouted. "Everybody stay put." Cloak flying, she twirled toward Paula. "This is a class that your late husband planned. We are carrying out his wishes."

With one hand, Paula grasped the bathrobe's lapels near her throat. "Can't you give a grieving widow some space in her own home?"

Kent stepped forward. "This building belongs to the Threadville Academy of

Design and Modeling. And the shareholders are . . ." He folded his arms like he was considering waiting all night for an answer.

"Antonio," Paula retorted. "And only Antonio. I'm his heir, so I own TADAM and this building. This is my home. Get out."

Behind me, I wasn't surprised to hear Vicki's voice. "I'm Vicki Smallwood, Elderberry Bay's police chief. Maybe I can help you sort this out." She didn't say it threateningly. A tone of kindness wrapped around the steel that was always at the core of her voice.

Paula stared at her, and then at the rest of us near her. "You! You haven't arrested those two women for their fatal attack on Antonio. They're in front of you, making a mockery of you and the law. Out!" She made a violent shooing motion. "All of you, out!"

"Wait," Loretta hollered. "Before you go, there's a sign-up sheet in the foyer for the rest of the Design 101 course. Many of you have vouchers for it that will save you a bundle. And if you don't sign up here tonight, you can do so on our website."

Apparently, Loretta wasn't planning to simply walk out of TADAM just yet.

She beckoned to Vicki. "And as a citizen of this village and an employee of TADAM,

160

I am requesting that the police chief come up here and mediate."

Kent bent one arm at the elbow, raising one hand above shoulder level in a lazy motion like he was voting with Loretta. "I agree. Maybe *you* can talk some sense into this woman, Chief."

Vicki sharpened the steel in her voice. "You three, let's reconvene your discussion in the kitchen." She made her way to the front of the room. "Everyone else, class is dismissed."

People in the audience gathered purses, notebooks, and phones. I sidestepped out of my row between chairs.

Paula yelled at Vicki to go away and, on her way out, to arrest Dora and me for murdering her husband.

Would-be fashion students cast me sympathetic glances and patted my arm.

I was more determined than ever to attend the Design 101 course. Ashley wanted to be one of the first to put her name on the list, but I whispered, "Let's allow the others to sign up first." To make room for them all, I pulled her down the hallway almost all the way to the kitchen.

Dora, Haylee, Opal, Edna, and Naomi joined Ashley and me. None of us were eavesdropping. That's why we all stood still with looks of fierce concentration on our faces.

"You're not evicting me," Paula shrieked. "This is my home!"

Vicki said firmly, "No one's evicting anyone."

Loretta chimed in, "I don't want anyone interrupting our courses. TADAM's on pretty shaky financial ground as it is." The shaking must have been contagious. It had crept into Loretta's voice, along with what sounded like barely controlled rage. "Antonio expected many more tuition-paying students to enroll in the school, and he borrowed heavily to restore this building — and to add that lavish director's suite you live in."

Vicki asked calmly, "Who owns this building?"

Paula shouted, "I do. It was left to me by my late husband."

Loretta corrected her. "The bank owns the building."

Paula retorted, "Lenders don't own a building unless there's a foreclosure. Antonio owned it, and now I own it. And anyway, the loans were for renovating. There's no mortgage to foreclose on."

Kent's voice held a note of wonder mixed with sarcasm. "Then the building itself must be collateral for the loan." He paused. No one said anything, and he continued. "Antonio told me that he and some silent partners owned TADAM, which of course owns this building. Antonio never mentioned anything about Paula inheriting even *his* share."

Paula muttered, "He never said a thing to me about any silent partners."

Vicki asked, "Paula, can you show me the deed to this mansion?"

"I don't know where Antonio put it."

Vicki said calmly, "I'll get someone to check with the land office. And they can find out whether TADAM is a corporation, a partnership, or a sole proprietorship, and who owns the school." Vicki's voice became louder, as if she'd turned her head toward us. "Okay, then how about you two, Kent and Loretta. Do you have legal papers showing you have the right to continue teaching in this building?"

"I have an employment contract," Loretta chimed. "In my apartment, a couple of blocks away. Kent lives in the same building. Do you have your contract, too, Kent?"

"Mine's in my safe deposit box in Erie," Kent answered. "I'll get it as soon as I can, but I teach classes here from ten to five tomorrow and the rest of the week."

Paula objected, "No, you don't."

Vicki heaved a sigh that was audible in the hallway. "Maybe none of you should use the TADAM mansion until after we find the answers to all of these questions. If the mansion is, as Paula says, in Antonio's name only, we'll have to wait until probate. If anyone questions the will, the courts can close this mansion for months or years, as long as it takes, and *no* one will be allowed to teach here or live here. Is that what you want?"

Silence.

Vicki wasn't done. "Each of you should consider hiring a law firm to represent your interests."

Paula gasped. "I can't afford that!"

Kent said, "Resolving the issue could still take years. And cost us a minor fortune."

Loretta's answer was terse. "Hiring lawyers is *not* an option."

Vicki said slowly, "Here's another possible solution, then. You can all agree right here and now that Paula can continue living in the apartment on the third floor, but only if Kent and Loretta continue operating the school as planned."

I could barely hear Kent's question. "How else do you propose to pay the bills, Paula? Taxes on the mansion, loan repayments, interest . . . If we stop teaching, the students will leave."

Paula sounded smug. "They've paid their tuition until June, and —"

Loretta cut her off. "They'll demand refunds."

"Well, they can't have them," Paula said, sounding less smug.

"Oh boy," Kent said. "Now you'll really need a lawyer."

"You're giving me no choice but to let you continue teaching here," Paula complained. "This is blackmail."

"How is it blackmail?" Vicki asked.

"Letting these people continue to come into my home and fill it with strangers." Paula's voice again, bitter. "You're making me pay for something that is legally mine."

"That's not exactly my definition of blackmail," Vicki said.

Paula stated again, "I own this school." She was sounding less sure.

Kent asked, "Don't you want your late husband's project to succeed?" His question might have placated her if he'd hidden his amusement.

Besides, he was heading toward emotional blackmail. Why didn't he and Loretta leave for more secure jobs? Maybe I was seeing the situation through my own selfish eyes. I didn't want Loretta to stay anywhere near Clay.

Vicki asked, "Paula, how did all those people get into the mansion tonight? I returned Antonio's keys to you, and you said you also had your own set. Did you leave the mansion unlocked, or did you let everyone in this evening?"

"I locked it, and I certainly did not let anyone in. I've been a basket case since Saturday night. I've mostly been sleeping."

Kent offered, "Loretta got here first and opened up."

Again it sounded like Vicki turned her head toward us. "*You* have keys, Loretta?"

"Of course." Loretta's answer was abrupt. "So does Kent. Antonio wanted us to be able to teach classes without him or Paula having to traipse all the way down from the third floor to let us in."

Vicki managed to sound puzzled, though knowing her, she wasn't. "But Loretta, on Saturday night, you didn't know how to lock up. You asked Clay Fraser to help. Then you let me use Antonio's keys to lock up while you watched. Why didn't you mention that you had keys then?"

Dora winked at me.

Loretta snapped, "I didn't have them with me."

166

Knowing that she'd be attending the reception in the TADAM mansion, she hadn't brought the mansion's keys with her that night. Maybe it made sense. TADAM students had been preparing the reception in the mansion when Loretta arrived, and she could have expected Antonio and Paula to lock themselves inside after everyone left.

"You had keys, Loretta, yet you didn't know how to lock the doors?" Vicki managed to make her question sound innocent.

"I didn't know every single step."

Right, Loretta would be totally helpless, especially when Clay was around.

Kent scoffed. "Insert key, turn key, remove key. Very difficult."

Fearing that my attempts not to laugh might be heard, I eased farther from the kitchen.

Hands over their mouths, Haylee, her mothers, and Dora tiptoed down the hall with me. Ashley scooted to the sign-up sheet and wrote her name. The rest of us signed up, too, but instead of leaving, we stood near the front door, even though at that distance, eavesdropping would be difficult.

We weren't given a chance. Vicki popped her head around the kitchen doorjamb. "You can leave now, folks."

Vicki and the state police communicated

about what went on in Threadville when Vicki was off duty. She should know that I'd told a state trooper about my suspicions regarding Antonio's death. She should also know that the people who knew Antonio best — his wife and his two employees — could have been the most likely people to have harmed him. And Vicki was proposing to remain in the mansion with those three people.

I made an exaggeratedly frightened face and raked one finger across my throat. "And leave you here alone with —"

Vicki's mouth twitched as if she were trying to hide her amusement. "I'll be fine, Willow," she said.

"There!" Dora announced. "We've all signed up for the course."

"Arrest them!" Paula yelled.

Haylee opened the front door. "I think that's our exit cue."

I hated leaving Vicki alone with three argumentative people, at least one of whom, I suspected, may have added candy-coated almonds to Antonio's stash of mints, and then hidden Antonio's medication from him in a deliberate attempt to murder the man. But even when not in uniform, Vicki usually had a radio and a weapon with her. And if any of the three adversaries had harmed

168

Antonio, he or she — or was it they? — would be foolish to attack Vicki. They might as well confess to having murdered Antonio.

Out on the front walk, Ashley checked her watch. "Perfect timing. I need to pick up my sister from band practice."

"Where?" Dora demanded.

Ashley pointed. "The conservatory."

"I'll come with you," Dora said. "Are you coming, Willow?"

"Yes."

Haylee cast an amused grin down at the woman she insisted on calling her grandmother. "I'll come, too."

15

Opal, Naomi, and Edna hurried down the sidewalk toward their shops. Most evenings, they convened in one of their apartments to work on handcrafts and sip wine. Gord sometimes joined them and was teased about his sewing ability. "Not sewing," he'd once corrected us while pretending to be miffed, "suturing."

Brandishing a clipboard, a teacher opened the conservatory door. "I see that you're picking up Isabella tonight, Ashley, but . . ." She peered at Dora, Haylee, and me. How could she see through the smudges on her glasses?

Ashley told her, "This is my boss and our friends. They're going to walk Isabella and me home. My dad didn't want us out alone at night."

The teacher held out the clipboard. "I'll need all four of you to sign in."

We did, then headed toward the conservatory's main room, where children were laughing and shouting. Apparently, band practice was over.

The runway was gone, and the only chairs in the vast space were arranged in concert band formation, not on the stage, but in front of it. The blue velvet stage curtains were closed.

Instruments in cases had been relegated to the sides of the glass-domed room, along with jackets, sweaters, and backpacks. A game of indoor soccer was going on in the middle of the conservatory's beautiful tile floor. The soccer "ball" was a wad of crumpled paper held together with rubber bands.

A miniature version of Ashley broke from the game and ran to Ashley. "Want to be goalie?"

Ashley only laughed. "It's time to go home." A few parents stood around watching the game and gossiping with a man I assumed was the band teacher. Other parents urged their kids toward the door.

Isabella begged, "Five more minutes?"

Ashley pointed to a trumpet case, a pink jacket, and a backpack that looked almost bigger than Isabella. "Now. Get your things."

I said quickly and quietly, "I'll go see if the TADAM students collected our garments from backstage."

Haylee said, "I'll help."

Dora must have recognized the conspiratorial expressions on our faces. She murmured, "I'll yell 'Thread!' if anyone follows you."

Haylee stopped. "Thread?"

"Can you think of something better?" She gave Haylee a shove. "Hurry."

Haylee and I climbed to the stage and pushed our way behind the blue velvet curtains. The area beyond the curtains was still lined in red-curtained dressing cubicles.

"I thought they were taking those down yesterday," Haylee said.

"So did I." I'd heard someone leap up onto the stage and say he was going to try to figure out how. Apparently, he hadn't succeeded.

We peeked inside cubicles. The clothing and shoes were still in them. When would the people who had bought the outfits receive them? Without Antonio, was nothing being done at TADAM besides teaching?

In my cubicle, I showed Haylee the briefcase with its odd bulge and the tissue-stuffed shoes. If the trooper I'd sent had seen the "evidence," he had neither taken it with him nor cordoned off the area to keep others out.

Haylee grinned. "We could move those things into the extra-large cubicle that Loretta was using as storage."

I let out an unladylike snort. "Not a good idea, since I told a trooper I'd seen them in my cubicle."

Out in the main room, Dora yelled, "Thread!"

Early yesterday morning, I had handled the candy package and the vial. Could I grab them, use one of the tissues to wipe away my fingerprints, and stuff the package and vial back where they'd been, before someone came and found us here?

A man asked, "Can I help you?" His voice was warm and polite, with no hint of suspicion in it.

We bumbled out between the polyester curtains. "We were in Saturday night's fashion show," Haylee explained. "We were checking to see if the garments were still here."

The man I'd guessed was the band teacher tilted his head. His eyes held a smile. "Are you the people who are supposed to clear out all this stuff? No big rush, but we'll need the stage before the concert on Friday."

I had finally recovered from being startled by his silent approach. "TADAM is supposed to take care of it."

The band teacher winced. "And their director died. No wonder there's a delay." He followed us to the stage.

Haylee swerved to the podium. "I think I left something here." She patted the shelf and pulled out a piece of paper. "I did." While I tried not to stare, she shoved the paper into her bag.

I backed away, gently poked my foot at one of the red curtains surrounding Loretta's storage area, and lifted the curtain an inch or two. I hoped to see one of Antonio's mints, which might mean I had kicked that, and not his medication, out of sight.

The part of the floor I could see was bare.

We rejoined Isabella, Ashley, and Dora. Isabella skipped to the main doors and won a race that the rest of us didn't know we'd entered. Ashley and Isabella led us out of the park along a pathway that took us past the back of the TADAM mansion. Trash cans, recycling bins, and old lumber and bricks were piled beyond the fence behind TADAM'S carriage house.

The path ended across the street from the apartment building that Macey, Samantha, and Loretta had entered. Early Sunday morning, Loretta could have been scooting back and forth using this shortcut while I was prowling around on sidewalks and steering clear of the sinister-looking TADAM mansion. Antonio had told us that Loretta would unlock the conservatory at nine yesterday. Maybe she had also unlocked it several hours earlier, and had wedged the door open. Maybe she and Kent had been inside the conservatory together, moving evidence that Antonio had been deliberately harmed into my cubicle. Or Loretta could have been planting the evidence while Kent kept a lookout.

On the other hand, Macey knew I'd stuffed tissues into the brown shoes, and she'd also been wandering around that night. Then again, maybe Loretta or Paula had seen Macey give me the tissues. Any of them could have gotten the idea of hiding the vial in a shoe and covering it with a tissue.

Haylee, Dora, and I escorted Ashley and Isabella safely to their front walk.

Ahead of us, two boys were kicking the paper soccer ball down the sidewalk. It rolled into the gutter. Leaving it there, the boys ran off.

Dora tsked. "Litterbugs." When we reached the ball, she scooped it up. Outside the post office, she was about to chuck it into the trash can.

I stopped her. "Who knows what might be in that ball? Maybe we'll find Antonio's fashion show script, along with a clue about who didn't like him."

"Ha," Dora said. "Who *did* like him? Besides, all you'd find would be fifty pages with nothing but the words 'lovely' and 'beautiful' on them."

I laughed. "You noticed that, too?"

Dora cupped a hand around her ear. "I'm not hard of hearing or of understanding."

Haylee patted her bag. "I'm dying to go where we can't be watched or heard so I can see if the page I found in the podium says anything besides 'lovely' and 'beautiful.' My place or yours?"

"Mine," Dora said. "Bring your dogs and cats, Willow."

We walked up Lake Street to my gate and down through the side yard.

By the time I ushered all four pets into Blueberry Cottage, Dora had a fire going in the fieldstone fireplace in the great room, and Haylee was boiling water for tea.

She stopped what she was doing, though, and with great drama, opened her bag and pulled out the sheet of paper she'd taken from the podium. "It's Antonio's list of seven threadly sins, along with our names.

Handwritten." She flipped the page over and slid it onto the table where Dora and I could see it. "Can you read what's written on the back?"

The printing was faint, as if the marker someone used had been nearly out of ink, and the letters were stringy and sheer in places, but the printing itself was forceful, and the message almost seemed to buzz with anger. I read aloud, " 'You won't get away with it.' "

Haylee asked, "Was that a warning *to* Antonio, or a warning *from* him that he didn't deliver?" She scrabbled in her bag. "Here's the slip Paula gave me with my name on it and the words *Ambitious Attire*. It looks like it was written by the person who wrote the list of seven threadly sins."

Dora checked the two pieces of paper. "Scrawled, you mean."

I bent to compare them. "The scrawls do look alike, and like the note I received telling me to wear *Distinguished Dressing* to the award ceremony. The scrawl also resembles Antonio's signature on the thank-you letter. But why would Antonio have written his list on the back of a warning, whether it was meant for him or someone else?"

Dora held the paper up to the light from the fire. "The warning's so pale you can't see it from the other side of the page. Maybe he thought he was writing the list on a blank sheet of paper."

"The printing on the warning doesn't look at all like Antonio's scrawl," I concluded. "So who printed the warning?"

Dora grunted. "That superhero female with the mess of auburn hair. She yelled at Antonio for accusing all of you of committing sins."

Haylee poured boiling water into the teapot. "If Loretta printed the welcome message on the easel, she probably did not print the warning. I'm not sure that Loretta can print without adding swirls or curls."

I thought back to the sketches that Antonio had given me, claiming he'd drawn them. "Someone printed instructions on the sketches that Antonio gave me for the outfits I was to make and model in the fashion show, and if I'm remembering the printing correctly, it was decorated with little flourishes. At the time, I believed him, but the printing of the instructions on those sketches was nothing like the scrawled list of threadly sins, and was a lot like the printing on that easel. Do you think that Loretta made the clothing design drawings, and Antonio was only pretending they were his?"

"Very likely," Haylee said.

Dora reminded us, "We didn't see who printed *Welcome to TADAM,* but we did watch Loretta draw the dress, and she printed a few words around the dress, here and there. With curlicues."

I guessed, "Maybe Paula wrote the warning, but would she print with anything like the bold flare of the warning? Despite the faintness of the worn-out marker, the warning looks like it was printed by an artistic, yet angry man."

"That pretty well describes Kent," Haylee said, as Dora and I nodded.

Sally-Forth and Tally-Ho sniffed at the paper ball on the coffee table, but cautiously, as if something might jump out of it. Mustache and Bow-Tie pawed at a basket of yarn between Dora's spinning wheel and her loom. I moved the basket to the top of one of the cabinets that Clay had built flanking the fireplace. Dora gave each cat a crocheted catnip mouse. After that, nothing in the cottage she rented from me was in danger from my cats, except their own dignity, but they didn't seem to mind.

Sally-Forth backed away from the paper ball and watched the cats roll around on the catnip mice. Tally-Ho galumphed up the stairs to the cottage's tiny second story, and thumped down again with a dog toy in his mouth. He deposited it in front of his sister, then ran upstairs again and came back with another toy, which he tossed around the living room. The cats continued their blissful and undignified rolling.

Dora set oatmeal cookies on a platter and poured the tea into pretty china cups — hers. I'd rented the cottage unfurnished except for Clay's many built-ins.

Clay. Everything reminded me of him. I was not going to think about him. I ate a cookie and sipped my tea.

We removed rubber bands from the ball. It unfurled into a heap of crumpled paper. The kids had outdone themselves collecting paper from, it appeared, their backpacks and the conservatory's recycling bins. Flyers advertising fertilizer and watering systems had been wadded with arithmetic worksheets and drawings of animals and autumn leaves. Kids had written notes to each other. *Zack likes you,* one said.

I felt almost nostalgic until I thought of Clay and Loretta in fourth grade. Back then, had someone written, *Loretta likes you?* And maybe Loretta had received notes saying *Clay likes you.* And maybe it had been true.

Maybe it was still true. Or about to be true.

Stop it, Willow.

Haylee was staring at me as if reading my thoughts.

"I'm not finding anything useful," I said. "Are either of you?"

Dora ironed one page with her hand, read it, and looked up at us. Her eyes were sad. "What happened to the innocence of children? Now they're blackmailing each other?" She read aloud, " 'Pay up or else.' It's typed, so maybe an adult, not a kid, sent it to someone."

Haylee reminded her, "Kids have computers and printers."

The piece of paper forming the core of the ball was stuck to a small label. We unstuck the paper from the label and the label from itself as well as we could without tearing it. It was a prescription from a doctor in Buffalo.

The patient's first name started with "AN."

We couldn't read the rest of the name, the name of the medicine, or the doctor's name, street address in Buffalo, or phone number. I hadn't told Dora my guesses about the almonds and allergy medicine. She concluded, "That must be the label from Antonio's heart medication! But where are his pills? Someone must have thrown them

out so he wouldn't be able to find them."
She frowned. "This is all circumstantial
evidence, isn't it?"

Haylee and I agreed. We had nothing
conclusive to report to Vicki or anyone else.

"Besides," I admitted, "Vicki's going to be
very annoyed if she discovers we removed
possible evidence from a crime scene."

Haylee corrected me. "A possible crime
scene. At this point, she would tell us that it
wasn't one."

The trooper I'd sent there must have
decided that.

Dora nodded in a birdlike way that reminded me of her daughter Edna. "And we
weren't the ones who removed this supposed evidence from the conservatory. I
liberated that paper ball from a gutter."

We finished our tea and cookies, and then
Haylee and I gathered my pets and escorted
them up the hill and into my apartment.

Haylee cuddled Mustache in her arms.
"Shall we take Sally and Tally for a walk
later?"

"Snooping where there is no known
crime? Vicki couldn't possibly object."

Haylee suggested, "Let's check out the
trash cans and recycling bins at the back of
TADAM's carriage house. Maybe we'll find
samples of printing or typing."

"Just lying on top of everything else, so we won't have to disturb anything."

Haylee set Mustache, who had begun wriggling, on the floor. "Don't be snarky. When Loretta arrived at Design 101, she came from the front door, while Kent came from the kitchen, so he could have been in the TADAM mansion before we got there, writing out *Welcome to TADAM,* and then silently sorting through bolts of cloth in some upstairs room. Both Kent and Loretta are artistic and can probably print in lots of styles."

"Maybe we'll be lucky and find that they autographed samples of their printing."

"You *are* snarky tonight." Her grin said she was teasing.

"Loretta inspired me."

Haylee snickered.

I became serious. "Meet you in front of The Stash around eleven?"

Because of the potential murderer in the village, I insisted that Haylee had to go home through my apartment and In Stitches instead of through my yard, and I watched from my front porch until after she locked herself inside The Stash.

I galloped down to my apartment.

No phone messages, from Clay or from anyone else.

I had almost two hours to kill before Haylee and I were going out. I climbed up on one of my bar stools and tapped my fingernails on the granite kitchen counter. Haylee and I planned to dig through other people's trash. If there had been no crime, we wouldn't be compromising a crime scene, and Vicki, even if she found out about it, could not object, much. Okay, she would find our behavior strange, but that was nothing new.

However, if we could demonstrate that there *had* been a crime, Vicki and the state police would need to know about it.

I suspected that the trooper I'd told about the candies and medicine vial had done nothing. It could be up to Haylee and me — and her sort-of grandmother, Dora Battersby — to figure out whether or not there had been a crime.

. I didn't want anyone getting away with murder, especially Loretta. For all I knew, she went around collecting men so she could kill them. What if Clay was next on her list?

Maybe we should tell Vicki about the warning that Haylee had picked up from the podium and about the threatening note and the prescription label we'd found among the pieces of paper that had made up the soccer ball.

And Vicki would . . . probably make fun of us and scold us.

Besides, at the class Vicki hadn't been dressed like she was on duty. My call would probably go to the state police, and they'd send out another trooper who would listen to our tale and then decide there was nothing he could or should do.

And maybe he would be right. Maybe Haylee and I wouldn't find anyone's printing in the recycling bins behind TADAM. Actually, that sounded like a very good outcome.

We would simply walk the dogs.

16

Dressing in black was a little silly when Sally and Tally were coming along on our sleuthing missions. Even if I sewed dark overcoats for them, their white-tipped tails would blow our cover.

However, my black jacket not only had a hood, it had plenty of pockets. Remembering the difficulty I'd once experienced while attempting to corral wayward trash, I poked a large garbage bag into one pocket. A handful of stoop-and-scoop bags and my phone, which would double as a flashlight, went into others.

At The Stash, Haylee was also wearing black. Both of us pulled our hoods up.

Haylee took Sally's leash. "I saw Vicki's cruiser a few minutes ago. With any luck, she's heading off to the rural areas outside Elderberry Bay and won't be patrolling here for an hour or more."

I hoped so. No matter how innocently

recognizable my dogs were, Vicki could take one look at our outfits and guess we were up to what she would think was no good.

Walking my dogs was never speedy. However, while we waited for them to sniff out clues, we snooped with our eyes. There wasn't much to see. Lawns and gardens were neat, and leaves were still on trees. The conservatory was dark inside with only a couple of floodlights outside.

A car crept up behind us.

Great. Vicki's cruiser. We whipped our hoods off our heads and waved. She flashed her headlights and turned toward TADAM.

Finally, Sally-Forth and Tally-Ho were ready to move on.

We listened for cars and looked for Vicki's headlights before plunging down the pathway toward the back of the TADAM mansion. The chain-link fence separating the TADAM grounds from the village park had shrunk in my imagination, but now it was easy to see that it was still five feet high. Not that we'd have climbed it, anyway . . .

I turned on my phone's flashlight app and lit the trash cans and recycling bins beyond the fence. "Those things don't look like they've been used for about a year."

Haylee pointed. "They have other bins, beside the back porch." She pulled at Sally, who appeared to be contemplating digging a hole for us underneath the fence.

We agreed that we weren't about to snoop closer to the mansion.

Afraid that Paula might be watching us at the moment, I glanced up. We were safe. The carriage house hid us from the mansion. We continued down the pathway to the next block. A pickup truck was parked across the street in front the apartment building I'd seen Loretta enter on Saturday night. The streetlight above the pickup was, to my way of thinking at the moment, too bright.

The pickup was red. The sign on the door said *Fraser Construction.*

Clay's truck.

I dug my heels into the ground, which forced Tally-Ho to stop.

Haylee and Sally-Forth kept walking.

I squeaked, "Let's go back the way we came!"

Haylee stopped but didn't turn around. "Why?"

"That's Clay's truck. And I think Loretta's apartment is in that building."

Haylee tugged Sally-Forth back to Tally-Ho and me. "It looks like lots of other people live there."

I tiptoed backward. "Macey does, and her

roommate, Samantha. But I saw Loretta go inside it early Sunday morning." My words sounded like they came from the depths of misery, which was not far from the truth.

Haylee tried to cheer me up. "Maybe another tenant is having her kitchen redone."

"And Clay is making a business call at nearly midnight? He works long hours, but not like this."

Both dogs sniffed toward Clay's truck and tried to pull us closer. I resisted.

Too late.

Whistling and carrying a large envelope, Clay came out of the building, trotted down the steps, and opened his driver's door. I tried not to notice how great he looked in his leather jacket and blue jeans.

Maybe he wouldn't see us, back here underneath trees in the park.

Sally barked excitedly, and Tally joined her. They strained toward him.

Clay threw the envelope onto the driver's seat, closed the door, and strode toward us. "Sally? Tally?"

Yipping, Sally pulled Haylee out of the shadows. Tally was never willing to let his sister, or anyone else, take the lead. By the time we reached Clay at the sidewalk, the two dogs were neck and neck, wagging their tails and insisting on his attention.

He crouched and rubbed their ears. "Hi, guys. I was afraid you'd gotten loose."

He didn't look up at Haylee and me. Embarrassed at being caught at Loretta's in the middle of the night, no doubt.

"We often walk them at night." I thought I faked a cheery tone fairly well.

He stood and gazed down at me. "I know."

I couldn't think of a thing to say.

Haylee, however, had no such problems. "What have you been doing here at this time of night?"

Clay glanced over his shoulder. "Loretta had drawings of possible renovations to TADAM's carriage house that she wanted me to pick up." His face almost expressionless, Clay stared directly at me again. "I worked late and got here only a few minutes ago."

Again, I was wordless, and again, Haylee spoke up. "Renovating the carriage house could be interesting."

If he had any enthusiasm for the project, he was hiding it. "I'd agree, but I like to know how I'll be paid before I undertake a project, and it's not clear to me that anyone at TADAM is in a position to pay for more renovations."

I managed to find my voice. "Paula,

Antonio's widow, had an argument about that earlier this evening with Loretta and the other teacher, Kent. Paula seemed to think she was inheriting the mansion and the school, and that Loretta and Kent should not have held a night school class there, and should go away and let Paula run the school by herself. Loretta and Kent pointed out that Paula wouldn't be able to pay her bills unless Loretta and Kent kept teaching."

The slight downward movement of Clay's chin could have been interpreted as a nod.

I faltered. "I suppose Loretta already told you about the argument." I'd have loved to have heard her side of it. Then again, maybe she and Clay hadn't done much actual *talking.* I didn't see any lipstick on his blue chambray shirt, but maybe his jacket, even though unzipped, was hiding telltale smears.

He continued to keep his expression from revealing his feelings. "She said something about it, enough to make me worry about being paid. Besides, as I hinted to you when we first went into the mansion, Willow, the contractor that Antonio hired to restore the mansion used only the cheapest materials. Even so, I'm not sure there's much left in the coffers for anything else. Antonio said something about renovating the basement and putting in a proper driveway as soon as they attracted more students and collected tuition from them." Clay spread his hands in another shrug. "So I have Loretta's sketches, but I'm not sure we can ever put them to use."

We. Clay and Loretta.

Haylee wasn't giving up. "It would be fun to see the sketches. And the inside of the carriage house, of course." She pointed at me. "Willow and I might have some good ideas."

Clay shoved his hands into his pockets. "I know you would. And Edna's mother would, too."

Haylee clapped her hands. "She'd love that!"

"And Ben," he added, "but I think we should wait until we're sure we're not wasting our time."

So much for getting a look at Loretta's sketches — and, more importantly, a glimpse of her printing.

Haylee backed up a step, and off the curb. "Ouch!" Much to Sally's excitement, Haylee hopped on one foot.

Clay and I asked in unison, "Are you okay?"

Obviously, she wasn't.

"I'm fine." Pain shot across her face. "I

only turned my ankle. I'll be better in a moment."

I grabbed Sally's leash before the enthusiastic dog could drag Haylee around and increase her injuries, if there were any. I knew Haylee well enough to guess she was faking them.

Maybe Clay didn't. He asked, "Can you drive a standard? You can take my truck and I'll help Willow walk these rascals home."

Haylee winced. "I can't, but it's my right foot. I wouldn't even want to drive my own truck."

"I can walk both dogs by myself," I said.

"Yes." Finally, he gave me one of his smiles, but it still seemed a little tentative. "And *sometimes* you don't need rescuing."

Once, he'd rescued the dogs and me. It hadn't been necessary, but it had been fun. This time he was rescuing Haylee, who probably didn't need it, either. I wasn't about to divulge her secret, however.

He offered, "I'll take you home, Haylee. First, let me bring the truck to this side of the street." He sprinted to his truck, jumped into it, tore off to the nearest intersection, and made a U-turn.

As if afraid that Clay could read her lips while zipping around in his truck, Haylee turned her face away from the street. "I'm okay, Willow. I just want another look at Loretta's printing."

"I figured."

"You should have been the one with the sudden injury."

"I didn't think of it." Dramatically, I stuck my nose up in the air and said loftily, "And even if I had, I wouldn't have stooped that low."

"Now I really *am* in pain."

"Here he comes. Stop smiling. Hobble."

Clay pulled up to the curb. In a flash, he was out of his driver's seat and helping Haylee into the truck. I envied her, sort of. On the other hand, I didn't really want to be alone with him until I could stop obsessing about seeing him with his arms around Loretta.

He closed the passenger door carefully and said to me, "See you at Haylee's place in a few minutes? She might prefer to have you help her go up into her apartment."

Maybe I'd get a look at those sketches yet. "Okay, but you know how these two can mosey."

"Take your time." He winked. "Maybe I should get Ben to come help her, instead of either you or me."

He was acting like he and I were still close, conspiring to throw Haylee and Ben together. I tried for a light tone, too. "We'll be there within the next hour or so."

With a wave, he ran back to his side of the truck and pulled out slowly, as if Haylee were as fragile as a hen's egg.

Fragile, right. He'd barely driven ten feet when the map light on her side of the truck came on. I couldn't help grinning. Haylee had lost no time checking out those sketches.

And maybe Clay hadn't been totally bamboozled by the flamboyant and artistic Loretta. I nearly giggled at the thought of his reaction if she'd been wearing her superhero/professional wrestler outfit while he was visiting her.

To my surprise, the dogs were willing to hurry. They knew which direction Clay and Haylee had gone and were undoubtedly eager to catch up with them.

Clay's truck was in the parking lot behind the stores on Haylee's side of the street. The pickup's interior lights were on, and Haylee and Clay were still in their seats. Haylee leaned toward Clay and pointed at a sheet of paper he held against the steering wheel.

He looked up, waved at me, and put the paper down, on the console between the seats, I guessed.

The dogs and I met him on Haylee's side

of the truck. He lifted her out. I *should* have been the one faking the injury . . .

On the pavement, she rested most of her weight on her left foot and some of it on our shoulders. "I feel silly for putting you two to all this trouble. I think my ankle's better already." At her building's back door, she thanked us. "I can manage the rest of the way."

Oh no, she wasn't going to fling me at Clay. "The dogs and I will come upstairs with you."

Clay gave us both a smile, told Haylee to put ice on her ankle, patted the dogs, and waved good-bye.

After his taillights disappeared, Haylee lowered her right foot to the ground. "He's so nice. I hate taking advantage of him."

"Well." I drew the word out. "That depends on how much time he spent with That Woman and whether or not she purposely harmed her boss. Did you get a good look at her printing?"

"It's like the way the welcome message on that newsprint pad was written, rounded with curls and swirls and other flourishes, very much like the printing on the sketches that Antonio gave me, and not square and angry-looking like the warning that said 'You won't get away with it.' "

"Which we think Kent may have printed."

"Exactly. Want to come through The Stash so I can watch until you're safely inside In Stitches?"

"Sally and Tally will protect me."

I walked the dogs around the block. At the front door of In Stitches, I turned around. Haylee waved at me from inside The Stash. I loved Threadville and the way we — most of us — helped each other.

After the dogs and I were inside and the door was locked, Vicki's cruiser went slowly down the street. I waved, but she probably didn't see me in the shop illuminated by only one night-light.

The dogs and I went to bed.

Despite the cats' nightly rumpus and my fears that Clay was about to find himself in Loretta's clutches, I managed to sleep.

There, I told myself in the morning. I was being rational and adult about Clay, and there was no point in confronting him. He was free to do what he wanted.

And I was fine with that. Just fine.

While the pets and I were enjoying our first backyard exploration of the day, Dora came out of Blueberry Cottage and handed me a platter of cookies. "Trade you these for a mug of your coffee. You make the best coffee."

"And you make the best cookies. Peanut butter, yum. Come upstairs to In Stitches while I brew some coffee."

Leaving the cats to take naps, Dora and I followed Sally-Forth and Tally-Ho upstairs.

The dogs settled down on their embroidered beds in their pen at the back of the shop. I couldn't help admiring that pen. It was huge, with plenty of space for them, their food and water bowls, and my desk and computer.

I remembered watching Clay build the beautiful oak railing, complete with a matching gate, surrounding the pen.

Clay.

Dora demanded, "Did you talk to Clay yet?"

"I saw him last night, briefly. Nothing's changed." I turned on the coffee grinder, effectively ending our conversation.

Dora wandered around, fingering fabrics, straightening packages of stabilizer, and putting spools of thread where they belonged. I started the coffeemaker.

A man in a dark suit climbed the front porch steps. Sally and Tally barked and wagged their tails.

I broke into a clammy sweat.

Dora glided to my side. "I've seen that man before. Surely, it's not . . ." She stared at him as if defying him to come inside.

"It is. Detective Neffting, from the state police."

"Last time we saw him," she whispered, "wasn't he investigating a murder?"

Closing my eyes as if I could make Detective Neffting disappear, I nodded.

17

I opened my eyes. Detective Neffting had not disappeared. He really was on my front porch.

He was not my favorite homicide detective. True, I'd met only two homicide detectives in my life, and I didn't know either one of them very well.

Detective Neffting reminded me of vegetables, but not in a good way. His almost chinless head was shaped like an upside-down garlic clove on a too-thin stem. His paunch was more like a potato. His eyes bulged like parboiled pearl onions, and were about as pale.

I wouldn't have cared what he looked like, though, if he hadn't always seemed eager to suspect me of horrendous crimes.

And now . . . what?

Lifting his knees high as if afraid of what the soles of his shoes might touch, he came inside.

Dora didn't say a thing, which was unusual for her.

His face inscrutable, Detective Neffting pulled a manila envelope out of a leather portfolio. "Can you help me with some questions, Willow?"

"Sure." I bit my lip to prevent myself from making a smart-alecky response. *What questions would you like me to ask?*

Neffting strode to my cutting table. "May I?"

I swept aside scissors, measuring tapes, and a couple of bolts of fabric. "Be my guest."

Dora stayed beside me.

Neffting slid a stack of papers from the envelope. The top one was from Saturday night's silent auction. Had he bid on some of the clothing? Maybe an outfit that I had made? I had to bite my lip again, and my tongue, or I might have laughed.

He pointed at the top sheet of paper. "Can you tell me who this woman is?"

"I can," Dora announced.

He gave her a cold look. "I'm asking *Willow.*"

Dora folded her arms and stepped back. I couldn't see her face, but I could imagine it. She was undoubtedly thinking of things she could say to deflate the man's confidence.

The photo featured Naomi in the first outfit she'd worn in the fashion show. Although I knew that Neffting had questioned Naomi about a murder last October and should have known the answer to his question, I gave him Naomi's name and told him she owned Batty About Quilts. The next three photos were also of her. With Dora sighing and huffing in her attempts to be silent, I also identified Edna, Haylee, Opal, Mona, and Ashley in each of their four outfits, and, finally, myself. Surely, he could have figured that out. Judging by Dora's grunts, she was dying to tell him to stop playing games.

Maybe because the reception had been cut short before people had progressed from cookies and wine to the auction table, not many people had bid on the outfits. The one that had won me the "award" for gluttony had received no offers. Maybe Neffting wanted to buy it.

I had to bite my lip, my tongue, *and* the inside of my cheek.

He fanned the four pictures of me on the table. "Can you tell me where these clothes are now, Willow?"

"Last I knew, they were still at the Elderberry Bay Conservatory, where the fashion show was held. TADAM students were going to gather them, clean and mend them, and then give them to the highest bidders."

Those pale eyes were unwavering. "Exactly where did you last see the clothes you wore in Saturday night's fashion show?"

"In a curtained-off cubicle backstage at the conservatory. We were told to leave the clothes in the cubicles where we changed. By now, TADAM students and staff should have collected them." Maybe someone had stolen the clothes since Haylee and I saw them last night, and Detective Neffting was now investigating thefts instead of homicides.

However, I suspected that Antonio had been intentionally harmed, and it was probably his death that Neffting was investigating. Instead of babbling everything I knew, though, I let the detective do the talking.

"What about the shoes?" He tapped the picture of me in my mud-hued Ambitious Attire dress and jacket. "For instance, these brown ones?"

My stomach began acting like it was on the down elevator while I was on the up. "They were lent to us — to TADAM, really — by Threadville's new shoe store, Feet Accomplished."

"And where are these brown shoes now?"

"They're either still in the cubicle, or in the TADAM mansion, or they've been returned to Feet Accomplished."

The coffeemaker beeped. Dora stomped to it. "Willow," she called, "coffee's ready." She held up the carafe. "Would you like some, sir?"

Neffting frowned down at the picture. "No, thanks." I wondered if he knew that he'd worn his charcoal pinstriped pants with a jacket from a different suit, a greenish one with black flecks woven into the fabric. He asked me, "Did you leave anything in those shoes?"

"Yes. Wadded-up tissues. The shoes were too big. Macey, one of the modeling students, gave me tissues to stuff into the toes to help keep the shoes on."

"Could you have left anything else in your shoes?"

"I didn't. But someone else did, between the time I left the cubicle Saturday night and went back into it Sunday morning."

"Sunday morning? Why did you go back then?"

I tapped the picture of myself in the revealing gown. "We were requested to wear our evening outfits to the reception Saturday night after the fashion show, and to bring them back and leave them in our cubicles Sunday morning. And when I did, I saw someone's allergy medication in the toe of one of those shoes. The medication hadn't been there Saturday night. I called the police about it and a trooper came and questioned me. I'd have taken him to see it and a package of candy-covered almonds inside a briefcase that someone had also put into my cubicle, but the trooper said not to bother."

Neffting's eyebrows rose as if he were skeptical of my story, and he also flushed as if he were feeling guilty or annoyed.

Dora plunked my mug of coffee on the table in front of me and took a sip of hers. "Mm," she murmured.

Neffting shuffled the papers and then pointed at the one of me in the Ambitious Attire outfit again. "You were carrying a briefcase."

"Everyone was, for that segment of the show."

"Where did you leave yours?"

"There weren't enough to go around, so I passed it to the next person in line who didn't have one."

"You're sure?"

"Yes, but when I dropped my evening outfit off in the cubicle Sunday morning, one of the briefcases — there must have been about eight of them in total — was in my cubicle. It bulged strangely, so I peeked in, and there was that package of candy-covered almonds. I explained it all to the state trooper, and he told me he was going to go check it out." Maybe this time, Neffting would tell me whether the trooper had followed through.

No luck. Neffting asked, "When did you put the briefcase into your cubicle?"

"I didn't. Why are you asking all these questions?"

Dora murmured an encouraging, "Mm-hm."

An image of Kent flashed into my head. He had taken the photos that Neffting was showing me. Before we'd left the conservatory Saturday night for the reception, Kent had headed toward the stage. Maybe to hide something temporarily until he had more time and could go back and move it to someone's cubicle?

And then, early Sunday morning, someone had been wielding a flashlight inside the conservatory, and the door had been propped open. Minutes later, I'd seen Kent on the street, near that door. Maybe he had come outside immediately after hiding things in cubicles, mine or someone else's.

206

If not mine, maybe seeing me in the vicinity had prompted him to go back inside and move the incriminating evidence into the cubicle I'd used. After taking all those pictures of us, he should have been able to figure out whose cubicle was whose by the outfits in them.

Loretta could have been coming from the conservatory, by a circuitous route, when I saw her enter her apartment building that night. But I'd seen that light inside the conservatory after I'd seen her go into her building. Maybe she'd gone back, taking the shortcut through the park.

I might have known that Detective Neffting would ignore our questions. Rocking forward on his toes, he half closed his eyes. "Let's go back to Saturday night."

Fortunately, that was impossible. Saturday night would never win awards as my favorite evening.

Though I gave him no encouragement, Neffting added, "To the end of the fashion show. Mr. Drudge —"

I asked, *"Who?"*

"Anthony Drudge. Apparently, when he decided to open the Threadville Academy of Design and Modeling, he began calling himself 'Antonio,' just one name." Neffting frowned in apparent disapproval. "His widow told us that Mr. Drudge believed the single name was more artistic and would attract more students."

Dora muttered, "Lothario might have been more appropriate."

Detective Neffting went on as if she hadn't spoken. Maybe he hadn't heard her, which was probably just as well. "At the end of the fashion show, Mr. Drudge said some unfortunate things to some of his models."

I suggested, "The seven threadly sins?" Antonio and his silly stunts were beginning to amuse me.

Neffting merely stared at me.

I corrected his earlier statement. "Antonio, um, Mr. Drudge didn't actually say those things to his modeling students, but to those of us from Threadville —"

Now it was Neffting's turn to do the correcting. "Elderberry Bay."

Dora proudly informed him, "*Everyone* calls this village by its nickname, Threadville."

I ran my forefinger across the photos Neffting had spread over the table. I gave up trying to call Antonio "Mr. Drudge." "Antonio made those comments to all seven of us in these photos, people from the shops in the section of Elderberry Bay known as Threadville. He said we'd each committed what he called a 'threadly sin.' Seven of them, altogether."

"Total nonsense," Dora stated.

Again, Neffting ignored her. He asked me, "What did *you* think of that, Willow?"

"It was clever, but it was also mean, because he was the one who had — so he said — designed the outfits and told us how to make them. This, for instance . . ." I picked up the photo of me in the mini-dress concocted of tiers of pale blue and white ruffles. "This was supposed to be a cocktail gown. I would never have worn that hideous thing outside of a costume party —"

"Or a fashion show." Neffting was fond of sticking to the facts, I noticed.

Dora had her own version of the facts. "You looked cute in that, Willow."

This time, I was the one who ignored her. "The fashion show was for a good cause, so I followed Antonio's instructions."

Neffting asked, "What was the cause?"

"Scholarships to TADAM."

Mug to her lips, Dora made a raspberry. I was a little surprised that she didn't spray coffee. "If I were young, *I* would not attend that so-called academy, if it really *is* a school," she said.

She'd been more than willing to go to the free class. I managed not to grin. "Anyway,

209

Antonio said the dress made me look fat, and therefore, I had committed the sin of gluttony."

Neffting tilted his head in a way he probably thought would look empathetic but was more likely to put him in danger of toppling over. "How did you feel when he said that?"

I warmed my hands on my coffee mug. "I was last in line, so by the time he got to me, I was expecting an insult. I pretended I thought it was funny."

He eyed me. "You were upset?"

"Not for myself, but he was unfair, especially to my seventeen-year-old assistant." I showed Neffting the picture of Ashley in her fabulous Ambitious Attire jacket. "Antonio said that Ashley couldn't do her own designing, which she very definitely *can,* and that she had copied other people. Again, he had given her sketches and told her what to make. Ashley's facing some challenges right now, and ordinarily, she might have laughed. But I was afraid she would be hurt and lose her self-confidence. Antonio doesn't — didn't — seem to know how to motivate young people. Ashley was thinking of applying for one of those scholarships."

Naturally, Neffting latched onto the one thing I should not have mentioned.

18

Neffting demanded, "You said your assistant is facing challenges?"

I rubbed a finger across the grooves of the ruler that was part of the cutting table's surface. "Her father lost his job, her mother had to go back to work, and Ashley has to look after her younger siblings even more than she used to. Knowing she might not be able to afford to go to college without a substantial scholarship, she's stressed right now."

Neffting wasn't ready to stop bombarding me with questions. "This is the Ashley who claimed that Mr. Drudge made unwanted advances?"

Dora thumped her emptied mug down onto the table. "He did. I'm not certain that he pinched Ashley, but he definitely pinched the girl with her, a student named Macey. I saw him do it, the despicable slimeball. Ashley pushed his hand away, but neither of them retaliated with any force."

This time, Neffting responded to Dora. "That either of you *witnessed.*"

I admitted, "The night before, at the rehearsal, I heard Macey slap someone in the dressing cubicle next to mine. A man responded, saying something like if she was going to be a model, she had to get used to people helping adjust her clothing. He had lowered his voice in a phony sexy growl, so I wasn't sure who it was at the time. Later, she told me it was Antonio."

Dora repeated, in even more colorful words, her opinion of Antonio.

Neffting acted like he hadn't heard her. "Did you see the man?" he asked me. "Were you able to make a positive ID?"

"No. I heard him head toward the podium, though, and a minute or two later, that's where Antonio was."

"And you're sure that this Macey said it was Mr. Drudge?"

"Yes."

"Could she have misspoken, or could you have misunderstood? There is a male teacher at TADAM."

I shook my head. "It was clear that we were talking about Antonio."

Dora chimed in, "I wouldn't put anything past that Kent guy, though."

"His last name is Quarrop," I said.

Detective Neffting asked Dora, "Did you see Mr. Quarrop touch anyone?"

She placed her fists on her hips. "No. But the man looks about to murder anyone and everyone at the drop of a pin or a needle."

Neffting wrote in his notebook. I made a mental note to try to find out why Neffting appeared to suspect Kent of something. Murder?

Dora was less reticent. "Why? Does Kent have a history? A criminal record?"

In my limited contact with detectives, I'd noticed that they almost never showed what they were thinking. I couldn't read Neffting's change of expression, a subtle narrowing of his mouth, but I suspected he was struggling to hide his surprise. Had Dora guessed correctly?

He asked her, "Why do you say that? Have you been checking up on him?"

Aha.

She managed to appear insulted. "Of course not."

Possibly mortified that he'd accidentally let us see the truth about Kent, Neffting suddenly changed the subject. "Willow, do you have allergies?"

"No."

"What about your assistant?" he asked.

"Not that I know of."

He took a clear plastic bag out of his leather satchel and held it up. A medicine vial was inside the bag. "Recognize this?"

"That looks like the vial I found in one of those brown shoes. Someone had taken out a tissue, put the vial into the shoe, and poked the tissue around it. But the tissue was sticking out, which was not the way I'd left it."

Dora leaned forward to peer across the table at the bag. "Has the prescription sticker been torn off it?"

He smoothed the plastic bag over white residue left from a sticker. "Could be. The medicine is not yours, Willow?"

"No. Why?"

Without answering, he shoved that bag back into his satchel.

Did Neffting believe my theory about Antonio's death? Could we have helped Antonio if we'd known to give him his medication? And had been able to find it?

Dora was nearly jumping up and down in excitement. "I know where the rest of the prescription sticker is!"

Apparently, Neffting wasn't used to coping with anyone quite like Dora. His eyes opened wider for a second before he controlled his expression to its customary neutrality. "Where?"

"In my cottage. Willow's cottage, really." She pointed at the back windows above the snoozing dogs. "We . . ." She faltered as if not wanting to admit we'd been snooping. "We picked up some litter, including a wadded-up sticker that looked like a pre-scription label."

"Where did you pick it up?"

"On Jefferson Avenue. Kids had been playing with a paper soccer ball in the Elderberry Bay Conservatory, and two of the boys kicked it down Jefferson, then left it in a gutter."

Neffting flipped to a new page in his notebook and wrote quickly. "The ball had been inside the conservatory?"

Dora nodded. "Lots of people saw it there, including my granddaughter, Haylee Scott, who lives across the street." She pointed at The Stash.

"And the prescription sticker was on this ball?"

"Inside it. We took the ball apart."

He again lost control of his face, but detectives probably allowed themselves to look inquisitive.

Dora tossed her head. Her short brown curls stayed in place. "I have a fireplace in Willow's cottage. I can use single sheets to

215

start fires, but a soccer ball's worth might cause a conflagration. There were other things we found that you might like to see, too. Haylee discovered a piece of paper in the podium that Antonio — Anthony Drudge — had used. Mr. *Drudge* had made a list of the seven threadly sins. A threat was hand-printed on the back of it."

Neffting repeated, "A threat?"

Dora turned to me. "What did it say, again, Willow?"

" 'You won't get away with it.' It wasn't signed. The printing was stark and brisk, like the person who had printed it was angry. Maybe he was, if only because the marker wasn't working well."

Dora pointed out, "The words by themselves were angry. The printing was very masculine, but stylish, as if an artistic man had printed it."

I retrieved the quarter sheet of paper with the words *"Glitzy Garb"* on it and gave it to Neffting. "I think the printing —"

Dora interrupted me. "The scrawl."

I went on, "I think the scrawl on this matches Antonio's list of our so-called threadly sins. I don't know what Paula's or Kent's writing is like, but Loretta decorates her printing with all sorts of little swirls and things."

Neffting asked, "Are you two handwriting experts?"

We both shook our heads.

Dora told him, "I'll show you the list with the threat on the back of it. You'll see what I mean."

"Maybe," he said. "I'm not a handwriting expert, either."

Touché.

Dora glared. "And you ought to see the prescription label, too."

Neffting asked, "Did it say what the medicine was?"

I held my hands out, palms up, showing I had nothing. "We didn't undo the sticker. It was all gummed together, and we'd have destroyed it. And we couldn't see a patient's name, either, only the letters A and N. Capital letters. The doctor's name, phone number, and address were missing, too, except for Buffalo, New York."

Neffting scribbled in his notebook. "I wish no one had removed those items from the scene, but when we're done here, I would like to see them, Mrs. Battersby." He wrote more, then closed his notebook, reached into his satchel, and pulled out another clear plastic bag. It contained a candy package, its top neatly cut off. Pastel candies had spilled from the package into the plastic bag. "Recognize any of this?" he asked.

Of course I did. "That looks like the package of Jordan almonds that I saw in the briefcase in my cubicle. That was the other thing besides the medicine vial that I sent a state trooper to see. The white Jordan almonds resemble the mints that Antonio was eating during the rehearsal on Friday night and at the reception Saturday night, and it appears to me that many of the white almonds were removed from the package you have there. Chief Smallwood and Gord, Dr. Wrinklesides —"

"Gord's my son-in-law." Less than a year ago, I'd never have expected Dora to sound this proud, of either her daughter or her son-in-law. Her months in Threadville had been good for her, for all of us.

I sent her a quick smile, then went on, "Chief Smallwood and Gord Wrinklesides found white candies in Antonio's pocket after he fell. I assumed they were the candies that Antonio had been eating."

I hadn't told Dora my theory about the almonds, but suddenly, she became even more animated. "Saturday night after Antonio collapsed, Gord asked Antonio's wife whether Antonio had heart trouble, and she said she didn't know, but our actions may have caused a heart attack. But the medica-

218

tion you just showed us isn't heart medication. It's to counteract sudden and severe allergic reactions."

Neffting stared at her as if she'd just confessed to murder.

She raised her chin. "Well, you *asked* Willow if she had allergies right before you showed her the vial. Besides, I haven't lived over seventy years without picking up a little knowledge. Nuts are a common allergen, even for adults. Antonio may or may not have heart trouble, but you'd think his wife would have mentioned his allergies. If that allergy medicine was his, maybe he was allergic to nuts, or maybe only to almonds. He could have accidentally eaten candy-coated almonds, thinking they were his usual mints."

I asked, "Wouldn't he have recognized the flavor?"

Dora shook her head emphatically. "Not if his first reaction to almonds was when he was a small boy and he hadn't tasted one since. I read about a case like that."

If she had read about it, a person planning to harm Antonio could have, also. I hoped Neffting didn't think that Dora's knowledge of these details meant that *she* had arranged his death.

I asked, "But wouldn't he at least have

noticed that the candied almond tasted different from his mints?"

Dora shook her head. "Try eating a bunch of strong mints and then placing something else in your mouth. All you'll taste is mint."

I persisted. "Wouldn't the texture be different? If he noticed that and then started feeling peculiar, like he was reacting to a nut, wouldn't he have taken his medicine?"

Dora answered, "Maybe he did notice the difference in the texture. And he must have recognized that he was having a reaction. Remember, he was feeling around in his pockets and saying, 'Where's my —' and 'Help!' before he collapsed?"

I turned to Neffting. "You're a homicide detective, aren't you?"

"Most of the time."

"Are you investigating . . . a death?"

He didn't answer.

"You are," I said.

Dora nodded.

"Antonio's?" I suggested. "Anthony Drudge?"

Neffting didn't answer.

I told him, "Despite what his wife, Paula, said, Dora did not hit him."

Dora picked up her empty mug again. "And neither did Willow."

I remembered to tell him another peculiar

220

thing I'd noticed on Saturday night. "After Antonio fell, his wife immediately jumped to the conclusion that he was dead, although according to Gord Wrinklesides, he wasn't. Could Antonio's wife have *expected* him to die?"

Dora wagged a finger at Neffting. "Who would be more likely to know about a man's allergies than his wife? She could have hidden his medication and somehow slipped him some of those candy-coated almonds."

I broke in, "He kept his mints in his jacket pocket. He was constantly popping those mints during the rehearsal for the fashion show, and Saturday night during the reception, he came too close to me, and his breath was minty."

Dora crowed, "So it was easy! His wife slipped a Jordan almond into his pocket along with his mints, and he unknowingly ate it."

I tapped my fingers against my cutting table. "When Gord asked Paula if Antonio had heart trouble, she said he might, and she didn't know if he had medication." I looked straight into Detective Neffting's eyes. "Wouldn't that have been the obvious time for his wife to state that he had allergies and should be carrying allergy medication? Don't you think the fact that she didn't mention his allergies could be incriminating?"

Detective Neffting merely stared at me, and I remembered another time when he hadn't seemed to believe my theories.

Unwilling to admit that I'd been eavesdropping on the argument between Kent, Loretta, and Paula, although I was sure that Vicki suspected that I had been, I worded my next question carefully. "Where did Antonio get the money to renovate that old mansion and open a school? Maybe he hasn't been making his loan payments, and the lender decided to teach him a lesson."

Dora squeaked, "We also found a warning in that wad of paper that said, 'Pay up or else.' That threat was typed. That could have been from the people who lent money to Mr. Drudge."

Neffting gathered the papers I'd given him and the sheets from the silent auction. "You watch too much TV. I'll take these things out to my car, then I'll meet you in your — Willow's — cottage, Mrs. Battersby." He left.

As soon as the front door closed behind him, Dora held up her index finger. "I think we guessed exactly what that detective was thinking."

"Maybe," I said with a lopsided frown.

"Except he thinks *I'm* the one who put the almond into Antonio's pocket and hid his medication."

"How could he? The killer is often the spouse, especially a wife if she's enraged by her husband's philandering, like Paula probably was. Paula should have known that he was allergic to almonds."

"We still don't know for sure that he was."

"Ha. That detective might as well have come right out and told us. They probably discovered during the post mortem that Mr. Drudge died from an allergic reaction, and they've decided the whole situation is a bit fishy."

"I think you're right."

Outside, Detective Neffting got into his cruiser and sat there as if he were writing notes.

Or waiting for backup to help him arrest someone.

19

I changed the sign on the door from *Come Back Later* to *Welcome.*

Neffting was still sitting in his car.

"Thanks for the coffee, Willow," Dora said. "I guess I'd better return to Blueberry Cottage before that detective comes to look down his pointy nose at the evidence we collected. Mind if I take a shortcut through your apartment?"

"Of course not." I might as well give her a key and let her supervise my life.

"Thanks. That hill in your side yard is too steep. I need your young man." She clumped down the stairs.

What young man? Dora could come and go through my apartment as she pleased, any time of the day or night, and she might never encounter the man she insisted on calling mine. I sighed.

Vicki's cruiser pulled up behind Detective Neffting's. Together, they headed for my side gate.

My phone rang. It was Mona. "I have the most fabulous idea!"

She's going to ask me to do something that takes all of my time. Get ready to say no.

"I've told that gorgeous hunk from TADAM that I want to buy all of the outfits from the fashion show that we seven Threadville ladies made."

"Gorgeous hunk?"

"You know, that guy with the sulky, damn-your-eyes look. Kent somebody or other."

Kent, a gorgeous hunk? To each her own.

Then I realized what else she'd said. "How can you buy all the outfits? It was a silent auction. The highest bidders are entitled to the clothes."

She let out a careless burble of laughter. "That would be me. I bid on some of them, but the auction was never properly completed, and now I've told Kent that I will pay two dollars over the top bids on *all* of the outfits that we made." Rumor had it that at least one of Mona's ex-husbands was looking after her very well, financially. Still, some of the outfits had received no bids, and Mona would be able to strut around in my Gluttony cocktail dress and matching bloomers for only two dollars. Lucky her.

I asked cautiously, "What are you going to

do with them?" *Resell them at a profit to the people who made them? No, thanks . . .*

"Kent — don't you just love that name? So distinguished. *Kent* said I can't have them yet. The police took the clothes we wore in the fashion show as evidence against that sourpuss who was married to that poor, sweet man who died."

Sweet? He'd been male, though, which had probably been enough for Mona. "Evidence against Paula?" And Dora and I weren't suspects? That would be a relief.

"Well, Kent didn't *say* that, but of course she did it. She couldn't have made it more obvious that she hated her husband for the way he ogled the rest of us. As if it were his fault that Threadville just teems with beautiful women, and *she* just let herself go!"

"But —"

Mona went on as if I hadn't tried to speak. "I know you think you're the only one in the world who can solve murders, but I intend to prove that Paula murdered her husband. Then we can have the outfits back."

"I think they keep evidence until after convictions, and sometimes for years beyond that, in case of appeals."

"Then you can make them all again! It

will be easy for you, having already practiced."

I didn't dispute her or point out that the other Threadville proprietors and I hadn't necessarily enjoyed making those outfits in the first place, and certainly wouldn't be thrilled about making duplicates. I asked, "Why do you want them? It's not like they were beautiful or elegant."

"That's just it!"

I was missing something. "Just *what*?"

"That hunky Kent is going to help me put on a play, and we'll donate most of the proceeds to TADAM's scholarship fund. What do you think of that?"

I think I may consider moving out of Threadville. "Do you have experience putting on plays?" I asked.

"I wrote one in elementary school and played the lead. How difficult can it be?"

That depends on whether or not you want people to enjoy it . . . "Why do you need the outfits we wore in the fashion show?"

"For costumes. And they'll only fit certain people, so we all have to be in the play! And guess what the play's title is!" Without waiting for my answer, she crowed, *"The Seven Threadly Sins!"*

There's another Threadville, in Mississippi. Maybe I can convince Haylee and her three

227

mothers to move there with me, and we can all open new shops . . . "But we're not actors."

"Not a problem! All you have to do is memorize your lines and act them out. Easy peasy. Besides, I'll help you. And I'll have most of the lines, anyway. You'll barely need to do more than you did in the fashion show — just go onstage and prance around. You hammed it up. You know how to act. You and Edna both do, and the others will learn."

"Mona, I'm sorry, but I can't take the time. When In Stitches is not open, I have custom machine embroidery orders to fill." I did my best to sound firm.

It did no good. "Don't forget the scholarship fund. I've told Kent that my one requirement before I pay for the outfits, if I can wangle them from the police, is that I am to be a member of the scholarship selection committee. At this point, the committee is only the widow, who will be in prison by the time the play winds up, that gorgeous Kent, and that woman with the hair."

"Loretta."

"Yes, her. I told him that I'd expect to get a scholarship for our little Ashley, and do you know what he said? He said that girl had a lot of talent, and he'd vote with me.

So, we have to do it."

And it would give us a chance to see more of him and find out if his printing was bold, stylish, and angry. Plus, as annoying as Mona could be, she was a Threadville proprietor, one of us, and we shouldn't leave the woman alone with Kent, much as she might like that, as long as we suspected he could be a killer.

"I . . . guess I can do it."

"Great! I'll tell the others that you're helping. Want to be assistant director?"

Gulp. "I wouldn't know a thing about it."

"No problies. *Your* hunk and his employees can build the set and be our stagehands. See what you can do to convince him, okay, before I tackle him?" She giggled. "Not physically, of course, but just give me the word anytime you change your mind about him, and I'll be happy to take over."

Yes, she'd made that obvious. And she apparently didn't know that Loretta was the one doing the tackling these days. I wasn't going to tell her, though. "He works long hours. He might like to do it but not have time."

"Nonsense. He built that haunted graveyard and chapel for that other gorgeous hunk, Ben. He'll make time for an important charity like this."

From the corner of my eye, I saw Thread-ville buses from Erie and from northeastern Ohio stop outside the shop.

"Today's Threadville tourists are here, Mona. We'd better stop chatting."

"They are? Okay." As usual, I didn't see any of the women head toward Mona's decorating shop, Country Chic. She kept saying she was going to offer courses and workshops, but after a couple of years in Threadville, she had yet to offer her first one. Nearly everything she sold was already made and decorated, and I didn't think she had a clue how to actually create anything herself, besides working up a yearning for every man between the ages of twenty and sixty-five.

The women from our morning embroi-dery class came into In Stitches.

"What are we doing today, Willow?" they asked.

"Crewel work."

Rosemary, who drove the tour bus from Erie, asked, "How can we do crewel embroi-dery with machines? Aren't you supposed to use thick wool yarn? That won't fit through the eyes of our needles."

Georgina, a frequent attendee who actu-ally lived within walking distance of the Threadville shops, guessed, "Bobbins? We're going to work upside down?"

Women clowned, pretending to stand on their heads.

I admitted, "I haven't tried it myself yet. Is everyone game?"

Of course they were. We chose flower designs that might have been in Jacobean tapestries and hooped our fabric right side down instead of right side up, with our stabilizer on top, in plain view for once.

We threaded bobbins with the heaviest weight of embroidery thread I'd been able to order. It was sort of woolly and came in many beautiful tones.

In machine embroidery, a little of the thread that goes through the needle is pulled around to the back of embroidery motifs so that the bobbin thread does not accidentally show on top.

But now we wanted the bobbin side of the design to actually be the top, so every time we changed to a new color of bobbin thread, we changed the thread in the needle to a matching color of normal weight, matte finish thread. I hoped that, when we turned over our embroidery to view it from the proper side, the thinner thread would hide among the heavier, woolly stitches.

We loaded our designs into our sewing machines and stitched them. They looked pretty from the top, which would eventually be the bottom, but we could hardly wait to take our hoops out of our machines.

My design didn't look really great, but some of my students who were extremely talented and patient ended up with floral motifs that they really liked. One woman had even managed to put her crewel embroidery on velvet, by pressing the velvet onto a sheet of my new super-sticky stabilizer on the bottom side of her hoop.

Before we broke for lunch, many people bought several spools of heavy embroidery thread.

Rosemary groaned. "Why do you keep doing this to us, Willow? I'm going to need lots more colors of this thread."

Sometime during the morning, Detective Neffting's and Police Chief Vicki Smallwood's cars disappeared from Lake Street.

In my afternoon workshop, we again practiced crewel machine embroidery. I turned down my machine's top tension and was happier with this version of upside-down crewel embroidery. Adjusting tension was always trial and error, and none of us particularly liked trial and error. We all wanted trial and perfect the first time.

Ashley came to work in the shop after school. During a lull, I asked if she had her notes from the night before. "And the sketches that Antonio gave you for your outfits?"

She rummaged in her backpack and pulled them out.

I pointed to one of the sketches that Antonio had given her. "Look at the printing on these sketches. Does it look like Loretta's?"

She studied the sketches, then paged through the notes she'd taken in our abbreviated night school class. "Yes, it does." She wrinkled her nose. "You were here with me when he gave me my sketches. He told me that *he* had drawn them. But we know for certain that he did not draw that dress on the easel last night, because we saw Loretta do it, and we saw how she printed words like 'shoulder seam' on the sketch. She must have drawn all of the sketches that Antonio gave us."

After we closed In Stitches, my animals and I had our suppers and a quick outing before firefighting practice.

Those of us who lived in downtown Threadville could have walked to firefighting, but we needed enough vehicles at the ball field for everyone, in case we were called to an emergency during firefighting practice. The dogs and I always went with

Haylee in her pickup truck, mainly because it was as red as the village's fire trucks, which seemed like a good idea, but that meant that I always had two largish dogs in my lap all the way to and from the baseball field.

Haylee parked and we all tumbled out. I took Tally's leash and gave Haylee Sally's. Firefighters jogged around the baseball diamond.

Ben strode toward us. Sally and Tally pulled us to him. He gave us a smile that would have melted anyone's heart. Sally and Tally wagged their tails even faster. Ben squatted down and rubbed their ears.

Behind me, I heard the hum of a large, well-maintained engine. Clay's pickup truck? Anticipation ran through me like sweet syrup. We were back to our usual schedule — firefighting practice, and then all going out together afterward. Everything between Clay and me would be fine.

Ben stood and stared toward the parking lot. The vehicle's engine shut off.

Although warned by Ben's sudden frown, I couldn't help turning around.

Clay's truck was beside Haylee's.

A vision in tight jeans and an even tighter T-shirt, Loretta climbed down from Clay's passenger seat.

20

Clay had brought Loretta to firefighting practice.

I didn't know what to do. My first two choices — becoming invisible or propelling myself into outer space — weren't exactly feasible, and no deep holes seemed about to gape open anywhere near me, either.

Luckily, I had mentors. My dogs might be uneasy in certain situations, especially when I was nervous, but this time they ignored my insecurity. Catching sight of Clay across the field, they charged toward him.

Haylee and I had the choice of letting go of their leashes, being dragged face-first to the parking lot, or charging along.

We charged along. Ben came with us.

Our speed as we ran across the field didn't give me much time to decide how to act or what to say, other than to remind myself that Loretta could be a murderer and I needed to learn as much as I could about her. And although Clay was ordinarily capable of looking after himself, he could be dazzled by Loretta's beauty and her obvious adoration of him.

Someone should keep an eye on the man.

Sally-Forth and Tally-Ho were obviously assigning themselves that job, so if they were my mentors, I would have to imitate them, and help protect him.

But that didn't answer the most crucial question. How should I act when we reached him? Aloof? Courteous? Again, I decided to take my cues from Sally-Forth and Tally-Ho.

By the time we reached Clay and Loretta, I was breathless and laughing, but at least I managed real smiles. Fortunately, Sally and Tally weren't the drooliest of dogs, and I maintained something resembling dignity. I didn't even pant.

As usual, Clay crouched to enjoy the dogs' thrilled greeting. It turned out that the dogs were a bit slobbery, all over his face.

Okay, that was enough of following their leadership.

Looking slightly pained, Loretta stood aside.

Clay stood. "Willow, Haylee, and Ben, you've all met Loretta. She's joining the volunteer fire department."

Great.

All three of us welcomed her. Since we spoke in unison, maybe no one noticed that my voice was a few rungs lower than sincere.

Clay asked Haylee, "How's your ankle?"

By the look on her face, I could tell she'd forgotten about her "injury." "All better," she said. "Thank you for the ice advice."

Wanting to giggle at how she had avoided saying that she had actually iced her ankle, I turned to Loretta and asked politely, "Were you a firefighter where you lived before?"

She dimpled prettily. "No, but I've always wanted to be one, even back in the days when I first met Clay." She tilted her head and looked up at him. "Didn't you bring a fire truck to show-and-tell?"

Clay looked puzzled. "I don't remember. Not a full-sized one, anyway."

She elbowed him. "You always did have something funny to say. Maybe I was thinking of your best friend. What was his name?"

Clay reached for Tally's leash. "Chief?"

Loretta clapped her hand on her forehead. "How would I forget that name?"

Noticing that Clay now had his leash, Tally lunged forward. Tally was especially fond of routines, and on Tuesday evenings at fire-fighting practice, Tally always raced around the baseball diamond with Clay. "We run laps, first," Clay called over his shoulder to Loretta as he loped behind Tally.

Sally was not about to be left behind, and all of us followed Clay and Tally, round and round the bases. Loretta didn't wimp out early, as I'd hoped she might, though she did seem more winded than the rest of us, who had been doing this every week for a couple of years.

However, Loretta wasn't the only one who couldn't quite catch her breath. The youngest firefighters were teenage boys, and they seemed to be having trouble not gawking at Loretta and her auburn curls, tight jeans, and tighter T-shirt. They vied with each other to offer to help her suit up in firefighting gear. However, the fire chief assigned Haylee and me the job, after the boys demonstrated, without too many blunders (the jacket goes on *after* the suspenders are placed on the shoulders), how it should be done.

Our fire chief was always happy to review the basics, and it didn't hurt any of us to be reminded of them. He stressed teamwork and always having each other's back.

Loretta squirmed. Was she paying attention to anyone besides Clay? I chided myself for being almost as bad, though in addition to being keenly aware of Clay, I was watching my dogs. Okay, I was paying more attention than necessary to Loretta. Maybe those tight jeans were causing her squirming.

After the chief had us show Loretta almost everything we kept stowed on our fire truck, he dismissed us, and we all headed for our vehicles. Loretta made a beeline for Clay's truck. Following her, Clay turned around and gave me a look that resembled a plea, as if he wanted me to somehow clamber into his two-seater truck with Loretta and him.

Hanging on to Tally's leash beside Haylee, who had Sally's, I merely smiled. Clay had brought Loretta. He could take her back.

Haylee drove the dogs and me into the center of Threadville and stopped her truck outside In Stitches. "Don't even *think* of not coming to Pier 42 with the rest of us, Willow," she ordered. "You can't just hand Clay to Loretta."

"Don't worry, I won't. I'm coming. Did you notice that I gave her a chance to tell us where she used to live, and she cleverly did not answer? I wonder if she really knew him in fourth grade. Let's see if we can get her to name the town where she first met Clay. He may be telling her that right now, though."

"I sensed caution on his part," Haylee said. "When you get a chance, ask him if he really had a best friend named 'Chief.' I thought he threw that out to see how she'd react."

"I wondered about that, too. Chief was probably his dog."

Laughing, Haylee drove off to park while I shut Sally-Forth and Tally-Ho into my apartment, and then as usual, Haylee and I met again near the entrance to the parking lot behind her and her mothers' shops, across the street from Pier 42.

Ben was waiting for us outside the pub. "The others have already gone in." He scrutinized me as if afraid I might burst into tears.

I smiled and shrugged. Why did everyone expect me to act like I owned Clay?

Ben opened the doors for us. Haylee went in first, then stopped in her tracks and made a noise that would not have seemed out of place in a farmyard. I half expected to see Clay and Loretta cuddled together in a booth in the back of the restaurant, but I followed Haylee's gaze and nearly made a few strange grunts, myself.

Mona sat with her back to us at a table for two. Her dining partner stared into her face. His eyes smoldered with dark intensity.

Kent.

Why did I suspect that Mona was not asking Kent leading questions about the possible murder of Antonio, also known as Anthony Drudge?

To our left, Clay sat beside Loretta in a booth next to windows overlooking the street. He grinned at me, stood, and let me scoot into the seat beside Loretta. Ben sat across from Loretta, and Haylee took the spot beside him, across from me. Clay slipped in next to me. It was a little crowded, so I edged closer to Clay. I couldn't help that, could I?

I was suddenly feeling much better about the situation, possibly because I was almost certain that Loretta was miffed at Clay for putting me between him and her.

Haylee and Ben gave me big smiles.

Pier 42 carried locally brewed craft beers on draft, and every Tuesday evening, each of the firefighters who was old enough to drink downed at least one frosty mug, along with an assortment of tasty, salty snacks.

As usual, we carried on a light banter, and Loretta joined in, often leaning forward so she could see around me and speak directly to Clay.

Haylee and I talked about our childhoods,

mine near Charleston, and Haylee's near Cleveland. Ben chimed in with stories about living as a boy in the Adirondacks. Clay said nothing. He appeared embarrassed, as if he didn't remember Loretta and didn't want to hurt her by telling her so. Loretta mentioned only generalities.

Finally, when all of our hints failed to yield answers, Haylee asked Loretta point-blank where she'd grown up.

Loretta slowly wrapped one auburn curl around a forefinger. "Lots of places," she finally said with barely concealed sadness. "My dad was in the army and we moved around a lot. That's how I lost touch with Clay." She let go of the curl and tossed the mane of hair over one shoulder.

It was a perfect opportunity for Clay to divulge where he'd lived in fourth grade.

Clay didn't take the bait. I knew that he'd spent most of his childhood in a suburb west of Boston. He'd lost the New England accent, though, so I didn't think anyone could have guessed. And, I noticed, Loretta didn't have a New England accent, either. But she didn't have any strong accent, and might have been honest about being an army brat.

Clay asked, "Anyone want something from the bar?" He unfolded himself from the seat.

Mona had appeared from the back of the restaurant. She grabbed his arm, looked past him at me, and demanded, "Did you ask Clay yet?"

Flustered, I couldn't remember what I was supposed to have asked him. "What?" Was I supposed to ask him if he was falling for the lovely Loretta? If I was reading him correctly, he wasn't. I hoped I was right.

Mona smiled up at Clay. "I'm putting on a play and I need you to build the sets."

Poor Clay looked almost desperate to escape. "I . . . um . . . what?" Maybe both of us becoming identically inarticulate would strengthen the bond between us. A girl could hope.

Mona offered, "Willow's going to be in it."

Clay looked down at me. An amused twinkle in his chocolaty brown eyes, he answered, "Then I guess I'd better help in my spare time."

"Of which he doesn't have much," Haylee contributed helpfully.

Mona stared pointedly at Ben. "Haylee's in the production, also."

Ben gallantly answered, "Then I'll help Clay, but he's the expert."

"I can nail boards together," Loretta said.

"And paint scenery." She glanced beyond Mona. "Can't I, Kent?"

I hadn't noticed Kent, eclipsed by the larger-than-life Mona. "She can draw clothes," he said.

Mona clapped her hands. "That's perfect, as Kent knows. The play I'm writing is about fashion and will be called *The Seven Threadly Sins.*"

"Antonio's little pun will live on," Loretta commented without enthusiasm. "Clay, I hope you will have time to do the renovations to the carriage house. We'll need to get together and plan —"

Clay was uncharacteristically abrupt. "I need to consult with my design team, first."

She began, "Oh, but I'm —"

Again, he interrupted her. "I wouldn't think of tackling the project without input from Haylee, Ben, Willow, and Dora."

Loretta gave him a blank look. "Dora?"

"Edna's mother," Clay supplied.

"That old woman who took a swing at poor Antonio and didn't recognize expensive crystal when she saw it?"

I corrected Loretta. "She didn't hit him. He collapsed and fell all by himself."

"And she's not old," Haylee said.

I added, "And no way was it crystal. It was glass. Cheap glass."

Clay provided the clincher. "Dora's a designer with years of experience."

Loretta sat back and folded her arms.

Mona turned to Kent. "Walk me home? This village doesn't always feel safe."

And being with Kent, a possible murderer, would be?

Haylee and I traded glances. "I should go," Haylee said.

I slid out of the booth to stand beside Clay. "Me, too."

Loretta followed me out of the booth. "Clay, we came in your truck. You're going to drive me home, right?"

He pretended to stagger. "Not right after a beer, and if no one wants more, I'll walk you home, then come back for my truck."

She gave him a brilliant smile. "If you have my sketches in your truck let's get them and then look at them together over coffee in my apartment."

"They're at my office," he said.

Mona led the way out, with Kent right behind her.

Loretta grabbed my arm and muttered, "You'd better follow Kent and your friend if you want her to get home safely."

I must have looked as startled as I felt.

She whispered, "Kent has a record for assault. Antonio knew about it and hired him anyway."

21

I wanted to ask Loretta if she felt unsafe working with Kent, but she budged past me and caught up with Clay, who was holding the door open for the rest of us.

Had Loretta been telling the truth about Kent? Dora and I had almost managed to worm information out of Detective Neffting that could have corroborated what Loretta had just whispered to me.

So why wasn't Loretta afraid of Kent? Maybe he was afraid of her, maybe for a good reason, like he knew she went around harming and sometimes killing people?

I shook my head. My imagination was running amok again.

At the street, Mona and Kent turned left, heading for Lake Street. Loretta could have gone that way, also, but she turned right, which, to be fair, was a more direct route to her apartment. Having said he'd walk her home, Clay went with her. Haylee, Ben, and

I caught up with Mona and Kent.

Maybe Mona's play would help us learn more about Kent and Loretta. How could I make the best of it? Encouraging Kent to show us the video he'd taken at the fashion show shouldn't be terribly difficult. I flashed a warning wink at Haylee, and then told Mona, "I'm still not sure I can act."

"Of course you can," Mona said. "Everyone is acting, all of the time."

"We're acting as ourselves," Haylee pointed out. "We have lots of practice at that."

"A skillful playwright will take that into account," Mona said. "I'm writing parts that will suit you."

Obviously having caught the message in my wink, Haylee dragged her feet. "I don't know . . ."

"If we could only see ourselves as others see us." I paused, then grinned and shook my head. "Maybe I'd just as soon not. If you took a video of the fashion show, Kent, don't show it to us." I kept my tone light and joking.

Mona pouted. "Kent, you videoed the fashion show, didn't you?"

"I set the camera up." His deep voice could have been the one I'd heard in Macey's cubicle, but she had told me later that she had slapped Antonio, not Kent. "I don't know if it caught the entire show. I spent the evening at Pier 42. Taking photos of the rehearsal was enough for me. I wasn't about to use up my entire Saturday evening as an unpaid babysitter for a video camera."

Interesting. A man who usually spoke in monosyllables, if at all, had delivered an entire monologue describing where he'd been the fateful night that someone had apparently set Antonio up to die. Had Kent rehearsed his alibi?

And he'd called himself an *unpaid* babysitter. I'd figured that Kent had printed the note that said *You won't get away with it.* Had he also typed the one that said "Pay up or else"?

Mona wrapped a hand around Kent's arm. "Everyone *else* got to watch the whole show, or at least the rehearsal, but those of us who were in it didn't see any of it! Could you arrange a showing for us, just us Threadville ladies, the people who are going to act in my play? That would really help me write a realistic play, and we'd all do a better job and raise more money for scholarships to TADAM."

Before Kent could answer, I butted in. "I doubt that he can. The police may have taken his video as evidence."

He didn't exactly confirm it, but he did say, "It's digital. I have a copy of the file."

Mona clapped her hands. "Great! Let's arrange a showing."

"Not at TADAM," he said.

Why not? He didn't want Paula to know about it? Or Loretta? But Loretta had already assigned herself to be part of Clay's set-building crew, so she'd likely find out about it sooner or later.

Kent didn't have a chance to give his reasons. Mona pointed up the sidewalk to her shop, Country Chic. "Come inside with me, Kent, and we'll see how we can re-arrange my shop and set up chairs for the showing of your video."

I nearly choked. Set up chairs in Mona's shop? As Haylee and I had discovered other times, two people in that shop along with Mona were already a crowd, putting her truckloads of fragile merchandise at risk.

Haylee suggested, "I have a classroom as part of The Stash, complete with a pull-down screen where we can show the video. We may be able to use my computer and projector."

Ben spoke up. "If not, we have audiovisual equipment at the Elderberry Bay Lodge."

"When can you show the video, Kent?" Mona asked.

"Any day after classes at TADAM."

"Do you have an evening class tomorrow?" Mona asked him.

"No."

"That's perfect!" Mona crowed. "Threadville shops close at six. How about tomorrow at seven thirty?"

We all agreed that was fine. Ben said he'd go early and help Haylee set up at her shop.

Yessss!

Mona made a big check mark with her finger in the air. "That's settled, then, but come in with me anyway, Kent. I need your input about scene changes. Ben can see these ladies home safely."

I considered objecting. No one should be alone with anyone even loosely associated with TADAM, and in my opinion, whether or not Kent truly had a record for assault, the man was, as far as I was concerned, a very likely suspect in the murder of Anthony Drudge, also known as Antonio.

On the other hand, Mona could probably look after herself, and she certainly did not want the rest of us around.

We said good night to the other two, then Ben and Haylee walked with me to the front door of In Stitches. After they were sure I was inside and had locked my door, they crossed the street to The Stash.

I didn't mean to be nosey, but I watched what happened next.

Nothing happened. Nothing interesting, anyway.

Haylee didn't get close to Ben. She waved at him, then went inside, and Ben loped back toward Pier 42, where his truck was.

Continuing to watch the street, I phoned Haylee. "It's a start," I told her. "He's never walked you home before."

I heard her take a deep breath. "He's adorable. He went hurrying off to save Clay from Loretta."

"That *is* adorable! Unless he's under Loretta's spell, too."

"Maybe she lived in Ben's town in *third* grade, and Ben has been in love with her ever since."

I snickered. "She didn't let on where she'd lived, did she? Didn't it seem like she's still trying to get Clay to tell her *where* she supposedly attended fourth grade?"

"It certainly did. And like she made up the entire thing as part of her murder plan. Antonio would eat the fatal almond while Clay was with her, and she'd use Clay as her alibi."

A dark figure strode up Lake Street. "Are you looking out your front windows?" I asked. "Who do you think that is?"

"Kent. He seems to be staring inside my shop. I'll wave."

I couldn't see her inside her shop, and apparently, Kent couldn't, either. He didn't wave, but then again, he wasn't exactly the friendly, waving sort. He turned his face toward In Stitches.

My night-light should have been enough to let him see me standing by the cash register. I waved.

Kent didn't return the greeting. He faced forward and continued south, walking quickly.

Clay didn't phone or text me, but why would he? Ben would have assured him that Haylee and I had gotten home safely.

I gave the animals one last outing, and then the dogs and I went to bed while the cats groomed themselves for their evening activities, which they would undoubtedly carry out on and near the dogs' and my beds.

Maybe Haylee and I should have taken the dogs out snooping. I would have been relieved if Clay's and Ben's trucks were gone from Pier 42. And if the trucks were nowhere near Loretta's, either.

On the other hand, if we had discovered Clay's truck within walking distance of Loretta's apartment, I might have been unhappier than I was *not* knowing how much time Clay might have spent with her.

I told myself that Clay had seemed reluctant to be around Loretta.

I also told myself that he could have been a little more reluctant. A lot more reluctant. He hadn't needed to invite her to firefighting practice. And he certainly had not needed to take her there in his truck.

But he was nice, and maybe she didn't have any other transportation.

She could have walked.

But he was kind . . .

I took all sides of the argument, round and round and up and down.

Falling asleep took a long time.

22

Shortly after the Wednesday morning students and I began our next upside-down crewel work projects, a bunch of college-age kids crowded into the store. Most of them looked wary, if not downright frightened. I spotted Macey easily, since she was the tallest in the group. She wiggled her fingers at me in a tentative wave that didn't prevent her from appearing almost as nervous as the others.

Paula, the recently bereaved widow, followed them in. She caught sight of me and paled. Was she surprised to see me in my own store?

But she pursed her lips with determination and kept coming, her attractive but very large quilted tote threatening nearby sewing machines. She joined me at the cutting table. "We're here for our field trip," she announced.

Field trip?

"The one my late husband arranged with you."

I was even more at a loss. Antonio had been in my shop, several more times than necessary, to explain what he wanted me to make and model for the fashion show, but he had never mentioned a field trip.

"I'm sorry for your loss," I managed. "Feel free to look around."

Macey and Samantha discovered Sally and Tally and leaned over the railing of the dogs' pen to pet them.

Had Antonio lied to Paula about arranging the field trip, or was Paula lying now?

I gestured toward the table where I'd set out the morning's treats. "You and your students, please help yourselves to cookies and cider." I had more downstairs in my apartment. "And if you have questions about our machines, what they can do, and how we use them to embellish our projects, feel free to ask."

Paula glared at me like I owed her something. "Antonio had it in his notes that you would teach our students to do machine embroidery."

In one field trip? Were they planning to stay all day? All week? The entire semester?

Always helpful, Rosemary edged up beside me. "How about if we form groups of a couple of us who have been coming here for years and some of these young folks, one group for each machine, and demonstrate the basics?"

I gave her a grateful smile. "Thanks!"

Rosemary and Georgina sorted everyone into groups and began demonstrating the easiest and perhaps most impressive part of machine embroidery — stitching the motifs on fabric. The basic designing details could come after my usual workshop attendees whipped up some enthusiasm in the young students.

I planned to oversee the process, but Paula cornered me near the table of cookies. "I guess I owe you an apology," she said begrudgingly.

I shook my head and gave a half shrug.

She stared at me as if waiting for a better response.

I tried. "For what?"

"They say that no one hit my husband." She took a deep, shaky breath. "But, see, I really believed that you and that other woman hit him. Your arms were up, like you had just hit him, and he fell down, and I thought he was . . ." Her voice dwindled to nothing. "But he wasn't, then. Apparently, what killed him was an almond. He was severely allergic to almonds. He knew that!

So why did he eat an almond?"

Again, I didn't know what to say. I couldn't tell if she was upset because her husband had died or because of something else. Did she suspect that the police were investigating *her* for possibly slipping her husband an almond and hiding his medication?

And were they?

Apparently, she didn't expect me to answer. She wandered off and hovered on the edges of the embroidery groups, but she didn't seem to be paying attention to the presentations that my exuberant workshop attendees were giving.

Customers came in. I helped them find what they needed.

Paula shut herself into the restroom. After she came out, she ignored the TADAM students and what they might be learning. Instead, she browsed through the shop. Who could blame her for touching and examining fabrics? I stocked lovely natural materials, mostly plain colors that we could decorate with embroidery. People came from all over to buy linen for tea towels, for instance. Pure linen tea towels were expensive and hard to find, and we could save by hemming them ourselves.

Our real goal, of course, was embroidering designs on them.

Eventually, Paula ended her tour of the store and stood slightly behind my right shoulder. Her frequent sighs could have been due to bereavement, not to boredom, especially if fidgeting were a sign of deep grief. Hoping to either distract her or entertain her, if that was what she needed, I led her to our most sophisticated sewing and embroidery combo and demonstrated its capabilities.

I didn't think she heard a word I said.

Shortly before noon, she called to the TADAM students. She gave me only the briefest of thanks and opened the door for the kids. With a shy smile, Macey thanked me. The other students did, too.

We broke for lunch, and then the afternoon students and I continued our exploration of machine crewel work.

Partway through the afternoon, I saw Paula and her students go into The Stash. Again, Paula carried that fashionable tote, as if Antonio's death had allowed her to emerge from her previous dull, brown, shadowy style.

I wasn't sure, but the group seemed like a different bunch of kids, although Macey again stood out because of her height.

Why was Macey attending field trips that

seemed geared more to TADAM's fashion design students than to its modeling students? Maybe Antonio's criticism of her modeling had hit her hard and she was changing her focus. Or maybe she was taking courses in both subjects.

Was Haylee as surprised as I had been by students descending for a field trip? Kent and Loretta had accused Paula of not being able to run TADAM without their help as teachers. Maybe Paula was hoping to send Loretta and Kent packing, and then let my Threadville colleagues and me teach the kids without being paid to do it. Threadville was a generous place, but not *that* generous.

Did Paula know much about fashion design or modeling? Kent and Loretta had implied that she didn't, and Paula certainly hadn't seemed interested in machine embroidery. At the fashion show and rehearsal for it, Antonio's descriptions of our outfits had lacked the details that anyone interested in fashion would have automatically mentioned. Maybe neither Paula nor Antonio had the necessary skills for running a fashion school.

Ashley arrived after school to help in the shop. "I won't be able to attend tonight's rehearsal for Mona's play," she told me. "I

260

have history and science papers due tomorrow."

I assured her that her homework was more important than Mona's play, which sounded iffy at best, and I sent her home as soon as the Threadville tourists returned to their buses, then locked the front door and finished tidying the shop.

A bolt of pale blue linen stuck up more than its neighbors. I tried to push it down onto the rack that was supposed to hold it in place.

It wouldn't budge.

Mystified, I stuck my hand underneath the bolt and pulled out a sheaf of paper folded in fourths. I unfolded the document and read the title of the top sheet.

THREADVILLE ACADEMY OF DESIGN
AND MODELING BUSINESS PLAN

What?

I rushed through the rest of my cleaning, then took the dogs and the business plan downstairs, where I gave the animals dinner and an outing. Finally, I plunked myself onto a stool at my kitchen counter.

Reading Antonio's business plan while eating wasn't the best idea I'd ever had. The more I read, the queasier I became.

Antonio had wanted his school to grow, a commendable enough ideal, and not terrible in itself. However, he had expected the Threadville Academy of Design and Modeling to spread all over Threadville. The current Threadville shops — those would be the shops owned by my friends and me — would be purchased and "repurposed" as shops selling the "excellent designs and one-of-a-kind garments" created by the TADAM students, while the apartments in the shops — our apartments — would provide student housing.

The current Threadville shops would be "fortunate" to relocate to a mall that Antonio would build outside the village limits.

How had he expected to accomplish all of this?

Aside from the probable astronomical costs of the project, we loved Threadville.

Haylee and her mothers had lovingly created it. Tourists came on buses to learn and buy. There was no way we would sell out and move to a mall, no matter how "modern and convenient, with parking spaces for several hundred cars and at least a dozen buses" the mall might be. A mall would not have the quaint flavor of our sweet little village. And even if it included lavish apartments for us, it would probably not be within walking distance of the beach and the riverside trail, either.

I thought Antonio had chosen Threadville because his academy would fit in, not because he wanted to take it over and force us out. His plan would have killed Threadville as we knew it. Maybe that wouldn't have mattered to him. He must have hoped that taking over our identity would make money — for him.

We owned our shops, with the help of banks. Maybe he'd figured that a great offer would make us move. However, I'd understood from my eavesdropping on the argument between Paula, Kent, and Loretta that TADAM was on shaky financial ground, and Clay had separately come to the same conclusion. So where had Antonio thought he would find the money to build a mall and buy our shops at prices that would tempt us?

I turned the page and read the figures carefully. Antonio had expected tuition from three hundred students by the end of this year.

As far as I could tell, TADAM had about forty students so far, fifty, tops . . .

Antonio had stated that each of the school's quarterly fashion shows would bring in thousands of dollars in admission fees.

Huh? From what I'd observed, the first "quarterly" fashion show had attracted maybe two hundred guests. Ticket prices had been modest, probably about enough to cover the rental of the conservatory and the food served at the reception.

Antonio had estimated that sales of the outfits modeled in the shows would bring in as much as a "lowball" five hundred thousand dollars each quarter. These outfits would be, he said, the equivalent of couturier designs.

I choked on a bite of green pepper. Had he thought that the Threadville shopkeepers would continue providing him with free outfits that he could sell — or so he claimed — for thousands of dollars each?

That was impossible. Couturier designs? What a wild exaggeration. From what I'd seen of the silent auction sheets that Detective Neffting had brought to In Stitches, the outfits that had sold after the first fashion show had been slated to bring in only a few hundred dollars, total. If the auction hadn't been cut short by Antonio's collapse, maybe another few hundred dollars might have been added. But that hadn't happened, and Mona's final bids would have added all of fifty-six dollars.

The one item in his business plan that might have come anywhere near hitting its revenue target was in small print at the bottom of the page. Antonio had planned to import inexpensive clothes, mark them up drastically, and pass them off as "designer" outfits to be sold in the TADAM shops lining Lake Street.

Except for that final bit of trickery, his "business plan" was a business pipe dream.

As I knew from my days as a financial consultant in New York City, many business plans were totally unrealistic. The people who wrote them and provided all the figures were trying to look their best — on paper, at least — and Antonio had been no different. He'd obviously written this one to score funds for his mall construction project.

Fashion design and real estate development? I'd never seen that combination before.

Had Antonio's schemes figured in his death? I wanted to take the business plan to Haylee, who was skilled at ferreting out creative accounting, but Ben had said he would go to The Stash early and help her set up audiovisual equipment for the fashion show video, and I didn't want to disrupt what might turn out to be the first time that

Haylee and Ben actually spent a few moments alone together. Sooner or later, Ben would realize he could love a new woman without betraying the memory of his wife, and I didn't want to be in the way when he did.

I folded the business plan and stuck it into my bag. Maybe I'd get a chance to show it to Haylee after we watched the video. She could help me decide whether or not to give the business plan to Vicki, who would know whether or not Detective Neffting should see it.

My phone rang.

It was Detective Neffting. "I'm at your front door, but it's locked. I need to talk to you."

23

A visit from detective Neffting was never exactly fun and was definitely not convenient at the moment, but I tried not to reveal my reluctance. "I'll be right up."

Mona, Haylee's mothers, and I had arranged to meet Ben and Haylee in The Stash at seven thirty, which was only a half hour away. Neffting could be quick, though, if he decided to wrap up his investigation of Antonio's murder right away and arrest the first person he came across, which, I feared, could be me, and then he'd haul me off in handcuffs and chains, and I would miss the video of the fashion show, anyway. Just possibly, my imagination was carrying me away.

I grabbed my bag, business plan and all, so I'd be ready to go to Haylee's after I talked to Neffting. Or to prison, if that was Detective Neffting's plan.

My dogs and cats wanted to come into the shop with me, but I managed to shut the door at the top of the stairway. They'd probably trot downstairs to their beds and snooze.

Detective Neffting wasn't shy about peering into the shop as I rushed to the door and unlocked it. He didn't smile. That wasn't unusual, but I took it as a bad sign, anyway.

I led him to the fabric cutting table, which was rapidly becoming an interrogation table. At least we could lean on it while we talked. Not wanting to appear the least bit threatening, I shoved all three pairs of scissors into drawers.

He merely raised one eyebrow. "I believe you told me that Anthony Drudge, or Antonio, as he'd been calling himself, pinched at least one young lady, and that bothered you."

"I hope it would have bothered you, too." I couldn't quite keep reproach off my face or out of my voice.

Perhaps I went too far. A trace of anger may have pulled at one corner of his mouth. "Of course it does. I believe you also told me that Mr. Drudge's comments about sins upset you, also."

"Not as much as pinching Macey. The threadly sins comments annoyed me, especially on behalf of my seventeen-year-old assistant, Ashley —"

"Who struck Mr. Drudge after he allegedly pinched the other girl, am I right?"

Why did he have to rehash my earlier statements when I was in a hurry? "Dora saw him pinch Macey. I only saw Ashley push his hand away from Macey's backside."

He scribbled in his notebook, then asked, "What other ways did Mr. Drudge upset you? Was there anything he said, did, wrote, told you, or that you heard about?"

"There was nothing in particular. He was generally annoying, like when he chomped on candies, especially over a PA system, and he was also very full of himself. Everything was about *him*."

"Did he make any proposals to you?"

"He offered me the chance to design and model those four outfits in his fashion show. The funds he planned to raise were supposed to go toward scholarships, so I accepted."

"Anything else?"

"Yes, but it was really minor. It was obvious that he was trying to be funny, and he made a rude suggestion into the microphone to the fashion show audience. He said that if I wanted to commit adultery — which I didn't, and don't — all that I would require was a married man, and he seemed to think he was the perfect candidate."

Neffting didn't look up from his notebook. "Anything else?"

"He was flirtatious backstage after the fashion show, but I made it clear that I wasn't interested, and he backed off."

"Did he mention anything about why, for instance, he chose to open a fashion school?"

"No. At first, I figured he had experience in fashion and design, and I guessed he had decided that a design and modeling school would be a good fit in a village nicknamed Threadville. But he didn't seem to know much about fashion."

Neffting said nothing. He was obviously waiting for me to continue.

"I don't know if anyone wrote the narration Antonio gave at the fashion show or if he ad-libbed, but he never used specific fashion terms. The closest he came were the words 'lovely' and 'beautiful.' If he actually knew much about fashion, he hid it well. Also, he reminded me of some of the would-be entrepreneurs that Haylee and I met while we were investment counselors in New York City, before we came to Pennsylvania. The aspiring entrepreneurs had an idea, a large dose of optimism, and some of them had more than their share of . . ." I paused, searching for the right words. "The ability to stretch the truth. Some of them started companies that failed, so they kept trying something new. Antonio's widow strikes me as fitting that mold, also. They don't — didn't — seem to have the right personalities to work for other people, so they opened their own company. TADAM may not have been the first. I wouldn't be surprised if either or both of them had been conning people out of money and running scams for several years." There, I'd said it.

He tilted his head to one side. "You knew them well?"

"I talked to Antonio a few times in the store. He'd mentioned that his wife was the school's administrative assistant, but I didn't meet her until the fashion show rehearsal."

"Yet you've made a lot of guesses from a short acquaintance."

"As I said, I'd met people like them before." I pulled my bag toward me. "And I found something today that supports my theory about Antonio and the founding of TADAM." I pulled Antonio's business plan out. "Someone stuck this under a bolt of fabric in my shop today. I gave it a quick read-through and was about to take it over to Haylee to see what she thinks." I handed the business plan to Neffting.

He unfolded it and looked at each page for a few seconds, long enough to get the gist. When he'd turned over the final page, he looked up at me, obviously waiting for me to say more.

I explained, "Haylee and I read a lot of business plans. The entrepreneurs hoped that our clients might invest in their companies." I stabbed a finger at the back of the last page of Antonio's business plan. "We would have turned this one down."

"Why?"

"The funds he expected to raise from the fashion show were ridiculously inflated. Also, he talks about tuition from three hundred students, but I haven't seen more than about fifty."

"Were you struck by anything else about the document?"

"The plan seems to be more about building a mall outside the village than about running a thriving fashion design and modeling school. But his plan of taking over downtown Threadville would never have worked. For one thing, none of us would have given in to pressure to move to a mall. For another, if a mall were built, the center of downtown Threadville would die. It would become only a college campus."

"Three hundred students would generate a lot of commerce."

"Which wouldn't be useful if there were no stores, or if the students had to drive out of town to shop."

"Tell me again how you came upon this document."

I backed to the rack of mid-weight linen and lifted the pale blue bolt. "It was stuck underneath this. I found it this evening." I shoved my hand underneath the bolt. "There's nothing there now."

"Did you put the business plan there?"

Had I been unclear? "No, I noticed that the top of the bolt was higher than its neighbors, and when I tried to push it down, it wouldn't go, and I found Antonio's business plan stuck there."

"When had you seen it before?"

"Never."

"How long could it have been underneath that bolt of fabric?"

"It had to have been put there today." I pushed the blue linen back into position, then ran my hand across the tops of the beautiful fabrics. "Last night when I closed the shop, the tops were even like they are right now."

"You're sure?"

"Positive."

"And Antonio Drudge did not personally give you that business plan?"

"He did not."

Neffting continued bombarding me with questions. "Did you hear about it before his death, or otherwise know what was in it?"

"No."

"How do you think that business plan got there today, four days after the man's death?"

"Someone put it there, and I think I know who. His widow, Paula, was here this morning. She brought a dozen TADAM students for what she called a 'field trip.' She said that Antonio had arranged the field trip with me. Maybe she believed that, but he hadn't."

"And you saw her place the business plan underneath that cloth?"

I smoothed the blue linen. "No, but she was carrying a large bag, and she was over here while I was over there." I pointed. "I could see Paula's head and shoulders, but not her hands."

He wrote in his notebook, then looked up at me again. "Why would she leave her late husband's business plan in your shop?"

I returned to my fabric cutting table. "It doesn't make sense, does it? Unless for some reason she was reading it and someone came close and she didn't want to be caught with it."

"She was attempting to read secretly in a shop full of people?"

"That doesn't make sense, either." Before he could agree, I blurted, "What if she arranged her husband's death?"

Neffting's eyes started to widen, but he let his lids droop and became very still.

I admitted, "I'm thinking aloud here. Nearly everyone who was backstage at the fashion show could have inserted a Jordan almond into Antonio's jacket. Someone kept moving the chair it was on into the way of the models —"

"Who?"

"I never saw anyone do it, though I moved it out of everyone's way at least twice. Most of us probably touched that jacket at one time or another. Antonio's assistant, Loretta, was backstage near that chair most of the evening, and so was Paula. She was nearest the chair at the end of the awards ceremony, which is when I accidentally kicked something away from under the chair. At the time, I assumed it was one of the candies, but it could easily have been that vial of medicine. Maybe I almost caught Paula in the act. So, let's suppose that Paula gave him a candy-coated almond and hid his medication . . ."

Watching me intently in a way that could cause the guilty to confess to a multitude of crimes, Neffting stayed quiet.

But I wasn't guilty, so I plunged ahead with my latest, not fully thought-out theory about Paula. "And what if Paula wanted to make it appear that someone else tried to kill her husband? Suppose she chose me as her scapegoat. She could have put the vial of medicine and the unused Jordan almonds in my cubicle. Then to make doubly sure you would suspect me, she could have told you that Antonio had shown his plan to me, and that I'd become livid about being shunted off to a not-yet-built mall outside the village. She could then have suggested that you should get a search warrant and look for that plan on my premises." I glanced across the street at The Stash. "This afternoon, she took a bunch of students to Haylee's shop. I haven't talked to Haylee since then, but I'm going over there after we're done here. I'll ask her if Paula claimed that Antonio had arranged a so-called field trip there. Maybe Paula hid a business plan in Haylee's shop, also."

Detective Neffting kept a poker face. Maybe I had guessed correctly about what Paula had told him about me. And maybe

276

Paula was now becoming his chief suspect in her husband's murder . . .

I asked Neffting, "If Antonio had a business plan that involved doing something sneaky against the people of Threadville, would he have shown it to us?"

Naturally, Neffting didn't answer.

I went on, "And if I had murdered Antonio because of his business plan, would I have hidden it in my shop? Wouldn't I have gotten rid of it long ago?"

"Criminals often make mistakes."

Well, that helped. Not really. But with any luck, he was referring to Paula, not to me.

Or maybe he was thinking of someone else. I suggested, "As Dora Battersby and I told you, a note that we found in the paper soccer ball and that she must have shown you was typed and said 'Pay up or else.' Have you figured out who Antonio's silent partners were, or who else may have lent Antonio money and then carried out the 'or else' part of that threat?"

"Mr. Drudge borrowed from legitimate banks."

"Banks? Plural? Let me guess. He kept taking out new loans to pay off old ones, and he kept taking out bigger and bigger loans."

Neffting did not refute my theory, except

to say, "He bought the TADAM mansion for a dollar, and by the time it was renovated, it could have been worth more than the amount he'd put into renovating it, which could have justified larger and larger loans."

"*Could* have. Also, might not have." I challenged him with my eyes, but he didn't back down and didn't explain.

He didn't haul me off in handcuffs, either. He asked, "You said you're about to go to Haylee's shop?"

"In a few minutes." I didn't want to tell him about the video we planned to watch. Even if he had a copy of it, he might want to confiscate the one that Kent had promised to let us see. "We're meeting to discuss a play that Mona wrote. She bought all the supposedly threadly sinful outfits from the TADAM fashion show and is planning to use them as costumes in a play she's calling *The Seven Threadly Sins.*"

He cocked his head. "Is that what's known as making lemonade from lemons?"

Vicki never laughed at his wisecracks, but I grinned. "I guess so. It's to be a fundraiser for the TADAM scholarship fund, and in return, she's going to be on the scholarship committee. That could give my as-

sistant a better chance at winning a scholarship."

"I see."

And I was sure he also saw that the good
citizens of Threadville were capable of a
little collusion.

But that didn't make us murderers.

He added, "Mona may have a long wait
until those costumes are released. So don't
rehearse *too* hard."

Neffting did have a sense of humor, but
still, he didn't come close to smiling.

"Okay. There's something else." I went to
my desk in the dogs' pen, took out the
sketches that Antonio had given me, brought
them back to the cutting table, and plunked
them down. "Antonio told me that he had
designed the clothes and drawn the sketches
for the outfits we modeled in the fashion
show, but on Monday evening in a class Loretta and her fellow teacher Kent gave, Loretta drew a dress. After seeing her style of
drawing and printing, I'm almost certain
that she made the sketches that Antonio
gave me, and that Loretta, not Antonio,
printed the design instructions accompany-
ing the sketches. Maybe she discovered that
he was pretending that her work was his."

"May I see?" He studied them carefully
and handed them back. "So you're saying

that his — we'll call it appropriation for lack of a better word — his *appropriation* of her designs made her angry enough to kill the man who hired her to draw those designs in the first place? A few minutes ago, you were telling me the widow killed him and is trying to cast the blame on you. Then you came up with a theory about moneylenders."

"It could be any of them," I said a little more heatedly than I meant to. "Or some combination working together. I'm just trying to tell you everything I observed around the time of his death."

"I appreciate that," he muttered.

His appreciation wasn't very convincing, but it was enough to encourage me to tell him more. "At first, Loretta was very angry at him for his seven threadly sins trick. Later, she hid her anger and tried to spin his behavior. She said he'd only been trying to cause us to be creative."

Neffting wrote in his notebook, then looked up at me. "Thank you, as always, for your theories about people, their motives, means, and opportunities. Now, give me time to talk to Haylee before you go barging over there. Feel free to talk to her about the business plan you found, but please wait until after I speak to her."

Barging? "Okay." But I did need to talk to her. We probably didn't want Neffting *barging* into The Stash and discovering that we had a copy of that video. If we had it yet.

Maybe we did have it. As Neffting crossed Lake Street toward The Stash, Kent left Haylee's shop. Neffting stopped him and removed his notebook from his pocket.

Quickly, I called Haylee.

24

Haylee answered right away. Her voice was full of smiles, as if she'd been joking with Ben. I dashed the smiles from her voice with the information that Neffting was on his way to talk to her, and she might like to hide that video.

With Haylee, I didn't have to go into long-winded explanations. "No problem," she answered immediately. "Ben will put Kent's thumb drive in his pocket." In all its glory, the smile returned to her voice. "There. He did."

Disconnecting the call, I hoped that Neffting wouldn't commandeer our phone records. He'd think that I had called Haylee to warn her about the business plan.

With any luck, she didn't know a thing about it, and her innocence would be plain to see, even to a detective used to searching out guilt.

However, I couldn't help some brilliant

smiles of my own. Haylee was with Ben, and she'd sounded very happy.

To keep anyone besides Ben from interrupting Neffting's and Haylee's conversation, I dialed Mona and told her the meeting was being delayed until eight.

"I'm in charge of setting rehearsal times," she reminded me in queenly tones.

"But we're 'rehearsing' in Haylee's store, and it's not free at the moment."

Naturally, Mona wanted to know why. I didn't dare say that Detective Neffting was there. Mona would undoubtedly develop a whopping crush on the man. Telling her that Ben was with Haylee would have an even worse outcome. "Customers stayed too long today," I managed.

"I'll call Kent!"

How could the surly Kent make anyone sound that thrilled? At least I got her off the phone in a hurry and could call Haylee's three mothers and stall them, too. Although they were concerned that a homicide detective was questioning Haylee, when I told them that Ben was also in her shop, they must have suddenly seen visions of beautiful grandchildren. They decided not to interfere.

Biting my fingernails, I peered outside. I

didn't see either Kent or Detective Neffting.

I hoped Mona wouldn't reach Kent. If he told Mona that Haylee was alone with two men, nothing would stop Mona from racing to The Stash.

After about twenty minutes, Detective Neffting finally strode out of Haylee's shop. He seemed to be staring straight at me. I waved and fiddled with my *Come Back Later* sign. Without acknowledging my greeting, Neffting turned, climbed into his car, and drove out of sight. I dashed across the street.

Haylee met me at her door and let me in. "Guess what the good detective found here!"

"A copy of the TADAM business plan?"

"How did you know?" Mimicking a balloon rapidly deflating, she whistled between her lips.

"I found one in my shop. I was about to bring it to show you when he arrived, and from the questions he was asking, I guessed he was trying to find out if I'd read the thing before Antonio died, and if I'd set out to murder him because of it."

"What does it say? I let Neffting keep the one he found here."

I fished my copy out of my bag and handed it to her. "Read it and you'll understand. Did Neffting have a search warrant?"

"No. He zeroed right in on a bolt of fabric that was sticking up a fraction of an inch higher than its neighbors and asked me if I would let him see what might be keeping it from sliding down. I said yes. And there was this folded business plan underneath it. I didn't want the thing and asked him to take it with him."

I burst out laughing. "That's great! That's how she — I'm assuming it was Paula — hid one in my shop. Now Neffting might believe me that Paula left them there. How likely would it be for *both* of us to hide Antonio's business plan under bolts of fabric before we went about our murdering ways?"

"Detective Neffting might believe anything of the two of us. Like we were conspiring to frame Paula."

"Arrgh. He might. Why did Paula bring a group of students to your shop today?"

"She said Antonio had arranged a field trip for his students here. He hadn't."

"She told me the same thing this morning. Where's Ben? Was he here when Neffting interviewed you?"

Ben's voice came from Haylee's classroom. "I was beside her the whole time the detective talked to her."

I followed Haylee into the large classroom she'd had Clay build in the back of her shop. Tables were set up in a rectangle so that everyone working on sewing machines or sergers could see each other, and they would all have lots of space around their machines, plus sufficient outlets in the floor. Good lighting had been carefully added, too, since windows were only along the wall of the room overlooking the parking lot behind the building. Now the blinds were pulled down, and a media screen had been unrolled from its ceiling-mounted case above the windows.

His back to the oversized screen, Ben grinned at us. A laptop computer, with a projector next to it, was open in front of him. "Here you go, you two sleuths," he said. "I've copied Kent's files onto Haylee's computer. The video from the fashion show was on his drive, plus a bunch of photos, probably from the same event. And don't tell that detective, but I also searched among deleted files and recovered documents that look like correspondence and archived e-mails. They're all on Haylee's computer now."

I pretended outrage. "You're as bad as we are, Ben."

With a boyishly innocent smile, he asked

me, "What's your e-mail address, Willow? I'll send the files to you, too."

Naturally, I told him. Not because I was snoopy, but because having more than one copy of important files was always a good plan.

"Okay," Ben told me. "They're on their way."

He clicked on a file, and the screen hanging from the ceiling displayed the conservatory, with chairs rowed up on both sides of the runway. The unlit podium was in front of the closed blue velvet curtains. We heard voices calling to each other, and then people began filing into seats.

A man put his nose almost on the camera lens. "I hope this camera's not turned on," he said.

All three of us laughed, and Ben paused the video. "It's all set."

Haylee didn't seem to be able to think of anything to do but smile at him. I scooted out of the classroom. "I'll go let people in."

"The door's unlocked," Haylee called after me.

"Then let's pretend I'm watching for them when I'm really just admiring your fabrics."

"Like Kent did," she shouted.

I popped back into the classroom. "Were you watching Kent every second?"

"No."

"Oh. So Kent could have left the business plan there."

"That's what I told Neffting. It could have been Paula, it could have been Kent, or it could have been the TADAM students who were here today."

Macey? I asked Haylee, "Did it happen today, for sure?"

"Yep. I straightened everything in the shop last night." She grinned up at Ben, who now stood beside her. "Want to have a look at the business plan with me while we wait for the others? It's not rocket science, but I suspect you'll understand it, anyway."

Before Ben and his late wife bought the Elderberry Bay Lodge, Ben had been a mechanical engineer in the aerospace industry. He returned Haylee's smile. "Let's have a look. Willow can signal us when we need to put it away."

"I'll yell, 'Thread!' "

"Thread?" Ben asked.

As I left the classroom again, I heard Haylee explain that Dora had come up with the word "thread" on Monday evening to warn us when someone was coming. Ben laughed.

I stood close to Haylee's front door and watched the street. It was quiet in Threadville at that time of evening, with hardly anyone coming from or going to the beach.

From the classroom, I heard Haylee's and Ben's murmurs and occasional words, like Ben's amazed *"What?"*

I was happy because they were obviously comfortable with each other and maybe beginning a more-than-friends relationship, but I was also a little jealous. What if Loretta kept working at it until she succeeded in wooing Clay away from me?

Mona walked up the hill, quickly for her, and crossed toward The Stash.

"Thread!" I called.

Mona opened the door, pranced in, and whispered loudly, "Is he here?"

"Who?" I hoped she wasn't chasing Ben, even though I didn't think she had a chance with him.

"Kent."

"No."

She turned her face toward the classroom as if sniffing in that direction. "I hear a man."

"Ben's helping Haylee get ready."

She sprinted through the store and into the classroom. "Hi, Ben." A pause. "Hi, Haylee. Ready for the first meeting between the director and cast of our first Threadville Theater production?"

I didn't hear Haylee's response. Edna and

Naomi came in and greeted me warmly. Next was Opal.

So. Since Kent hadn't stayed, and Ashley wasn't coming, we were all there.

Unless, I thought wistfully, Clay showed up.

I told myself that if Clay came to the showing, Loretta probably would, too, and we did not need to have the entire set-building crew watch us make fools of ourselves on the runway.

With my head up, I marched into the classroom, reached for the light switches near the door, and sent Haylee a questioning look.

She nodded.

As I turned the lights down, Mona ordered, "Dim the lights for us, Willow, so we can get started." Mona was In Charge.

Hiding a grin, I slipped into a seat next to Edna.

Mona cooed, "Start the video, Ben!"

We watched people seat themselves in the conservatory.

Mona edged forward. "Can we fast-forward to see ourselves?"

Ben answered, "We could, but we might miss something you'd like to use in your play."

Mona wriggled back in her chair. "You're

so clever, Ben."

He certainly was. He knew that the rest of us wanted to watch the video for clues about who might have deliberately harmed Antonio, and that we didn't want Mona telling Kent about our sleuthing.

The stage curtains parted. In her off-white silk pants, top, and flowing jacket, Loretta stepped out through the gap, gave the gathering crowd an assessing look, and shoved a sheaf of papers into the podium. Had she written the entire script, including the seven threadly sins commentary, or was she only the gofer?

Seeing Antonio emerge between the curtains gave me a weird feeling. He didn't know — no one knew, except his killer or killers — that he had only about three hours left to live. Smiling toward the audience, he shielded his eyes against the lights, then waved a piece of paper as if greeting someone. Or everyone, perhaps. He smiled directly at the camera. He pulled the papers out of the shelf where Loretta had put them, placed them on top of the one he'd been carrying, squared them on the podium, switched on the reading light, and tapped the mike. It was live.

Paula burst out through the curtains, grabbed Antonio's jacket by the shoulders, pulled it off, and rushed offstage. Antonio grinned into the audience. They were still talking, but it was easy to understand what he purred into the microphone. "Women! Always trying to undress me!"

Ick.

Antonio pushed the curtains aside and hurried after his wife. The microphone didn't pick up the stage-whispered argument that I had witnessed between the couple, which was probably just as well. Her comment about his addiction probably wouldn't have gone over well with the audience.

Without his jacket, Antonio returned to the podium, read his welcoming remarks, and launched into describing us as we tripped down the runway.

The students were fine, and the Threadville ladies didn't do too badly, but I had to cringe at seeing myself, especially in that ruffled confection with my long legs sticking out like toothpicks beneath it.

Mona sat forward, breathing quickly whenever she was onstage.

Finally, the fashion show ended, and Antonio started his "awards ceremony." The looks of surprise on our faces when he first announced that we'd been guilty of seven threadly sins made us all laugh. Everyone singled out before Ashley had recovered quickly from Antonio's jibes and played along with them, but when Ashley's turn came, we saw the color drain from her face and watched her dart toward the opening in the curtains. Always attuned to others' feelings, Naomi frowned in sympathy and followed the girl offstage.

Mona laughed when I made my comment about childery. "I put that remark into the play," she announced.

I gave her a weak smile. I hoped the play wouldn't turn into a play about a murder, with a stork-like woman in a Bo Peep dress as the villain. Neffting would probably decide that the person whom Antonio had forced to wear such a silly dress had to have arranged his death.

At the end of the awards ceremony, the models bunched up near the curtains. The chair holding Antonio's jacket had prevented everyone from making a graceful exit.

Macey was last to disappear behind the curtains.

People in the audience stood, talked, laughed, and began leaving the conservatory's domed main room.

Mona ordered, "Turn up the lights, Willow."

I wanted to watch the rest of the video, but a copy was on Haylee's computer, and Ben had e-mailed me one, so I obeyed her.

She stood and tugged her tight, stretchy dress farther down her thighs. "We're done here for now. Our next rehearsal is tomorrow night at nine. Kent says we can use the carriage house behind the TADAM mansion for our rehearsals and for the play. Isn't that fantastic?"

Haylee and I traded grins. "Fantastic" could be a good word for rehearsals and a play held in a building that had to be dim, dusty, and possibly about to fall down.

And what about Loretta's plans for turning the carriage house into an apartment? Loretta and Kent had been united when they'd been arguing with Paula, but once they found out about each other's plans for the carriage house, would they fight? And in the process, divulge secrets that would lead us — I meant the police — to the person who had killed Antonio?

Mona stared hungrily at Ben. "Your truck is parked near my shop, so you might as well walk me home on the way. Threadville is just not safe!"

Ben glanced at Haylee, who didn't look at him but seemed to be holding her breath. He thrust his hands into his pockets. "Sure.

And everyone else who is going that way . . ." He let the unended phrase act as a question.

Haylee's mothers and I all jumped up. Opal said, "Let's all go together."

Mona showed a dimple. "But I'm the farthest away and the nearest to his truck, so he has to see me home last."

Maybe she could have been more obvious if she'd tried harder.

Ben turned to Haylee. "I'll come back afterward and help you tidy everything up."

"This place looks tidy enough," Mona stated. Compared to the usual clutter of merchandise in her shop, Country Chic, anything was tidy. But Ben had helped with the audiovisual equipment, and of course he'd want to make sure everything was put together again correctly. He may have brought some of the equipment from the Elderberry Bay Lodge, besides.

Mona asked, "What about the video? I need to give that back to Kent."

Haylee said, "Kent was going to pick up his thumb drive at our next rehearsal, which you said is tomorrow night at nine. At the carriage house?"

Mona laughed, a sound that was both shrill and hollow. "Yes, at nine at the carriage house. I may see him before that, though. He and I have to plan those rehearsals, you know. That's why the rehearsal can't be earlier than nine. I'll take the thumb drive."

Ben pulled a red thumb drive out of his pocket and gave it to her.

He ended up walking us all home, except that none of us went to our own shops. We all accompanied Mona to Country Chic. Unlocking her front door, she inspected her porch as if expecting someone to jump out at her from among garden gnomes, bistro tables, and trellises. "No one's here," she said. "Maybe he'll be along later."

Edna, who occasionally lacked tact, said, "Kent's boss was killed. Kent could be a murderer."

Naomi added, "You shouldn't be alone with him."

Mona tossed back her hair. "Well, I *have* been alone with him, and nothing happened."

I refrained from consoling her but couldn't quite control a snicker.

Mona glared at me and corrected her earlier statement. "Nothing *bad* happened."

Opal tried. "He could be dangerous."

Mona stared at us as if we all, including Ben, had flown in on broomsticks. "For your information, I know for a fact that Kent did not murder his boss."

25

I asked Mona, "how can you *know* that Kent didn't murder Antonio?"

"He told me. Several things. One, as he told Ben, Haylee, you, and me last night, he wasn't even at the fashion show that evening. He set up the camera, then went to Pier 42 until he had to go to the TADAM mansion and check that the students and caterers had everything ready."

Edna burst out with, "But Antonio collapsed at the reception. Kent was at the reception. I saw him there."

Mona had an answer for that, too. "Kent believes the poison or whatever it was that killed Antonio was administered earlier. It took time to work."

That theory was similar to mine, which didn't mean that Kent was *not* the one who had put a candy-covered almond or two into Antonio's pocket.

Mona must have noticed our skeptical

expressions. She raised her index and middle fingers. "The second reason I know that Kent didn't kill Antonio is that he is investigating the murder himself because he's afraid the police are going to try to pin it on him."

"Exactly," I said. "And maybe they're right. Maybe he's only trying to cast suspicion on someone else." Like by leaving that business plan in Haylee's shop, for instance. Maybe he was the one who planned to tell Detective Neffting to obtain a search warrant for a shop — Haylee's, this time. Maybe both he and Paula had tried the same trick, in different places. Maybe they were working together. I doubted that they had separately come up with identical plans.

Mona shook her head. "No, you still don't get it. The police might have a reason to assume that Kent was guilty of murder. But he wasn't."

That was too much for me. "What reason?"

"Antonio hadn't paid him. Or anyone. And that includes that redhead." She nodded as if expecting us to suddenly point fingers at Loretta as a murder suspect.

Not that I didn't want to.

Opal demanded, "Then why did they continue working for Antonio, Mona?"

"Antonio told Kent he was *going* to pay him. Eventually. How would Kent get paid if he left TADAM? Antonio had also assured Kent that the fashion show would bring in so much money and so many more tuition-paying students that everyone would be paid."

Ben asked, "And Kent believed him?"

Mona nodded. "At first. But then he began doubting and made a big mistake."

I was sure I wasn't the only one holding my breath and hoping that Mona would tell us more.

She did. "Poor Kent got impatient and wrote threatening notes to Antonio. He never should have put such things in writing. He says he didn't sign them, but I know a lot about solving crimes. They can trace who wrote those notes."

You won't get away with it.

Pay up or else.

Maybe Kent had printed the first note and typed the second.

Mona waved a hand in front of her face. "But it doesn't matter. We need to find the real murderer quickly so we can get those outfits back to use as costumes in our play, and Kent and I are afraid that the police will come after him." She lowered her voice. "This is confidential, so don't go telling anyone, especially not the police. Kent was wrongfully convicted when he was in his early twenties. He has to figure out who killed Antonio before the police dig up his old criminal record and think he was Antonio's murderer."

Was Kent's criminal record due to the assault that Loretta had told me about, or something else? Whatever criminal record the man had, the police probably already knew about it. Unless . . . I asked, "Was his conviction overturned?"

Mona stamped a foot. "No. That's the problem. Don't you see? A model accused him of assaulting her, but he was only draping fabric on her and barely touched her. The girl wanted attention and made a capital case of it."

I asked Mona, "Why did Antonio take the risk of hiring a teacher with a record of assaulting a model? In a fashion design and modeling school?"

Mona gave me one of her superior, haughty looks. "Didn't you understand what I just said? Kent wasn't guilty. He was wrongfully accused and convicted." Her eyes went suddenly dreamy. "Poor Antonio. He was not only handsome, he was a good man, a fair and just man. He believed Kent, and he gave him the chance he needed."

She took a deep breath. "So you see, Kent would never have harmed Antonio. Kent loves fashion design. He wants to design clothes just for me. Isn't that darling?"

Actually, it was worrisome.

She didn't seem to notice our exchange of glances and clearing of throats. "Kent needed to prove he could be in the fashion industry without being unjustly accused." She glowered up the hill in the direction of TADAM. "But things have gone all wrong for Kent. First, his employer died. May have been killed. And then, to make matters worse, another model here in Threadville, a TADAM student, has just accused Kent of touching her."

Almost breathless, I asked, "Another model? Did he say who?"

Mona's forehead puckered. "Some name like a department store. Blooming? Blossom?"

"Macey?" I supplied.

Mona nodded. "Yes, that's the name. Poor Kent suffers from terrible luck, probably because of his good looks, and we wouldn't want to compound his problems by going around speculating that he murdered someone, would we? He could end up with another wrongful conviction."

Naomi answered, "We certainly wouldn't

want to see anyone being wrongfully arrested."

Edna folded her arms, making her look quite formidable, despite her tiny size. "But nothing you have said actually clears Kent's name. Be careful."

Ben added, "Don't be alone with him."

Mona smiled up at him. "Want to be my chaperone?"

Ben brushed that off with a light quip. "Maybe we all should be."

Opal reminded her, "Whether Kent is innocent or not, there could be a murderer in Elderberry Bay. Lock your doors."

"I'll be fine. You all worry too much." Mona went into her shop. With an exaggerated flare, she twisted the dead bolt.

26

Although Haylee's mothers and I would gladly have let Ben return to spend the rest of the evening alone with Haylee, Edna summed up what I'd been thinking. "We have work to do. We'd better watch that video again and figure out where everyone was, and when. Especially Kent. Mona is obviously besotted. What she said makes me even more suspicious of him."

Ben, Edna, Naomi, Opal, and I hurried toward The Stash.

Naomi glanced over her shoulder. "I hope Mona doesn't look out and see us not going back to our own shops, after all."

"You can bet she's watching the street," Edna said. "But she'll be looking for Kent. I would not want to be alone with that man."

"Me, neither," said Ben.

We all laughed. Ben was taller than Kent and more muscular. He could probably look after himself.

"If you have allergies, though," I told Ben, "don't let anyone know what they are."

He pulled at the handle of The Stash's front door. "Haylee told me what you suspect about Antonio's killer and the almonds and allergy medication. So don't worry. If I develop any allergies, I'll keep them a secret."

The door was locked, but Haylee dashed out of her classroom and opened it for us. Although her smile was wide, she blushed and didn't look directly at Ben.

She had it bad. And who could blame her?

After we were all inside, she carefully locked her door. "We're not going to want surprise visitors."

Either Edna or one of Haylee's other mothers had managed to whisper to her that we would return, or she had guessed. In her classroom, she'd already put out sheets of paper and pencils for each of us.

She went to her computer. "I thought we could watch the show again, all the way through, without stopping to discuss it. If you glimpse something you want to see better, make a note of it, along with the time, which will show at the bottom of the screen. Then we'll go back through the entire thing, pausing whenever anyone wants to. Okay?"

It was already nine thirty, and watching it two more times would take us until nearly eleven thirty, but we all agreed.

Ben asked, "Should I call Clay to join us? And what about your mother, Edna? She wouldn't want to miss this."

Edna pretended to draw a big X on her pad of paper. "My mother can already find too many ways to get into trouble."

I burst out with, "We can't call Clay. Loretta could be with him. We don't really want her helping us analyze who might have stuck candy-covered almonds into Antonio's pocket and removed his medication. Loretta could have done it."

Ben frowned at me and shook his head. "I doubt that Clay would be with her, but I won't call him. Too bad. Clay's very observant."

Opal nodded. "He has a good head on his shoulders."

Edna chimed in, "Except around that redhead."

My thoughts, exactly.

Naomi brought us all back to the subject. "What should we be looking for in the video?"

I answered, "Anyone who had access to Antonio's jacket."

Haylee nodded. "Who was near it, and when,"

Edna groaned. "All of us were, at one time or another."

Ben added, "Maybe we can eliminate some of the people as suspects."

Edna burst out laughing. "All of *us*!"

I dimmed the lights. Ben started the video.

While we watched, pencils scratched on paper.

Suddenly, after the fashion show was over and the audience began leaving the conservatory, the blue velvet curtains swayed. Kent thrust his way out between them. He marched down the runway, crouched, rested his weight on one hand, then vaulted down to the conservatory's floor. With two quick strides, he reached the video camera, and then the picture went black.

I turned on the lights.

Edna spoke first. "Paula was just out of view almost the entire time. She used her clipboard to hold the curtains back for us, and I could see at least a corner of the clipboard every time someone went between those curtains."

Haylee tapped her pencil against her chin. "Are we sure that she was the only one doing that? Did Loretta have a clipboard?"

We all agreed that we hadn't seen Loretta

with one, and that the few times that a hand had appeared on the video holding a clipboard, the hand had looked more like Paula's.

"Nail polish," Haylee summarized. "Loretta's was red that evening, and if Paula was wearing any, it was a more subtle shade."

I asked, "Did anyone see Kent, either backstage or in the main room of the conservatory, between the time he set up the camera and later, when he shut it off? After the show, Kent came backstage from, it appeared, outside. He passed Antonio, who was again wearing his jacket and was on his way out of the conservatory and probably heading straight to TADAM."

Ben pointed his pencil at the blank screen. "He was near the back of the rows of chairs before the fashion show, when Clay and I arrived with Dora Battersby, but I didn't see him again."

None of us had seen him during the fashion show. "Maybe he told us the truth," Haylee concluded. "Maybe he did stay away."

"There was an area at stage right that was sectioned off by red curtains like the ones surrounding our cubicles," I said. "Kent could have spent at least part of the show in there. He could have come out and put candies in Antonio's pocket when we were either in our cubicles or out on the runway, so none of us saw him. However, he was definitely coming from the opposite direction when I saw him rush past our cubicles. That conservatory has other rooms besides the main one, though, and that red-curtained storage area could possibly have been accessed from the ramp that winds around behind the backstage." I stared at the screen again, even though it was blank. "Loretta disappeared into that larger cubicle and came back several times. Did Paula, also?"

"I saw Loretta come out of there," Haylee said, "but no one else. She retrieved those white briefcases and other props. But every time I was near the stage curtains, Paula was, too."

"Someone kept moving the chair that Antonio's jacket was on," Opal contributed. "They kept putting it where people coming in off the runway wouldn't see it and could bump into it and knock the jacket off."

Edna nodded. "It was like whoever planted the almonds in Antonio's jacket pocket wanted to make certain that as many people as possible handled it."

I groaned. "He — or she — succeeded."

"I moved that chair away from the curtains at least once," Opal said.

"Me, too," Naomi added.

It turned out that all of us had pushed the chair away from the curtains, bumped into it, knocked Antonio's jacket off it, or picked up the jacket and hung it on the chair.

Edna said, "I think every student in that fashion show also touched his jacket."

Including Macey, who had told me that she'd slapped Antonio in her cubicle, but had apparently told the police that Kent *had been the one touching her.* But I only said, "As I told Detective Neffting, I saw Paula near that jacket immediately after the awards ceremony, which was when I accidentally kicked something that could have been the vial of medicine out from underneath the chair."

Edna nodded quickly. "It's often the spouse." She gazed at her sparkling engagement and wedding rings. "Sad."

"Paula moved that chair into everyone else's way," I said. "Did anyone else do that?"

Edna looked up from admiring her rings. "Once when I was in line to go out onto the runway, Paula pushed that chair so far that it bulged the stage curtains, and she had to pull it away. And that's on the video, too, seen from the audience's side of the curtains."

Ben fingered the keys of Haylee's laptop. "Did you write down the time?"

Edna consulted her notes and gave him the exact time in the video.

Ben reset the video, and I dimmed the lights. Sure enough, the curtain bulged for a second, the clipboard held one curtain back, and Edna, wearing her Distinguished Dressing outfit, pranced out onto the runway.

I summarized, "That bulge in the curtains is close enough to the clipboard that Paula could have been holding the clipboard with one hand and moving the chair with the other."

Naomi closed her eyes briefly, then reopened them. "When Ashley and I went backstage together right before the awards ceremony ended, Loretta had her hand on the back of that chair, and it was tight up against the stage curtains again. Loretta quickly let go of the chair, and we edged around it without knocking Antonio's jacket off. Maybe Loretta was only trying to regain her balance — she was sort of tilting sideways — or trying to move it out of our way, instead of into it. Paula was glaring at her."

"As usual," I said. "Paula seemed to glare at everyone, including her late husband, before he was late, that is."

Naomi said, "Loretta seemed upset about what Antonio was saying. She told Ashley that Antonio didn't mean it about threadly sins, and of *course* Ashley had created her own design. But if you ask me, that Loretta is a fake who will say whatever she thinks people want to hear."

Edna leaned forward. "Ben, talk to Clay. Tell him that redhead is a fake."

Ben gave Edna a devilish grin. "Your mother has already warned him."

I made a weak sort of groaning noise. Maybe no one heard it. We were all pushing our chairs back.

Ben asked Haylee if she needed help putting her classroom in order.

Say yes, Haylee.

"No," she said. "There's really nothing to do."

I caught Naomi and Opal exchanging disappointed looks. We all, including Ben, trooped to the front door. Haylee let us out, stayed inside, and locked the door after we left.

"We'll walk you to your truck, Ben," Edna offered.

He laughed. "I can look after myself."

Opal explained, "But you're parked in front of Mona's shop."

Naomi finished the sentence. "And we should go see if Mona needs our help with anything."

Ben ambled with us. I wasn't certain that Mona would want us interrupting a possible rendezvous, but when we arrived at Country Chic, all the lights were out. If Kent was with her, they were in her apartment above the shop. We didn't see lights up there, either, and none of us wanted to pry.

We started up the hill toward our own shops. Ben came with us. *Going to Haylee's after all?* But he only said, "I'll watch until you're all safely inside."

After I went into In Stitches, I peered out at him. He turned and strode back toward his truck.

Although it was nearly midnight, I called Haylee. "Want to go for a walk with me and the dogs?"

"I'm ready," she said. "But maybe we should go to Pier 42 for a few minutes, first, and ask if Kent was there on Saturday night."

"When does it close?"

"Why would I know the closing time of local bars? Except I do know. It closes at one."

I laughed and hung up.

Dressed alike again in the black jeans and hoodies that would raise Vicki's eyebrows if she caught us, Haylee and I met in front of The Stash and strode down Lake Street to Pier 42. Even this late, the pub was noisy and crowded, but we found two stools together at the bar. It was tended by Ray, a big man with a thatch of brown hair that resembled the fur on a teddy bear's head. We each ordered a small mug of craft beer. When Ray brought them to us, I asked him, "Were you working here Saturday night?"

His dark eyes seemed to snap. "I work here every night."

"Did you happen to notice a short, muscular man wearing a black T-shirt?"

"Angry-looking dude?" Ray asked. "The one who talked to you when you were leaving here with the other firefighters last night?" He pointed toward the back corner near the hallway to the restrooms. "He'd been sitting over there with Mona?"

"That's the one," we said.

"Yep, he was here Saturday night. Ordered a pitcher of beer and drank it himself, all but the two or three inches he left in the bottom of the pitcher." Ray's upper eyelids nearly covered those black eyes. "A waste of good beer, if you ask me. But he said he had to rush off. Something about filming a fashion show and getting the reception ready afterward, in that old mansion — you know, the one they fixed up in a huge rush and turned into a school?"

I asked, "Did you notice what time he arrived and when he left?"

Ray shook his head. "Sorry. But he was here a long time. Kind of funny, I thought, for someone who claimed he was working the whole time, when what he was actually working on was most of a pitcher of beer."

We finished our beer, left Ray a nice tip, and hurried back to my yard. Blueberry Cottage was dark. For once, Dora Battersby wasn't spinning, weaving, knitting, or reading. Or watching my back door so she could chat while I let my animals out. I opened the patio door, leashed the dogs, and handed Sally's leash to Haylee. Sally and Tally strained toward the cottage, probably hoping for their usual handouts from Dora, but after I locked the door, Haylee and I urged them up the hill to my side gate, instead.

On the sidewalk, where our talking wouldn't disturb Dora, Haylee asked quietly, "Want to climb into my truck and go see if Clay's truck is parked in his driveway?"

"No! Would *you* like to make certain that

Ben's truck is back at the Elderberry Bay Lodge?"

"Definitely not."

"I really like him," I said. "He fits in with the rest of us. But maybe that's not a point in his favor."

She laughed. "I like him, too. He's a good friend. With the emphasis on *friend*. And I'm afraid that's the way it's going to be for a long time."

We guided the dogs south, away from the lake. "Maybe not so long. He seems to find it natural to go where you are and help with whatever you're doing." *Meanwhile, have I lost Clay, even as a friend?* I didn't want to suggest it. Haylee would only contradict me, which could give me false hopes. Logic, I knew, was not my strong point.

The conservatory was dark, but lights on the pathway surrounding it showed yellow police tape encircling the building. "It seems a little late to tape that off as a crime scene," I muttered.

We stayed on the pathway.

When we were behind the TADAM mansion's carriage house, a sudden succession of loud thumps and grunts made us jump.

The noises came from inside the carriage house.

27

Yipping, the dogs pulled us toward the back of the carriage house.

I couldn't hear anything besides barking.

Afraid we might interrupt a lovers' rendez-vous, I pulled Tally back toward the street. Sally always wanted to go wherever her brother went, so she and Haylee came along.

When we were far enough away to be inaudible to anyone in the carriage house, I stopped and asked Haylee, "What was thumping and grunting inside the carriage house?"

"An animal?" She didn't sound convinced.

"Sally and Tally bark like that when Clay is near . . ."

"And you think he could have been back there with Loretta? In a moldering old carriage house? Give me a break. Give *him* a break. Even if he liked her, and I'm sure he doesn't, at least not *that* way, give him credit for having some class."

She could always make me laugh. "I guess you're right. We probably heard raccoons or cats or dogs."

"Maybe we should go back and try to figure out what was going on inside the carriage house."

Knowing we would never hear other noises around the dogs, we took them back to my apartment and shut them inside. Then we pulled our black hoods over our hair again and strolled toward TADAM.

I whispered, "Maybe the raccoons or possums will have left by now."

From near the yellow-taped conservatory onward, though, we said nothing. We stopped near the back of the carriage house, held our breath, and listened.

The moon had set several hours ago, and only a few stars glimmered through the haze. Lights above the pathways behind us cast a feeble glow on the rear of the TADAM mansion, its grounds, and its carriage house.

Something moved near the mansion's back porch.

Haylee grabbed my wrist and pointed.

First, I thought the small black-and-white animal was a cat. Then I did a double take and was very, very glad we had taken the dogs home.

"Back away slowly," I said. "Skunks don't

see well. We're far enough away that it may not feel threatened."

We started to edge backward, but thumps and grunts came from inside the carriage house again, and one of the grunts sounded like a muffled call for help.

Haylee and I stopped in our tracks. The skunk sniffed the base of a trash can and waddled slowly away, toward the next house and, fortunately, farther from us.

Were skunks inside the carriage house, too, possibly surrounding someone? Whoever it was had taken up frantic thumping again.

I called out, "Hello?"

Again a muffled cry. This time, it sounded like "Help me!"

Haylee made her hands into a megaphone. "Don't move! There's a skunk."

The pounding only became louder and faster.

"Bang twice if you need help," I yelled.

The pounding stopped. There was one loud and decisive thump, and then a second one. Then nothing.

"We're coming," I shouted.

No more thumps and no more bumps.

We were no more interested in scaling the chain-link fence than we had been on Monday evening. Lengthening our tiptoeing stride until we were almost at the street, and more importantly, far from that skunk, we began running.

Haylee sniffed. "What's that smell?"

At first, it resembled bruised greenery. Then it resembled bruised greenery mixed with a particularly smelly petroleum product. And then . . . we both recognized it.

"Skunk," we said together.

Although it smelled atrocious, the spray had not hit us directly. We turned right, then right again at the next block. The closer we got to TADAM, the more the skunk spray reeked.

I wanted to go home and take a shower, but I suspected the smell was going to cling to the insides of my nostrils for quite a while, shower or not.

It was after one. The TADAM mansion was totally dark, and there were no trash or recycling bins beside the curb. If Paula was upstairs in her apartment, she'd turned out the lights.

A ghostly, creaking noise made us grab for each other. The mansion's front door opened slowly, a few inches, then just as slowly, creaked shut again. We didn't hear it latch.

Using our phones as flashlights and keeping our eyes open for the skunk and any of its friends and family that might still be fully armed, we tiptoed past one side of the mansion on one of three narrow concrete tracks that must have originally been poured for a horse and carriage. The wider central track would have been for the horse. The outer ones, spaced more or less correctly for more modern vehicles, could still serve as the mansion's driveway. When the concrete had been fresh and damp, grooves had been gouged across it, presumably to give the horse and the carriage wheels traction, but over the years, all three tracks had cracked and heaved. They threatened to trip us or turn our ankles.

With great care, we approached the mansion's back porch and flashed our lights on garbage cans beside it. No skunks, cats, dogs, raccoons, or possums. Except for the stink that burned our eyes and throats, everything was serene. No noises came from the carriage house, either.

Years ago, two large wooden doors would have swung open to let horses and carriages into and out of the carriage house. A hefty wooden plank spanning the width of both doors kept them closed. Beside them was a smaller door, the one I'd seen Loretta and Clay use.

My heart seeming to beat inside my bitter-tasting mouth, I tried that door. It opened. No thumps or crashes or muffled calls for help, only a few skitterings like mice or squirrels.

Skunks would not move that quickly, would they?

The stench of skunk was worse than it had been outside.

Streetlights from the park provided the only light, and it was filtered through dirt and cobwebs covering the building's windows. As far as I could tell, there were only two of them, one on each of the side walls.

I felt around for the switch I'd seen Loretta use. It was old-fashioned, with two round buttons. I pushed the top one.

With a snap, it hit home and three bulbs on cords dangling from rafters came on. Although the bulbs were dim, I had to shield my eyes.

It was no wonder that Loretta wanted to renovate the structure. It was large, solid, and there was a loft above our heads, over the front half. It could become a cute cottage after the stink of skunk wore off.

And I understood why Kent thought it could be turned into a theater, also, though it was small. The hayloft could be a balcony for some of the audience.

Thump.

Beside me, Haylee gasped and rushed forward. "Are you all right?"

Obviously, the woman beyond the stall near one back corner of the carriage house was far from all right. Gagged and bound with strips of what looked like extra-wide white adhesive tape, she sat against the wall. The thumps we'd heard had been caused by the back of her head banging against the structure's interior tongue-and-groove paneling.

She bopped the wall with her head again, which seemed to cause her eyes to go expressionless, then she focused on us and her eyes widened in apparent terror, and she shook her head violently.

It took me a second to recognize the wan brown hair and sloping shoulders.

Paula.

28

Haylee and I both knew not to touch anything, including Paula, unless we needed to rescue her or protect her from injury. I dialed 911 and described what we'd discovered.

"Are you hurt?" Haylee asked.

Paula's slim shoulders lifted in a shrug.

"Can you breathe all right?" Haylee asked.

There was a pause, another little shrug, and then the slightest of nods. Her mouth was covered, but her nose was free.

The emergency dispatcher said that an ambulance and police officer would be there soon and asked me to stay on the line.

I told Paula, "I know you're uncomfortable. We could try to free you, but it would be best if the police could see you as you are." I hoped Vicki was on duty, or if she wasn't, that her backup was nearby.

About the only thing we could do while we waited with Paula was take pictures with our phones. So we did, of Paula and of the interior of the carriage house, including the door that hadn't been locked when we arrived.

Beside Paula, a strip of the strangely wide white tape was stuck to the rusting handle of a lawn mower. The strip was about twelve inches wide and about two feet long. What was it, something to do with fashion design? Or maybe a theatrical prop used to resemble bandages? Duct tape could be bought in normal paper-sized sheets in all sorts of colors, for creating fashions and accessories, so maybe it came in larger sizes, also, like foot-wide rolls.

We'd left the door open. Stray breezes didn't seem to dissipate the skunky odors much, but they could possibly blow the tape onto me and stick me to the lawn mower. Edging between it and Paula, I carefully bent closer.

Pieces of scrunched-up paper lay behind the lawn mower. A checked design on the paper looked familiar. A grid for measuring? Maybe the strange white stuff really was duct tape.

And then I saw a label on plastic packaging, and I knew what was covering Paula's mouth, hands, wrists, the hems of her jeans, and her ankles.

Stabilizer, the new super-sticky stabilizer, exactly like what I sold at In Stitches.

The crumpled packaging partially hid a pair of dressmaker's shears. I had a pair like that, and so did Haylee, Opal, and Edna. Naomi had given them to us. She'd thought that having our names engraved on the outside of one of the blades would make it easier for us to keep track of our own pairs, but obviously, someone's had gone missing and had ended up beside Paula. It wasn't the first time that a pair of them had been left at a crime scene. Unless I moved the packaging, I wouldn't be able to tell whose shears they were, but I wasn't about to touch anything.

Maybe the scissors didn't belong to one of us, and maybe the super-sticky stabilizer hadn't come from my shop, either. We were on the property of a fashion design school, after all, where things like stabilizer and dressmaker's shears should easily be found. I'd seen Kent wielding a similar pair, with longer blades than any of us owned. Maybe these were his.

He'd been obvious in his scorn for Paula. But why would he do this to her? Had he murdered Antonio, and now he feared that Paula had figured it out and was about to tell the police? If so, merely immobilizing her didn't make sense. Maybe he'd planned to return later and . . . what? Load her into a vehicle and take her away?

Had something interrupted him?

Maybe the skunk had made a direct hit and forced Kent to delay his murderous plan. Maybe he was attempting to scrub the stink off himself and his clothes.

Worse, he could be hanging around outside, and we wouldn't know it. He might smell like a skunk, but so did the carriage house and everything in it, including us.

I snapped photos, then straightened and turned to Haylee, who was looking worried, as if she'd been thinking similar things about Antonio's murderer and Paula's attacker. "Have a look at this," I said. "Maybe you'll know whose scissors these are."

She couldn't tell, either, and agreed with me that the "tape" was actually stabilizer with the paper backing removed from its strong adhesive.

A siren became louder and louder. I ran outside and around the mansion to the street in time to meet Vicki leaving her cruiser. The emergency dispatcher let me go. I gasped to Vicki, "I'm glad you're here."

"I'm not. You stink. What did you do, run over a skunk?"

"No, but Paula's bound and gagged in the

carriage house, and a skunk may have sprayed her. We didn't touch anything."

"We?"

"Haylee's keeping Paula company."

"Paula?"

"Antonio's wife. Widow. His murderer may have come back for her. We'd better get back to Haylee. She could be in danger." Something like hysteria fluttered through my voice.

Frowning, Vicki strode to the carriage house. I was right behind her, but afraid that a murderer — Kent, Loretta, or even Macey — might leap out at us from the overgrown privet overhanging the trio of crumbling concrete tracks that served as a driveway.

Vicki seldom swore, at least in my hearing, but when she caught sight of Paula, she let out a streak of words that made the insides of my ears burn.

She bent and peered at Paula's lower face. "What kind of tape is this?" she asked no one in particular.

I explained, "It's stabilizer. We use it in embroidery." I pointed behind the lawn mower. "Her assailant tore off the backing paper and threw it down. That exposed the sticky side, and it is *very* sticky."

"So the adhesive is strong?" Vicki asked.

"Yes, and so is the stabilizer."

"Do you know how to get it off skin?"

"I've only pulled it off my fingers, which wasn't easy and hurt a lot, but I've never had that much skin covered with it, so no."

Vicki turned back to Paula and said in a gentle voice, "We'd better let the emergency technicians remove that stuff when they get here. They'll have a better idea how to do it without tearing your skin." Then she took out her notebook. Writing, she didn't look up at Haylee and me. "You two can get out of this stinking building, but don't go far. I'll want your statements later, after I make notes and take pictures."

"We took some ourselves," I volunteered.

"Print them for me when you get a chance." She peered past us toward the mansion. "Meanwhile, how about sitting on the back porch steps there, until I can get to you? Don't discuss this with each other or with anyone else."

Obviously, she didn't want us comparing our stories and making things up. Not that we needed to. Very likely, we would both tell her the same things, anyway.

We went outside and sat on the second step of the porch with our feet on the concrete path leading to the carriage house.

I didn't know what to fear most, Kent or

Loretta bursting out of the mansion's back door with another roll of super-sticky stabilizer, or a super-stinky skunk coming along and using us for target practice. I murmured to Haylee, "Maybe if another skunk wants to investigate the trash cans, it won't bother spraying us because we already reek."

Haylee covered her mouth, but her laugh was probably still audible to Paula, who would not be amused by our having a grand old time on "her" back porch while she sat in possible pain.

Another siren blared its way to us, and I jumped up and dashed to the street. Bright lights shined down the driveway. Carrying tool kits, the two technicians, a man and woman, ran from their ambulance.

The woman held her nose. "They didn't tell us we needed to wear gas masks."

"Skunk," I said. "It didn't get me, but it might have sprayed the victim." I pointed. "She's in the carriage house with Chief Smallwood." The technicians sprinted away from me and into the carriage house.

I rejoined Haylee on the porch stairs.

A few minutes later, the female technician came out, rested a foot on the bottom step, leaned an arm on her raised knee, and bent forward to talk to me. "Chief Smallwood said to ask you if that sticky stuff is water soluble."

"I don't think so."

The tech yelled toward the carriage house, "Dunking her in the lake is not an option, Chief." Then she ran in the opposite direction, toward the front of the mansion.

Haylee restrained another giggle. "That must have reassured Paula!"

The technician returned, bumping a gurney along the uneven concrete driveway.

Less than a minute later, Paula, sticky stabilizer, stinky skunk, and all, was on the gurney and being wheeled to the ambulance.

Vicki darted over to Haylee and me. "They can honestly say the patient is stabilized."

Haylee and I tried, without great success, to stifle our laughter. I started to stand, but Vicki, who had somehow managed to keep a straight face, said, "Stay there." Equipment jingling, she trotted around the side of the porch and disappeared toward the front of the mansion.

Haylee whispered to me, "I hope Vicki doesn't expect us to wait here until she goes all the way to the hospital in Erie with Paula."

I muttered, "Me, too." For one thing, it

was nearly two. For another, the entire vicinity stunk, though maybe not as much as it had before Paula was wheeled away. Maybe I was becoming used to the smell.

Worse, though, was the creepy feeling that a murderer might lunge out of the mansion behind us.

Vicki returned with a state trooper who carried a big roll of police tape in one hand and covered his nose with the other.

Vicki turned to us. "Come on, you two, let's leave this to the staties and get out of here, for all the good it will do. We're probably going to carry this stink around with us for a few weeks."

We followed her to the front of the mansion, where her cruiser had been joined by the state trooper's. I told her, "When we first arrived after hearing the thumps that turned out to be Paula banging her head against a wall, the mansion's front door was ajar and creaking in the breezes."

Vicki stared up at the porch. The door opened slightly.

I joked, "Maybe a skunk wandered in and is peeking out at us."

Vicki made a disgusted face. "I see why you're obsessed by skunks tonight. I mean I *smell* why."

"The aroma is dissipating," Haylee said.

"It was worst inside the carriage house."

"Yes," Vicki agreed. "So I was the one who had to stay in there while you two were lounging around on a back porch."

I retorted, "Where a murderer might have been ready to leap out at us."

She cocked her head. "Why do you say that?"

I sputtered, "It's obvious, isn't it? Antonio was given almonds in the hope that he would die, and now his widow has been attacked."

She studied my face, but all she said was, "Haylee, can you wait right here on the front steps while Willow comes to my cruiser and gives me her statement?"

Haylee glanced up toward the front door, which, as far as we knew, was still unlocked.

Vicki relented. "No, better yet, sit on the trunk of the statie's cruiser so I can see that you're safe."

Vicki pushed empty coffee cups, maps, and stray pieces of paper off her front seat so I could sit there.

"I'll make your car stink," I objected.

She sighed. "No worse than I will. Get in."

I did. In front of us, Haylee folded her arms and leaned against the state trooper's fender.

Vicki radioed someone to check on the mansion's front door and put tape around the front porch, then turned to me. "What happened?"

"We were walking the dogs and heard thumps coming from that carriage house. The dogs barked. We couldn't tell what was going on, so we took them home and came back, expecting that the raccoon or whatever might be long gone. That time, though, we thought we heard a muffled call for help. We saw a skunk, just minding its own business, but we had to run around the block to the front of the mansion to get closer to the carriage house, and the skunk sprayed almost as soon as we left. It was almost like that smell was chasing us. When we got to the mansion, we noticed the front door swinging open." I pointed at the mansion's large front porch. The young trooper who had been at the carriage house was now stringing tape from column to column. Apparently, he'd given up on holding his nose.

I turned to Vicki again. "The carriage house door was unlocked, too. We went inside and turned on the light. When our eyes adjusted, we could see Paula, bound and gagged."

"Anything else?"

"A piece of the stabilizer that Paula's attacker wrapped around her was hanging from the handle of a lawn mower, as if Paula's attacker had prepared everything in advance, but didn't need that last piece. It was big, about two feet long, and a foot wide."

"I saw that."

"I peeked behind the lawn mower and saw the packaging from the stabilizer. It could have come from just about anywhere, including TADAM, but I sell that brand and size in my store. And I could see the handles and part of the blades of a pair of dressmaker's shears back there, also. They looked like the ones Naomi gave the rest of us, but I couldn't be sure, and if they were engraved, I couldn't see the part that was engraved. You would expect to find many pairs of dressmaker's shears at a fashion design school, and as you may remember, Kent was using a pair with very long blades at the Design 101 course."

"And you have pictures you're going to print for me, of Paula and the stabilizer and scissors and anything else that seems relevant?"

"Yes."

"Okay, go out and tell Haylee I want to talk to her. Stick around and I'll drive you both home. My car can't get much smellier."

I clambered out, signaled to Haylee, and took my turn leaning against the state trooper's car.

Vicki's interview with Haylee didn't take long, then Vicki opened her cruiser's back door for me, shut me in, and went off to confer with the state trooper. During the short time that Vicki was gone, my legs and feet began going numb in that cramped space. Maybe riding in a cruiser had not been a worthy goal, after all.

Vicki drove us toward Lake Street. I said between the heavy steel mesh separating the back seat from the front, "It's possible that Paula's attacker was sprayed by that skunk, so maybe all you have to do is go around finding people who stink."

Her cackle was witchlike. "I don't have to look far for that, do I? Might as well arrest you two right here and now."

I corrected myself. "Somebody *else* who stinks."

She turned the steering wheel and heaved a huge sigh. "I'm not likely to smell anything *but* skunk for a long time. But you both told me you smelled the skunk after you heard the head-banging. A long time after, if you took time to walk the dogs home. I'm guessing the attacker was long gone by the time the skunk delivered his message."

"That makes sense," I said. "Poor Paula. That skunk somehow went into the carriage house and added insult to injury."

Vicki pulled up in front of In Stitches. "There are holes in that building big enough for skunks, and who knows what else, to get in. Maybe Paula was blocking the way to its den." She shuddered. "That woman got the worst of everything tonight." She turned to look at me. "I guess I'd better open that door for you, Willow, or you'll be riding around with me all night."

"That'd be okay," I teased, "if you opened all the windows and drove very fast. The circulation to my feet stopped about two blocks ago."

But she let me out, and Haylee was able to open her own door. Vicki drove off, and Haylee and I said good night and headed for our apartments.

Not wanting to odorize In Stitches any more than I had to, I went around to the patio and let my animals out. All four of them thought that sniffing me was more intriguing than doing their duties, and I was beginning to worry that Tally-Ho might mistake my legs for a fire hydrant that had been anointed by a skunk, but he finally wandered off to water a bush, instead. All of them followed me inside with more eagerness than usual.

Maybe my pets would love me more and follow me everywhere if I wore skunk cologne all the time.

I stripped, showered for a very long time with lots of soap and shampoo, then threw my outfit into the washer. It was about three when I was finally ready to crawl into bed. Except for my hair, I wasn't too overly skunky. I checked my phone. A text had come in when I was on the line with the dispatcher, and in the excitement in the carriage house and afterward, I hadn't noticed it.

Clay had asked me to text him when I got home.

It was late, but I did, and I wasn't surprised that I didn't hear back from him until the first thing in the morning. He called while my animals and I were eating breakfast. "Any chance of getting together this evening after work?" he asked.

29

I still smell like skunk.

"Sure," I said. *Maybe I could take three more showers before meeting him . . .*

"It's supposed to be warm. How about if I bring a picnic we can eat on the beach? Your dogs can join us."

We'd be outside in the fresh air, and I could try to keep him away from me, and upwind. "That sounds great. What should I bring?"

"The dogs. Meet you at one of those tables at the west end of the swimming beach?"

"Near the cottage colony?"

"That's it. I can park close to the beach with my truckload of picnic. How does seven sound?"

Truckload? Who else was coming? "Great."

"See you then." His voice held its usual warmth. After we disconnected, I didn't know whether to dance and sing in anticipation, or worry that he had invited a crowd, including Loretta.

I looked down at my dogs. Their beautiful brown eyes brimmed over with adoration. "Maybe I can blame you two for the skunky smells." *Nice way to reward the darlings for their unconditional love.* They wagged their tails.

Maybe I didn't stink. I pulled a hank of my hair to my nose and took a deep breath.

I did stink.

Maybe no one would notice. I took the dogs and the morning's coffee, cider, and cookies upstairs. I unlocked the front door of In Stitches, turned the embroidered *Come Back Later* sign in my glass front door to *Welcome,* and sat down at my computer.

Georgina was the first of the morning class to enter In Stitches. "I smell skunk," she said.

So much for no one noticing. The day — and the evening — should be fun.

Georgina glanced past me to the dogs in their pen. "What did you two get into?"

They wagged their tails, and I had to confess that I was the one who had been too close to a skunk. Other women came in and asked questions, but I didn't elaborate. I didn't think Vicki would want me telling last night's story. I felt a brief moment of sympathy for Paula, and what she must have suffered with that stabilizer stuck to her skin while a skunk gave her the full force of his opinion of her.

Had Antonio's killer attacked Paula? If so, it was no wonder that she'd looked terrified.

Had the killer returned later to do something even more drastic to Paula and been stopped by a militant fur ball? And then we'd come along and saved her from the killer?

Kent? And did he still reek? I imagined him staying away from TADAM today because he couldn't rid himself of the smell.

"Wash your hair in tomato juice," Rosemary suggested.

Georgina objected, "That might turn it red. Take a bath in hydrogen peroxide mixed with baking soda."

Another woman piped up. "That would be too corrosive. I've heard that vinegar works."

I laughed. "I can think of better ways of getting pickled." Like this evening, on the beach with Clay and a bottle of wine . . .

Again, we worked on upside-down crewel work. I wasn't watching what Rosemary was doing, so I didn't see her project until she took her hoop off her machine, turned it over, and shouted, "Ta-da!"

Everyone in the store laughed, and I had to, also. Using thick thread with hairs wisping from it in the bobbin, she had embroidered a darling and rather fuzzy skunk. "I made use of the fragrance permeating your shop," she explained.

During lunchtime, word must have gone around Pier 42 that embroidering skunk designs would be appropriate at In Stitches. At the afternoon workshop, three more women chuckled over what they insisted on calling "scratch and sniff" embroidery motifs.

After school was over for the day, Ashley came in. Her smile was the widest I'd seen on her face in a long time. "Skunk!" she shouted. "Did the dogs get sprayed, Willow?"

"Not the dogs," I said. "But I went too close to where a skunk had recently been."

Ashley made an exaggeratedly pouty face. "I have some bad news for you. I've decided I don't want to go to TADAM. I'll probably go away to college, so I won't be able to keep working here after next summer."

"I'll miss you, but I really don't think TADAM has much to offer you."

"And there's good news." She clapped her hands. "My dad was offered a job, and it's nearby. We won't have to move." She hopped around in a little dance, and so did everyone else in the store, including me. From their pen, Sally and Tally yipped gleeful songs of their own.

After our customers left, Ashley helped close the shop. I asked her, "Do you remember the curtained-off storage area behind the podium at the fashion show?"

She nodded. Her shining brown curls bounced. "Loretta kept those briefcases back there."

"Did you see anyone else going into and out of that storage area?"

"Paula, for sure. Kent may have gone there after the fashion show. I don't think he could have been in that storage area during the rehearsal. He was at the foot of the runway taking our pictures. But right after the show itself, I saw him rush through the backstage, like he was in a hurry or angry, but I didn't see where he went."

That agreed with my memory, except I had seen where he went — directly onto the stage. And the video had shown him bursting out between the curtains.

However, that didn't prove that he hadn't slipped a candy-coated almond into Antonio's pockets, only that he'd had fewer chances to do it than Loretta, Paula, and the rest of us.

"Macey told me something suspicious about Paula," Ashley told me.

"You've been talking to Macey?"

"She hardly knows anyone here. She's lonely. She's very nice."

Seems nice, I thought to myself.

Ashley continued, "We both like to run, and it's good to have a running partner. Safer, too. But I wasn't with Macey when she went out jogging a few hours after Antonio collapsed. She said she saw Paula come out of the conservatory. That surprised Macey. She thought Paula would still be in Erie with her husband. So what was Paula doing roaming around at that hour?"

"Vicki drove Gord and Paula home around one thirty."

"Why would Paula go back to the conservatory?"

I wish I knew.

After Ashley left, I sat down at my computer.

Ben had sent Haylee and me copies of files that he had retrieved from Kent's thumb drive.

Kent had sent e-mails to Antonio. Kent had asked to be paid, politely, at first, and then more firmly. Antonio had answered that Kent could either stay at TADAM or take his chances with the sort of reference that Antonio would give him. Antonio had made it clear that although he'd been ignoring Kent's criminal record, other schools wouldn't.

Ben wrote to Haylee and me, "I think we should turn these files over to the police. What do you two think?"

I sent a message agreeing with him that we should, and that I would call Vicki. I did, and asked Vicki if I should forward her the files. She said she'd come see them.

While I waited, I phoned Mona. "Are you all right?"

"Why wouldn't I be? You don't have to worry about me being in danger from Kent. He's a great guy. Except he never showed up for his thumb drive last night. Maybe he'll come tonight."

Vicki's car pulled up outside my shop, so after giving Mona another warning, which I knew she would ignore, about staying away from anyone who'd had anything to do with Antonio, I said good-bye.

Vicki stomped into the shop. "Do I smell skunk?"

I made a show of sniffing in her direction. "I suspect you do. And you were smelling it before you came in here."

"Tell me about it." She patted her stomach. "These vests aren't washable. All I could do was dab at it with a damp cloth."

I couldn't help laughing.

She gave me the evil eye. "AND I had two smelly people in my cruiser last night."

"Did you go to Loretta's and Kent's apartment building last night to sniff out if either of them had been sprayed?"

"That would be one for the record books — go to a judge in the middle of the night and ask for a warrant to search for the remnants of skunk spray. Besides, if I'd gone snooping around apartment buildings or anywhere else, all I'd have smelled was myself. In addition, it wouldn't have proven a thing. Lots of people ended up smelling like skunks last night. Me, for instance, and the investigators from the state police."

"Investigators?" I asked. "Plural? So they think Paula's attack could be connected with Antonio's murder?"

30

Our police chief cocked her head. "Do *you* believe the attack on Paula had something to do with the murder of her late husband?"

"Yes, but I'm not an officer of the law."

She opened her notebook. "Good to hear you admit that. I'm going to write it down in case we ever become confused about it in the future." But she didn't write anything, and I heard the teasing note in her voice. "Where are these files you said you found?"

"Ben and Haylee dredged them up." I led her to my computer and showed her the correspondence between Kent and Antonio.

"Anyone could have written that stuff," she pointed out. "Why are Haylee and Ben interfering?"

"Haylee and Ben are naturally concerned because initially, Paula accused Dora Battersby and me of murdering Antonio. Paula has since apologized, saying she now knows that Antonio wasn't killed by someone hitting him, but still, what if the state police are investigating Dora and me instead of the real culprit?"

"Maybe one of you *is* the real culprit. Maybe you didn't like being called a glutton and Dora didn't like Edna being accused of greed."

I scoffed. "Neither of us would harm anyone."

Vicki scrutinized my face for uneasy seconds, then returned her attention to my computer screen. "How did Haylee and Ben unearth these e-mails?"

"They were on a thumb drive that Kent lent us so we could watch a video of the fashion show. A few minutes ago, Mona told me that Kent has not picked up the thumb drive from her yet."

"The staties have the video of the fashion show."

"Kent had another copy. Maybe he's not picking the thumb drive up on purpose. Maybe he doesn't want the investigators to see the correspondence he had with Antonio, so in case anyone searches his apartment, he's keeping it hidden by letting Mona hold on to it. He had deleted the file with the correspondence in it, but Ben was able to open it. If he could, the state police could, and Kent might have known that."

She scribbled in her notebook.

When she looked up, I said, "Mona had already told us that Kent had a criminal record, for touching a model, and that a TADAM student had accused him of the same thing. Mona couldn't remember the student's name, but I suggested Macey, and Mona thought that was the girl's name."

Vicki asked, "The Macey I met?"

I nodded. "That one. The one that Antonio pinched. As I told you, I heard Macey slap someone in her cubicle right before the dress rehearsal, and I guessed from his artificially lowered voice that it could have been Antonio, but I wasn't sure. It could have been Kent. However, later Macey told me that she had slapped *Antonio.* If she's now saying that it was Kent who touched her before the dress rehearsal, she's changing her story. I don't know about you, but that sounds suspicious to me."

Vicki did her usual thing of avoiding answering by changing the direction of her questions. "Describe what Macey did after Antonio pinched her at the reception."

"I didn't see him actually do it. Ashley squealed, and then I saw her shove Antonio's hand away from Macey's rear end."

"Did you see Macey touch him?"

"No."

"Not even push him away?"

"No. Did you find her fingerprints on, say, that smooth, shiny belt buckle he wore?"

"We don't have the fingerprint results back yet."

"Who did you fingerprint? Everyone at TADAM?" They hadn't fingerprinted me or any of my friends, as far as I knew, and Ashley would have told me if they'd fingerprinted her.

Vicki wrote in her notebook. Whenever she ignored my questions, I suspected that she was too professional to tell me I might be right. Police officers could be a pain.

I suggested, "Just because I didn't see Macey slap Antonio or bat him away doesn't mean that she didn't."

Vicki continued writing without looking at me.

I guessed aloud, "Maybe Macey changed her story about who touched her at the rehearsal because she was afraid of being accused of harming Antonio. After the fashion show, I saw Macey leave her apartment building and jog toward the lake. A short time later, I saw Kent outside the conservatory. This evening, Ashley told me that Macey said that while she was jogging that night, she saw Paula come out of the conservatory in the wee hours of Sunday morning."

"Hearsay," Vicki scoffed. "Circumstantial."

I defended myself. "I thought you'd like to know so you could ask Macey herself."

"Okay, sure, but we probably already got that information from her." She jotted something in her notebook, anyway.

I pressed on. "However, if Macey was out in the wee hours of Sunday morning, she could have been in that conservatory, also. She could have planted the evidence in my cubicle. She could have made up her story of seeing Paula come out of it."

"You're really fond of jumping to conclusions, aren't you, especially if you can contort those conclusions to fit into one of your many theories."

I defended myself. "All of them — Paula, Kent, Loretta, and Macey — were near the conservatory around one thirty. One of them could have put the candy-coated almonds and the vial of allergy medicine with my things. Didn't you drop Paula off at the TADAM mansion around that time? Maybe Antonio's key ring included one for the conservatory."

"Where *do* you get all this information?"

"Edna knew when Gord came home and that you'd dropped him off before you took

Paula to TADAM."

"And you were out wandering the village at that hour, too."

"Yes, but even if I, for some strange reason, had planted the evidence among my belongings, why would I have gone out of my way to report finding them there?"

"Some investigators might say you were trying to deflect suspicion from yourself."

"My fingerprints are probably on the candy package and on the medicine vial, and maybe even on the briefcase. That proves I didn't put them in my own cubicle. If I'd been trying to implicate someone else, I'd have wiped off my own fingerprints." I didn't mention that I would have wiped them if I hadn't heard someone coming.

Vicki stared at me like I'd flown in from outer space. "Maybe. But if you'd been trying to implicate someone else, you might have left all the earlier fingerprints in place."

I shook my head as if to clear lingering skunk fumes. "You give me too much credit. Someone, not me, attacked Paula last night, and I'm betting it's the same person who arranged Antonio's death. Were they able to remove that stabilizer from Paula's skin?"

"Yes. Her skin was a little red. It may burn or itch, but she'll heal."

"So? Who did she say attacked her?"

Just as I feared, Vicki didn't answer my question. Instead, she asked, "Has any of your stabilizer gone missing?"

I slapped my forehead. "I was tired after that late night. I forgot to check."

My inventory was computerized, so it was easy to tell how many rolls of that kind of stabilizer I should have. I went into the storeroom and counted, then came back out to the rack where I displayed it. I counted twice. Three times. I heaved a big sigh. I didn't want the assault against Paula to be connected to In Stitches, but it was. "One roll is missing," I admitted.

"Could you have taken it yourself, maybe downstairs to work on a project?"

"No. I keep good records."

"I thought so. What do you imagine happened to it? And when?"

"I can't tell when, but the theft had to have been recent. I ordered that kind of stabilizer for the first time a month ago. I'm guessing it went missing yesterday when Paula and her students were here. I believe that Paula hid a folded sheaf of papers, Antonio's business plan, underneath a bolt of fabric. Either she or one of her students could have taken the roll of stabilizer. I didn't watch all of them the entire time they were here. And she was carrying a bag big enough to hide it in."

"What about your other customers?"

"My regulars have never shoplifted, although I suppose stranger things have happened. And I didn't creep around spying on new customers."

She glanced up at my white cathedral ceilings. "No security cameras?"

"No."

"Maybe you need some."

"Close the barn door after the horse is stolen? Luckily, stabilizer isn't as expensive as a horse."

She stroked the top of a sewing machine. "How much is a roll of that kind of stabilizer?"

I told her and she whistled.

I justified it. "Aren't the things we need supposed to be expensive, to prove that we're doing something important?" I added in sly tones, "Like police cars and equipment?" Acting afraid that she was about to swat me with her notebook, I scooted to the cutting table and opened a drawer. Of course my engraved scissors weren't there. I kept them downstairs in my guest room closet. At least, that was where I'd last seen them. I asked, "Were you able to figure out whose scissors those were?"

"Three guesses."

"Mine should be downstairs. Paula took her students to Haylee's shop yesterday, also. Someone left a business plan there. Kent visited The Stash later. Paula or her students or Kent could have hidden the business plan and/or picked up Haylee's scissors."

Vicki merely tilted her head and raised an eyebrow.

"They were Haylee's," I concluded. "Engraved with her name."

Again, Vicki refrained from either affirming it or denying it. Looking down at her notebook, she asked, "Was Kent in your store yesterday?"

"Not unless he was here while Rosemary took over during my lunch hour." Rosemary often worked in the Threadville shops while we had our lunch breaks. In return, we gave her an employee discount plus wages. She spent more in our shops than she earned, however, so it was a win for everyone.

"Can you give me Rosemary's name and address?"

"Sure. She lives in Erie."

"All the better for the staties. They're based there."

Was Kent guilty of both Antonio's death and the attack on Paula? Maybe both cases would be wrapped up this evening. I asked,

"Did the scissors have fingerprints on them?"

Vicki didn't answer.

"I guess that means they'd been wiped," I hazarded.

Again, no answer from Vicki. Did that mean I'd guessed right?

I tried another question. "How about the plastic packaging for the stabilizer?"

"Wouldn't you expect your fingerprints to be on that?"

"Yes, and maybe the prints of anyone who handled it before it was shipped to me, and from customers who examined it. But what about inside the packaging? Someone ripped the backing from the stabilizer, wadded up the backing, and tossed it on the floor. Did they wipe off every fingerprint? Or from the stabilizer itself that they pressed over Paula's mouth and around her wrists and ankles?"

"That's a little more complicated. The lab's working on it. We won't get those results soon, either."

"Let me guess. The doorknob on the carriage house had been wiped, but they found nice clear prints on that. Those will be mine."

"Should I send the fingerprint tech to take your prints?"

"You can. I have nothing to hide."

"Where were you and Haylee at nine last night?"

31

Did Vicki think that Haylee and I had ganged up on Paula? My answer was a little heated. "Neither Haylee nor I would have bound and gagged anyone, with stabilizer or anything else. We were in The Stash with Opal, Naomi, and Edna."

Vicki reminded me, "Those three are Haylee's mothers, and they treat you like a daughter, too."

"We were also with Ben Rondelson."

"Would he lie for you or Haylee?"

"I doubt it." Why would Vicki suspect that Haylee and I might have attacked Paula? Surely, Vicki knew we would never do anything even remotely like that. Had Paula blamed us? I guessed, "Paula may have heard our voices outside the carriage house when she was banging her head against the wall. Maybe she somehow connected us with the attack. But it had obviously happened earlier, or she wouldn't have been inside the carriage house banging her head against a wall." I tapped my fingernails on the butcher block counter. "How did she get into that predicament without noticing who put her there?"

"You're sure she didn't know who put her there?"

"If she says it was Haylee and me, she certainly did *not.*"

Vicki only watched me. Was she waiting for a confession?

She was going to wait a long time. I suggested, "What if . . . Paula somehow managed to wrap herself in stabilizer?"

Still, Vicki said nothing.

Okay, if I had to do all the talking, I would. "It doesn't make sense for a murderer to immobilize Paula and trust that she'd still be there when he came back to . . . do whatever he'd planned to do to her."

"He?"

"Or she. If Paula had figured out who killed Antonio, and then Paula threatened that person, wouldn't the murderer have silenced Paula right then and there? Or at least made it harder for anyone to find her? That stabilizer is sticky. The adhesive is strong, and the stabilizer itself is tough. But I suspect that anyone with any strength at all could have gotten out of it. Paula was neatly sitting against a wall, in as comfortable a position as possible under the circumstances. Her hands were bound on her lap, not behind her. Again, comfortable. And there was that long piece of stabilizer stuck to the handle of the lawn mower, easily within her reach, as if she'd prepared it before she got her wrists and hands stuck together, and then she'd found that she didn't need it."

"That could have been the way the attacker worked," Vicki responded. "If you were going to stick someone together with stabilizer or duct tape or anything like that, you wouldn't want to be wrestling with the sticky stuff at the same time you were wrestling with your victim."

"I don't like your use of the word 'your.'"

"One's."

"And you didn't write down a word of my theory."

"*Theory,*" she repeated. "No, I didn't."

"So, should we try it?"

"We? Are you planning to assault a police officer, or have one assault you?"

"Neither. I'll put some of it on myself to see if I can do it, and then get out of it. Did you find out from the EMTs how to get the adhesive off skin?"

"Nope."

I pictured myself arriving at Clay's picnic with stabilizer around my ankles, wrists, and hands, and frowned. "I'll stick the stabilizer to my socks and the hems of my jeans, which was how Paula's ankles were bound together. But this is not my preferred use of my expensive super-sticky stabilizer."

"I'll make a note of that." But she didn't. Instead, she took photos of every step while I removed a roll of stabilizer from the rack, opened it, cut a four-foot-long length, peeled off the backing, then carefully wrapped the sticky mess around my ankles.

"Lucky thing for you that you're a police officer," I muttered. "Or I might accuse you of planning to post those pictures on social media so you and your friends could get a good laugh."

She took another photo. "The only *friends* who will see them are in the state police."

"How's Toby Gartener? And why isn't he the detective on this case?"

"He's fine. He wasn't on duty when Antonio's death was ruled a possible homicide, so he didn't get the case."

I patted the stabilizer into place. "There."

She asked in a sweetly encouraging voice, "Aren't you going to try gagging yourself?"

"No way. I'm going to see if I can pull my

ankles apart without *touching* them with my hands. Or banging my head against a wall."

"She didn't have that much of the stuff on her ankles."

"Thanks for telling me that now that I've immobilized myself."

"No problem. If this experiment doesn't work, I'll suggest that some rookie state troopers should try it, with only the amount of stabilizer Paula had around her jeans."

First I tried to pull my ankles away from each other. It was harder than I'd guessed. As I'd already told Vicki, that stabilizer was tough. I looked up at Vicki.

She held her hands up. "Keep trying."

"I wasn't going to ask for help," I said with as much dignity as a person sitting on the floor with her ankles bound together with super-sticky stabilizer could.

I tried pulling one foot toward my bum, but both feet moved together.

I rubbed my ankles up and down against each other, and before I had to humble myself to ask Vicki to pass me some scissors, the stabilizer began rolling onto itself and coming unstuck from my jeans.

Within minutes, I was free, and I hadn't used my hands.

"Ha!" I shouted. "Paula could have rescued herself. But she didn't. Either she's the biggest wimp on earth, or she planned the whole thing, planned that she'd be discovered like that, and then she'd blame Haylee and me. I'm guessing that she'd already told Detective Neffting that we must have seen Antonio's business plan and had killed him because of it. And this was after she'd hidden copies of his business plan in our shops. She's trying to add more 'evidence' that we killed Antonio." I raised one dramatic finger. "And why would she do that?"

Vicki only shook her head. She was still not writing in her notebook. But she did take a picture of me in that heroic pose.

If she wasn't going to answer, I would have to. "To deflect suspicion from herself, because *she's* the one who made certain that Antonio's medicine wouldn't be near him when he ate the almonds she placed in his pocket!"

Vicki didn't write any of it down. Instead, she headed toward the front door. "See you, Willow. Stay out of trouble."

I bent down and tried to pull sticky goo off my jeans. "Wah! I'm not sure how to get the rest of the adhesive off my clothes."

"You're the expert on fabric and fashion." She aimed her camera at my gummy ankles, snapped several pictures in rapid succession, then left.

"Thanks!" I called after her.

She turned and waved.

I went downstairs to my apartment and put my jeans and socks in the laundry room to worry about later. I had just enough time for a quick shower with lots of lather in my hair. Knowing my hair would stink most when wet, I dried it thoroughly and then braided it in a tight braid in back.

In clean jeans and a sky blue sweater that Opal had knit for me, I leashed the dogs and took them out the patio door.

"Yoo-hoo!" Dora called from her porch.

I went closer.

"I smell skunk," she said. She wagged her finger at the dogs. "Did you two get into mischief?"

"They didn't," I answered. "Haylee and I did. Last night."

"Your dogs are on leashes. Where are you off to? I'd say I hoped it was to make up with your young man, but you're going to have to wait until you smell better. That redhead may have the advantage over you at the moment."

I had to confess to Dora that the dogs and I were on our way to a picnic with Clay. "He's bringing the food."

She folded her arms and a dreamy expression crossed her face. "No man ever brought *me* food. Have a great time. But don't go near him."

I laughed. "Since you detected the smell from so far away, I guess I'd better stay on the opposite end of the beach from him."

She made shooing motions with both hands. "Run along. And have fun."

I took the dogs out the back gate so we could walk along the hiking trail. I wanted to hurry to Clay, but the dogs had to sniff every bush and tree along the wide, shaded trail.

They didn't speed their pace much when we reached the sand at the shore of the lake, either, but I told them we might be late to see Clay. Hearing his name, they perked up their noses and their tails and let me lead them to the harder sand at the water's edge, where we jogged.

Clay was already sitting at a table, which he'd covered with a cheerful yellow and blue plaid tablecloth and what looked like enough food for ten people. Was it a good sign that only two bottles of wine were visible?

My plan of not going close to him was ruined by the dogs, who yelped and rushed toward him, their tails waving madly. Dogs had to be leashed while on the beach, so I had to go along.

Letting them sniff his hands, Clay looked up at me with a rueful smile. "Better not come too close," he said. "I smell like a skunk."

32

Clay had given me the perfect opportunity to confess that I smelled like a skunk, too, and it wouldn't matter if I came closer to him. Instead, I fastened the dog's leashes around the leg of the picnic table, scooted onto the bench across from him, and blurted, "What happened?"

He pointed at the bottles of wine. "White or red?"

"Red."

"We're having cold fried chicken."

"Red."

He grinned. "Good choice. I went a little heavy on the spices."

"You made it yourself?"

"Yes."

"It looks heavenly."

He removed the cork from a bottle of Shiraz. "And probably smells like skunk."

I repeated, "What happened?"

"Loretta asked me to come over last night

and pick up more sketches. She'd gone over to the TADAM carriage house to check on her measurements, but she saw a skunk go into the carriage house, so she stayed outside. And then it sprayed, and Loretta was still too close."

I had to give him points for honesty.

But I wouldn't give Loretta any. Had she really been planning to check on measurements? Or had she wrapped sticky stabilizer around Paula earlier, and then gone back to do something horrid to the woman? Maybe I'd maligned Paula by telling Vicki that Paula could have tied herself up.

Clay's jaw tightened. "Loretta is one of those huggy types, always flinging herself at people and hugging them like they're her long-lost friends. I backed away, but not far or fast enough."

'People' had been Clay, and only Clay, as far as I'd noticed. "But aren't you? Her long-lost friend from fourth grade?"

He handed me a glass. "Cheers." We clinked.

"Cheers," I repeated, though if Loretta was always flinging herself at Clay, I didn't feel particularly cheerful. Except that Clay was a witness that Loretta could have been in Paula's vicinity around the time that

Paula ended up with sticky stabilizer all over herself.

Had Haylee and I interrupted Loretta as she was about to do more harm to Paula? Maybe Paula had been too scared to discover she could get out of her predicament by herself. And she'd been confused, too, if, as I'd guessed, she'd told Vicki that Haylee and I had ganged up on her. Maybe she'd thumped her head a little too hard against the carriage house wall.

Clay handed me a platter of crispy, perfectly browned fried chicken. "Loretta *says* I'm her long-lost friend. That's why I wanted to talk to you."

I bit succulent meat off a drumstick. "Yummmmm . . ." I closed my eyes. Any man who could cook chicken like this had to be kept. And kept safe from skunks. Like Loretta.

He spooned potato salad onto my plate. "I don't think I met her before the reception at TADAM on Saturday night."

I wasn't terribly surprised, but my mouth was too full for me to say anything. The potato salad was delicious, also.

He handed me a large piece of corn bread. "I didn't think I had, so I asked my mother. She keeps everything I ever brought home from school, and she scanned the class picture from fourth grade. There was no one even vaguely resembling Loretta. No one with hair like hers. Do you think she colors and curls it?"

The corn bread was moist and tasty. "The color and curls look natural, but I'm not sure. It's beautiful, however she came by it. *She's* beautiful."

"It's only a facade. It's not important." He saluted me with his wineglass. "I like beauty best when it's inside, also." He smiled into my eyes.

"Thanks, I think."

"Why do you think she lied about knowing me before?"

I might as well return the compliment he'd just given me. "Haven't you ever looked in a mirror?" I began regretting that I'd chosen to sit across the table from him instead of beside him.

"I've never had a woman absolutely throw herself at me like that. It's an interesting approach, but it didn't work for me. At least not when *she* did it."

An invitation? I was tempted to jump up and sit next to him, very close.

But I wanted to hear more of what he had to say. I stayed where I was. "Why would she lie about knowing you? Maybe she knew another kid with your name in fourth grade."

"We could give her the benefit of the doubt on that, but she couldn't have known *me*. My mother checked the class list. There were no Lorettas. And I have not told Loretta where I grew up or the name of my grade school, and she has never said either one."

"Did you have a best friend named Chief?"

"You caught that, did you? I did, but Chief never brought fire trucks to show-and-tell. He wasn't allowed at school. He was a German shepherd."

I couldn't help snickering. "Maybe she thinks she remembers. What do they call that, false memories?"

"I don't trust her." He thinned his lips. "Antonio's death is being investigated as a possible homicide. I can't help wondering if Loretta set him up somehow to die, and then made certain she was with me when he collapsed."

"I wondered the same thing."

"You didn't tell me."

I helped myself to more potato salad. "She didn't seem to be threatening you." *Except with lipstick.* "Besides, if she was a fake, I knew you would figure it out."

He stared at me for long seconds that made me blush and squirm. "She put that lipstick on me deliberately, almost the first moment we met. She ran right up to me and pressed her face into my shirt. I'd have dodged her if I could have in the crowded kitchen. But that lipstick made you think I was interested in her, and I didn't help my case by not explaining it to you and everyone else who was present when she offered to remove the stain. And you've been keeping your distance from me ever since."

I gave a noncommittal shrug. "You and I would still be . . . we *are* friends."

He opened his mouth as if to say something, closed it, then opened it again and asked, "And we're a design team, right, along with Ben, Haylee, and Dora Battersby?"

"Right."

"So you'll all protect me from her."

"If you want us to."

"I suspect you would even if I didn't want you to. Dora, especially. She's already warned me that Loretta was . . . *on the prowl,* I think she said."

I couldn't help laughing.

Clay grinned, stood up, and pulled his picnic basket closer. "I brought cake for dessert. Devil's food with fudge icing, my mom's recipe."

"We're *definitely* a team." I scooped up the rest of my yummy potato salad.

He cut us each a square of delightfully chocolaty cake. "Loretta wants to meet me tonight at eight at the carriage house to go over her plans again. But as I said on Tuesday, I'd need the rest of my design team there."

I paused with a piece of cake on a fork halfway to my mouth. "You're meeting her at the carriage house at eight this evening?" So much for a long walk on the beach after the delicious picnic.

"Please say you can come along, or I'll have to postpone it."

"Um, we're supposed to have a rehearsal there at nine. Kent wants to turn the space into a theater."

"Kent and Loretta can battle that one out. I'm not doing any work on that place until I know for certain that I'll be paid. But if we have two reasons to go there tonight, I guess we'd better."

"There's one smallish problem."

"If you can't make it tonight, we'll do it another time. No problem."

"It's not that. Last I knew, the TADAM carriage house, and TADAM, for all I know, is a crime scene."

"Still? Because of Antonio?"

"That was just the mansion, but the carriage house was taped off last night."

He was even more adorable when his eyebrows came together in a puzzled frown. "What happened?"

I told him the entire story, about Haylee and me finding Paula and calling for help. "And Paula had been sprayed by a skunk."

He threw me a keen glance. "Was Loretta there?"

"We didn't see her."

He pulled at a wrinkle in the plaid tablecloth.

I had to be fair, even though it was Loretta we were talking about. "I suspect that Paula bound and gagged herself, before the skunk sprayed."

"Bound and gagged herself? Why would anyone do that?"

I told him about the business plans we thought Paula had left in our shops. "I'm not sure, but I'm guessing that Paula told Detective Neffting that Haylee and I had read those business plans before Antonio died, and that if he wanted 'proof' that we could have read them, the police should search our shops for them. And of course copies were in our shops, because she had put them there."

"That's bizarre."

"She was probably afraid the police suspected her of harming her husband. And they probably do, for good reason, and so she's been thinking of ways to throw suspicion on Haylee and me, which, to me, makes her seem guilty. Paula was the most likely person to know what Antonio's allergies were, and to be able to slip a candy-coated almond into his pocket. And to know where he kept his allergy medicine, so she could hide it."

"And she staged an attack on herself in the carriage house, and a skunk came along? That's a first. A skunk administering justice."

"Unfortunately, that skunk was pretty indiscriminate about the justice it administered."

He made a pretense of sniffing his arm. "You can say that again."

I merely grinned.

He caught on. "Wait. You said you and Haylee were nearby. Did you get sprayed, too?"

"We didn't need to be *sprayed*."

"You mean I'm not the only one at this table who stinks?"

"Thanks, Clay! But no, you're not."

"Why are we on opposite sides of the

table, then?"

I smiled. I wasn't sure I was capable of anything else.

He unfolded his lanky frame from the picnic bench, came around to my side of the table, and held out his arms. "Come here, Willow, please."

I stood too quickly, bopped my knee on the table, and had to hop to catch my balance. He reached out, grabbed my arms, and pulled me toward him. "Willow . . ."

It was too much for Tally and Sally. Wagging their tails and barking, they leaped to their feet and nudged their way between Clay and me.

But that wasn't the only interruption. From the other side of a row of willow trees separating the beach from the parking lot, a woman shouted, "Clay, where are you?"

Loretta.

Between our knees, Sally and Tally barked.

Clay swore, grabbed my chin, pulled my face toward his, and planted a swift and oddly fierce kiss on my lips, then pulled away and murmured, "We'll continue this conversation later, okay?"

I could barely gasp, "Okay."

He whispered, "I'll get rid of her." Dodging long, trailing branches of weeping willows, he dashed away.

33

"What are you doing here?" Loretta called to Clay.

"Beach." Clay was not usually terse.

"The beach! Just what I need. I'm so upset!"

The next thing I knew, Loretta was brushing aside willow wands and heading straight for the table. She was in her tight suede shorts again, and the tank top and boots. She wasn't wearing the cloak, the tights, and the wide belt, and she looked a little less like a superhero or a professional wrestler.

I wasn't sure what she did resemble, however. Not Clay and me in our jeans, sweaters, and flip-flops, or the couple strolling along the beach in long pants and jackets.

The dogs barked and wagged their tails. Behind Loretta, Clay held his hands out in a helpless shrug. I caught the message.

There was no way he could have prevented her from coming out onto the beach without manhandling her or being rude. His deep brown eyes seemed to burn into my skin.

Loretta stopped walking at the sight of me and the picnic-laden table.

She smiled. "Gluttony?" Then she sobered. "That Antonio. What a tease. What a terrible tragedy." She eyed the chicken, potato salad, corn bread, and cake. "You may not be tempted by gluttony, Willow, but looking at the feast you've prepared, I am." She actually sniffed toward Clay. "I know you'll excuse my skunky smells, Clay, since I'm pretty sure you didn't do as good a job of getting rid of them as I did after I accidentally rubbed some of it off onto you."

Accidentally? Right.

Clay and I traded glances. He winked.

Clay probably knew that I'd be unable to completely repress my early training in Southern hospitality. "Join us," I offered. "There's plenty."

Loretta lost no time plunking herself down on the bench. I was glad she hadn't sniffed in my direction, or she might have noticed that I smelled skunky, too. Letting her think that my skunky perfume had come from Clay might be a sort of fun revenge. On the other hand, to what lengths might

Loretta go to eliminate a rival? While knowing the answer to that might help pinpoint who had arranged Antonio's death and maybe attacked Paula, I didn't want to find out the hard way what Loretta might do.

Call me conniving, but I couldn't help asking her, "Where did you meet up with a skunk?" Maybe she'd say something that would prove that she'd attacked Paula.

She lowered her head coyly and looked up at Clay from the corners of her eyes. "As I told Clay, I went near the carriage house last night hoping to do some measurements, and apparently a skunk was inside. It came out and attacked me."

That was not, as I understood it, how skunks ordinarily behaved, unless they felt threatened. "Attacked you?"

"You know. Lifted its little tail, and then . . . Did you know that you can't outrun skunk spray from a determined skunk?"

"I guess that makes sense."

"Their spray is very forceful."

If she'd been inside the carriage house when the skunk sprayed, she wasn't about to admit it. I was no closer to knowing for sure whether she had wound the sticky stabilizer around Paula or whether Paula had done it to herself.

Meanwhile, Clay had been digging around in his picnic basket. He set a plate, napkin, wineglass, and cutlery in front of Loretta.

Clay had brought too much food for two of us, and extra utensils, too? But he truly had not seemed to expect Loretta.

She glanced at her watch. "I guess there's time for me to eat quickly before you and I go to the carriage house, Clay. Kent wants to use it as a theater for our threadly sins play before we convert it to an apartment. He said that Mona and the rest of you" — she flicked a glance at me — "will be along at nine for a meeting or rehearsal or something."

Clay sat down beside me. Across from us, Loretta gazed at the beach and the lake. "What a beautiful spot." Her words came out girlishly wistful. "I hope TADAM can stay here after what happened."

I passed her the platter of chicken. She helped herself to a drumstick and bit into it. "This is wonderful, Willow. You could tempt anyone into gluttony." She heaved a huge sigh.

If I'd told her that Clay had prepared the feast and invited me, I would have sounded catty. Besides, if she discovered what a good cook he was, she would probably throw herself at him even harder. If Clay wasn't going to tell her who had actually prepared the meal, I didn't need to, either.

Clay offered wine. Loretta asked for white. He opened the bottle and poured some into her glass. "When you got here this evening, Loretta, you said you were upset. Why?"

"It's terrible, but not surprising, I guess. Antonio's widow, Paula, has been arrested."

I stared openmouthed at her, but Clay asked, "Why?"

"Apparently, the police figured out that she killed Antonio."

"When was she arrested?" I asked.

"A couple of hours ago. I got a call from her lawyer. She must have realized they were closing in on her, so she faked an attack on herself to make it look like someone else had been out to get both Antonio and her. After the police put all of that together, it was a piece of cake." She bit into corn bread. "Speaking of cake, I hope I have room for some of yours, Willow, after all this other delicious food."

Clay still didn't admit that he had been the chef, and I only nodded. Immediately after talking to me, Vicki must have told Detective Neffting that Paula had stolen the stabilizer and stuck it to herself. And the police had put that theory with other evidence that they must have found, and had arrested Paula for Antonio's murder.

Loretta must not have heard about Haylee's and my involvement, or about where Paula had faked the attack. I told her, "Haylee and I happened along after Paula's supposed 'attack.' It was in the carriage house. Last I knew, that area was still a crime scene, so we won't be able to go there tonight."

Apparently, Loretta had saved room for cake. She cut a large piece for herself. "Once the police discovered that Paula had made the whole thing up, they took the yellow tape down. They'd already gotten enough evidence."

One thing about Loretta's story struck me as odd. Paula hadn't seemed to like Loretta. I asked, "Why did Paula's lawyer call you?"

"Paula wanted clothes from her apartment."

"And her apartment is not a crime scene now that they've charged her?"

"The entire mansion is. So I bought a few toiletries and canvassed the TADAM students in my apartment building who are about her size for a change of clothes. The state police took her to Erie. I didn't want to cancel Clay's and my meeting — we need to get started on the carriage house renovations — so one of the students is driving the things to her."

I asked, "Do you know if Paula spent much time in the carriage house before last night?"

Loretta shook her head. "She refused to go near it. She said it was creepy."

For once, I agreed with Paula. "And it seems to be the home of at least one skunk."

Loretta waved her hand in front of her face. "It's terrible. I only walked near the back of the TADAM mansion last night, and I probably still stink. But the smell will leave the carriage house eventually. Despite a few holes where the siding rotted near the ground, the carriage house is substantial, right, Clay?"

"Substantial enough."

His obvious lack of enthusiasm did not prevent Loretta from gushing, "The income from renting it as a cozy cottage will be helpful to TADAM's bottom line."

I didn't need to look at Clay to know what he was thinking. If TADAM's bottom line was a problem, where would the money come from to renovate the carriage house? I changed the subject, slightly. "Do you have any idea why Paula killed her husband?"

She tapped an expertly manicured finger against her wineglass. "I figured it out long before the police did. Paula was a woman scorned. They'd only been married about half a year, but Antonio didn't want to give up his bachelor lifestyle. He was always either having affairs or attempting to. His insensitive comments to you over the PA system about adultery were probably what put her over the edge. Plus he kept making moves on the female students at TADAM."

Clay asked, "What are you going to do now, Loretta? Who owns TADAM?"

Loretta answered, "Apparently, Paula was mixed up about Antonio owning it by himself. She even signed the papers that made her his partner in the business. She is one confused lady. But in the end, it works out the same. She'll be the sole proprietor. Which will do her a lot of good in prison."

I commented, "I heard there were silent partners." Loretta tossed her head, shaking those auburn curls around and making them glisten in the reddening sun. "Antonio told us that, but apparently, the money he — I mean he and Paula — got to start TADAM and renovate the mansion was actually from bank loans."

"And to buy the property? A mansion, a carriage house, plus a large yard?" Clay had already told me the answer to that, but I wanted to hear if she knew.

She did. "The buildings needed repair,

and the village wanted to unload the property and get some tax revenue from it. I think Antonio bought it very cheaply. That was part of the appeal for him."

I asked, "So if Paula now owns the business, are you and Kent out of a job?"

"Not yet. Paula's lawyer, who is also TADAM's lawyer, suggested that since I was the assistant director, I should try to keep the place going while Paula fights her case, and that is what Kent and I intend to do."

She looked at me with clear and guileless eyes. "I shouldn't say this, but neither Antonio nor Paula knew much about fashion or about running a school. They heard about the mansion being for sale for next to nothing if the new owners would renovate it, and they figured that Threadville would be a good place to open a fashion design and modeling school." She drew a shaky breath. "And they were right, but things just didn't work out. Antonio shouldn't have been allowed near female students, for one thing, and he shouldn't have hired someone with a record like Kent's, either, but Kent assures me that he was wrongfully convicted, and he promises not to touch any students. I guess that Paula knew only one way to keep Antonio from running around on her and embarrassing her by being charged with assault." She shuddered. "Horrible. So unnecessary, and now Paula's going to spend the rest of her life paying for it." She swirled wine in her glass.

I said, "She took drastic steps."

Loretta stared out over the waves. "Abused wives often do."

I asked, "She was abused?"

Loretta finished her wine. "I suspect so, if not physically, then verbally."

Yes, I could see that. Antonio had been fond of saying mean things to people, and who knew what he might have said or done to his wife when no one else was looking? It all fell into place. His arrogant belief that other women would welcome his advances . . . The way Paula had glared at him . . . Her nervous demeanor . . . Her immediate use of the word "murder" and yelling at Dora Battersby and me for killing her husband although he wasn't dead . . . Her hedging when asked about his medication . . .

Even after only six months with Antonio, Paula must have felt trapped in an unbearable relationship. "It's all very sad," I said.

"Yes," Loretta said. "Antonio meant well, really. He just wanted to succeed, and he wanted people to like him."

I thought aloud, "Paula must have liked him enough to marry him. And yet the two of them destroyed each other."

Loretta centered a lid on the container of potato salad. "It's like a Shakespearean tragedy, isn't it? I guess the least we can do is to make a success of TADAM in Antonio's memory. Starting with Clay and me assessing the carriage house. We should get going, Clay."

She could try to leave me out all she wanted, but Clay had made it clear that he and I, just the two of us, had a private "conversation" to continue, one that had begun with a fierce kiss that still burned my lips.

Loretta stretched out one shapely leg. "These boots weren't made for walking, and I was wearing them all over the village just now. I'll never be able to hobble back to the carriage house. Can you give me a ride, Clay?"

"Sure," he answered. "I'll drop you off, then go put the leftovers away." He looked at me. "After you walk your dogs home, Willow, I'll meet you at your place."

"You can put the leftovers in my fridge and collect them after we assess the carriage house." Loretta's voice flowed like honey.

He turned her down. "I'm going to Willow's, anyway, to see if Dora Battersby wants a ride."

Loretta pouted. "Is she in the *Seven Threadly Sins* play? Those people are meeting later, after we're done. At nine."

Clay was patient. "Dora's a member of my design team. Willow is, too, and you're coming with me, Willow, right?"

"Yes." I tried to look unexcited, but something like triumph or anticipation could have shown in the smile I did not quite manage to suppress.

"But, Clay, your truck has only one passenger seat," Loretta pointed out. "You can't give Willow and that other woman a ride at the same time."

He deftly packed containers into his picnic basket. "Then Willow can drive my truck, and I'll walk."

Loretta gave me a hard look. "Don't either of you women have vehicles?"

Didn't Loretta? I didn't quite answer her question honestly. "Everything in Threadville is within easy walking distance of everything else. Dora and I will probably walk with Clay."

"Isn't Dora too . . . old?"

I defended my spry friend. "Not that old. She walked to and from the TADAM mansion the night of the fashion show. Want help carrying any of these things to your truck, Clay?"

"No, thanks."

"I'll help him," Loretta informed me.

She didn't give up easily.

And neither did I, not after that kiss and the promise it had held.

After a backward glance at me, Clay led the way, holding willow fronds back so Loretta could pass between them.

I unfastened the dogs' leashes from the leg of the picnic table. "You two have been sooo good," I crooned. "Let's run down to the lake, and you can splash on our way home."

They lapped up several mouthfuls of water before they were ready to run along the hard sand with me, all the way back to the park between Lake Street and the mouth of the Elderberry River. We jogged across grass, then along the accessibility boardwalk, and onto the unpaved hiking trail that ran upriver for miles. We went only a block, though, to the gate to our backyard. I let the dogs in, latched the gate behind us, and unfastened the leashes. Sally and Tally tore around, and then were happy to go inside to greet the cats.

The evening had become too chilly for the

flip-flops I'd been wearing for picnicking and wading in the shallows. I put on warm socks and sneakers. Since I didn't plan to do any snooping, I pulled a pale blue jacket over my sweater.

Clay knocked on the patio door, and I let him in, complete with the picnic basket. "Here's your lunch for tomorrow," he said.

"Yummy. Thanks!" I gave him a peck on the cheek.

"Hey!" he complained. "Not fair when my arms are full."

Smiling, I turned around and led him to the counter nearest the fridge. "Set the basket here, and let's unpack it."

He did, and handed me containers of potato salad, chicken, corn bread, and cake.

I found spaces in the fridge. "There's more than enough for one person for lunch," I said. "Maybe you'd like to come here for supper tomorrow night and we can polish it off?"

His warm smile nearly undid me. "I'd like that. It turned out the beach was a little too public. That Loretta! She doesn't know when to give up."

Flustered by the affection in his eyes, I said, "Leave the dishes in the sink. I can wash them after I get back."

"I'll come with you and help."

Suddenly, washing dishes had become a romantic activity.

I unpacked the dishes into the sink and pushed the basket out of the way.

"Now," said Clay, "about that conversation we were about to start when Loretta interrupted us." He pulled me into his arms.

But it turned out that even the inside of my apartment was too public. The cats leaped onto our shoulders and meowed in our faces. The dogs wormed their way between our knees again.

And that's when the tapping started.

34

I looked past mustache, who was teetering on Clay's shoulder. "We'll have to continue this conversation later, *again,*" I whispered into Clay's cheek. "Dora's peeking in."

Clay tightened his arms around me. "So? Let her."

Giggling, I squirmed away and opened the door.

Dora marched in. "Sorry to interrupt whatever you were doing with your *friend.* He phoned me a few minutes ago and said he was calling a sudden meeting of his design team, in the TADAM mansion carriage house. *I'm* ready to go."

"We were just heading that way," I told her. "Clay's letting me drive you in his truck, and he's walking there to meet us."

"We could all fit in your car," she pointed out sensibly. Then she made a face of pure revulsion. "Your skunky smell is horrible. Would you two mind if I didn't come along?

It's giving me a headache. Besides, I really want to finish the place mats I'm weaving."

I teased, "That's your real reason for not coming along!" I suspected, though, that she wanted to give us more time alone together. I had to admit, "The carriage house probably smells worse than we do. I think the skunk sprayed inside it last night."

She pushed the dogs inside and backed out to the patio. "Sometimes I think you folks have no sense. Enjoy!" She headed down the hill toward Blueberry Cottage.

Clay and I followed her out, and I locked up. Although we could walk to the carriage house, Clay drove us there.

He stopped in front of the TADAM mansion. "I called Ben to come to the design meeting, too, and he was going to call Haylee."

"Subtle."

He gave me a teasing smile that made me forget to breathe. "I do what I can. Ben and Haylee should be along in ten or fifteen minutes. I should leave room for him to park, and anyone else who might drive here tonight." He leaned forward to stare past me at the three-track "driveway" leading toward the carriage house. "Might as well use the driveway. There was a fair amount of junk in that carriage house that will need to be removed before Mona can use it as a theater. Maybe I can enlist Mona and the rest of you to help me load some of it into my truck and take it to the dump."

Would that be before or after our dish-washing date? Either way, the evening was shaping up to be very romantic. Or something.

He backed down the driveway. Tendrils of unclipped privet, lilac, and forsythia brushed the truck.

As Loretta had told us, the police tape was gone from the carriage house. Lights were on inside it. I hopped out of the truck and met Clay at the back. He was carrying a manila envelope. He pulled the carriage house's person-sized door open and let me enter first.

Loretta's voice came from a back corner, near where Paula had been sitting the night before. "There you are." She stood. She looked cold in the tight shorts and tank top, but maybe the tall boots helped keep her from shivering. "I think I found where the skunk goes in and out."

I pinched my nose. "I hope it's out, not in, but it smells like it's in."

"It sprayed Paula in here last night," Loretta explained, though I knew that. "The smell lingers a long time." I knew that, too.

Clay pointed near the door. "I'll use some of those concrete blocks to plug the hole."

I helped him. The blocks were an old style of dense concrete, and surprisingly heavy. Loretta poked around in other corners. I hoped she wouldn't scare up any skunks or other furry critters. I wanted to suggest we should simply leave the carriage house alone until the smell went away. Even if the actors consented to work inside it, would audiences stay after they'd taken a whiff?

The piece of super-sticky stabilizer was still on the handle of a lawn mower. "Don't go near that white thing over there," I told Clay, "unless you want a lawn mower attached to you for the rest of your life."

He laughed. "That was how I felt the summer I was thirteen and started my own yard work company." He raised his voice. "Did you hear that, Loretta?"

"The summer you were thirteen?" she repeated. "I wish I'd known you then. You must have been adorable."

It was undoubtedly true, but I didn't enjoy hearing her talk about him in that syrupy tone.

He corrected her. "I meant did you hear what Willow said? Not to go near that white stuff hanging from the lawn mower? It's very sticky."

"I heard." She knocked against a broken pitchfork that went clanging down onto a pile of other rusting gardening implements. "Paula wrapped the stuff all over herself and couldn't get loose." Loretta peered into the carriage house's one stall. "What shall we turn this stall into, Clay? Wouldn't it be fun to repurpose it into something cute? With these half-height walls, it could be a cozy dining nook."

And the tenant could feed his or her guests hay.

We'd closed the skunk's passageway as well as we could with the concrete blocks, which cut off some of the fresh air. I ran back to the door and opened it as far as it would go. The big swinging doors, though, were not only blocked in the closed position with a long two-by-ten across the outside, they had settled into the ground, and to free them, we'd need to dig for hours.

Where were Ben and Haylee? I couldn't blame them if they'd decided not to join us in this putrid place. The ten or fifteen minutes weren't up yet, however.

Clay picked up his manila envelope and tapped it against the leg of his jeans. "Loretta, didn't you draw a bathroom just about where you're now proposing a dining nook?"

She giggled. "Half walls? I don't think so. Oh! How about topping the half walls with glass blocks to let in lots of light but still allow for privacy?"

"If that's what you'd like," he said in a totally neutral tone. "We'd need to shore up the walls beneath the glass blocks to hold the weight."

"You could do it, Clay." That woman could really gush. "Or panels of frosted glass. Did you bring my sketches? Is that what's in the envelope?" She stared hungrily toward his hand.

"No. I brought something else you might like to see. Which school was it where you knew me in fifth grade?"

I knew she'd said fourth grade, and I was certain that Clay knew that, also.

She flashed her cute dimples at him. "That's just it. I can't remember the name. Wasn't it one of those common school names, like Roosevelt?"

"Harry S. Truman?"

She studied him for a second.

Clay looked totally honest and innocent.

"I think that was it," she said slowly, "but I was young and had no idea who Truman was. All those old presidents' names sort of got mushed together in my mind."

Clay opened the flap of the envelope. "I'm

sorry I don't remember you from those days."

She pouted. "No, you weren't noticing girls yet. It was the great tragedy of my young life."

Give me a break.

"And my mom scanned and e-mailed me the class photo." He pulled a photo out of the envelope. "I printed it. I couldn't find you in it. Can you?"

She practically galloped to his side. "Let's see! Where are you?"

He pointed to a tall, thin, serious boy with dark brown eyes.

"I'd know you anywhere, Clay. See why I fell for you?"

"No," he said.

Yes. I couldn't see anyone with curly auburn hair, or anyone who resembled her at all, except one girl with her hair pulled back in a ponytail. "Is that you?" I asked.

"Maybe," she said. "I had jeans and a sweatshirt like that."

So did nearly every other girl in the picture.

"No, that's Velvet," Clay said. "She was my next door neighbor."

"Velvet?" Loretta said. "What a name. Sounds like she could have been one of the residents of that stall over there."

"Don't you remember her?" I was sounding like something else that may have resided in that stall over there, but one that meowed instead of whinnied.

"Of course I do. Let's see if I can pick out Chief." She pondered the picture. "Isn't this fun?" she asked.

Fun? Maybe. Informative? Definitely.

She apparently gave up on recognizing Chief, which was just as well, since there were no German shepherds in the picture. She pouted. "I don't see myself. Maybe I was out sick that day." She snapped her fingers. "No, I remember now. Aren't class photos taken early in the year, like September or October? We moved there near the end of fifth grade, and I was at Truman only during May and June of fifth grade."

Moved "there." *Once again, she'd avoided naming the town.*

Clay slid the photo into the envelope. "Too bad. I guess I should get my mother to send me the next year's photo."

Loretta shook that mane of hair. "No. We moved away that summer."

The woman had an answer for everything.

"Let's go up to the hayloft," she said. "To see if we can put a tiny bathroom up there and still have room for a bed and a closet.

Wouldn't it make a spectacular sleeping loft?"

Clay pushed gently at one of the thick wooden posts holding up the loft.

"It's sturdy enough," Loretta urged him. "Look at how well the stairs are built."

We followed her to steep wooden stairs leading to a landing halfway to the loft. The planks were thick, solid wood.

Clay walked around the downstairs and tested more posts. None of them seemed to budge. He peered up at the joists underneath the loft and at the underside of the loft. He took his time.

Fidgeting, Loretta prodded at the outer walls as if examining the inside of the building's tongue-and-groove cladding for signs of dry rot or insect damage.

Finally, Clay announced his decision. "I think it's safe for one of us to go up there. I'll be careful. Willow, get ready to call 911 if I fall through a hole."

I could tell he was joking, but Loretta again said that she was certain it was safe.

Staying close to the wall, he climbed the stairs until he was out of sight.

Loretta ran up the stairs after him. "See?" she crowed from the loft. "It's perfectly safe, even with two of us walking around."

Clay called down, "Willow, don't come up here."

Loretta objected. "What a thing to say! She's tall, but despite what Antonio said, she's not *that* fat, and she can't weigh *that* much."

Thanks for the compliment. I wasn't fat at all. Maybe, someday, I would have to watch what I ate, but between rushing around inside In Stitches and my frequent long walks with my dogs, that day had not yet arrived.

Clay answered, "Willow weighs hardly anything, but I'd just as soon not have another person up here. Two of us may be pressing our luck." He raised his voice. "And stay out from underneath the loft, too, Willow. Okay?"

"Sure." I moved all the way to the back wall near the stall. From there, I could see only the top of Loretta's head. She was near a shuttered window in front. Years ago, when the stall had an occupant, hay would have been loaded through that window, stored in the loft, and pitchforked down to the horse as required. Clay was beside the railing. He took a measuring tape out of his pocket. With his arm extended, he couldn't quite reach the peak of the ceiling. He checked the tape and wrote something in a notebook.

"Aren't you going to measure the floor, too?" Loretta asked.

"We already know the entire floor's dimensions," he said. "You measured them from downstairs."

"I did?"

"You noted on your sketches where the posts are."

"Oh," she said, "I guess that would work, wouldn't it?"

"For a ballpark figure, which is all we need at the moment, yes. But I'll measure the area where I can stand up without banging my head on the ceiling."

"Thinking of living here?" Did she know how flirtatious her teasing sounded? Probably.

"No, but you wouldn't want your tenants knocking themselves out, either."

"No one is as tall as you are."

Gush, gush, gush. I wanted to run outside and breathe air that was untainted by skunks and Loretta's insincere praise.

But Haylee and Ben should be along soon, and at least Loretta was entertaining.

Floorboards creaked beneath her as she investigated the inside of the building's front wall. All I could see of her was the top of her auburn curls, then she must have bent over, and I couldn't see her at all.

Clay's measuring tape twanged. If I'd been up in the loft, I'd have helped him hold the other end of it. Loretta could be missing an opportunity. But I supposed that since I was below them, on the dirt floor, she figured she was scoring points by being closer to him.

He made notes, then moved to the railing and hooked the end of the tape over the edge of a floorboard.

Suddenly, he went still. I knew him pretty well. Something had surprised him. He glanced down at me, put a finger to his lips, and pulled a white square from between the floor and the bottom of the railing. He stood, studied the white square for a moment, turned his upper body toward me and away from Loretta, and slipped the white square underneath his T-shirt.

"Did you find something?" Loretta pounded toward him. "Let me see." Her voice was sharp.

"Just my note—"

"No, that envelope. That's *mine.*" She reached toward him. "You were always good at keep-away on the playground in fifth grade, too."

Fourth grade.

"You never met me before Saturday

night." His words were firm.

"You just don't remember." She elbowed him.

Clay tilted toward the railing. It did not quite come up to his knees. Arms and legs flailing, he toppled over it and landed with a horrible *thunk* on the packed earth floor of the carriage house.

35

Completely still, Clay lay on his stomach with his arms and legs in strange positions.

His shin should not be bent like that.

I pulled myself out of an immobilizing, wide-awake nightmare. Screaming Clay's name, I ran the three steps to him, squatted, and felt his wrist for a pulse.

Above me, Loretta shrieked, "No!" In those heeled boots, she pounded down the stairs.

Clay's pulse was strong. I squeezed his wrist and gently placed my other hand on the back of his strong, tanned neck. I wasn't sure whether I was trying to comfort him or myself.

Loretta's incongruous knee-high boots appeared next to his stretched-out arm. "Clay darling!" she wailed. "What *happened*?"

She didn't know that in her rush to snatch the envelope he'd been trying to hide underneath his shirt, she'd knocked him off balance, causing him to fall and break his leg, and maybe his skull and his back, too?

She grabbed at his shoulder and his waist. "Help me turn him over," she ordered.

"No. I have first aid training. Don't move him. We could make his injuries worse." I spoke with both authority and desperation.

"Shouldn't we give him mouth-to-mouth, check his heart or something?"

"No. He's breathing. Don't touch him." Okay, I was being a little ferocious. I didn't own the man, but I would protect him. Or any other injured creature.

Glancing toward the door, Loretta pulled her hand out from underneath him. "I'll go for help. I'll drive his truck." She groped in his pants pocket, extracted his keys, and jumped to her feet. "You call an ambulance and stay with him."

"Find Haylee," I ordered. "She should be on her way here, possibly walking. Bring her here as soon as possible. She has first aid training, too." I added, "Can you drive a standard?"

"I'll manage."

I wasn't sure she would, but I was not about to leave Clay and drive his truck around searching for help. His face was turned away from me. I stroked his arm with one hand and fumbled for my phone with the other.

I heard Loretta stomp to the door and slam it shut behind her. She must have been panicking. I would have to open that door for fresh air again, later. But at the moment, skunk odors were not my primary concern.

"Willow . . ." Clay's whisper was so soft I barely heard it. "Call 911."

"Yes," My fingers were already hovering over my phone's keypad. "You'll be okay."

"I am," he said.

He didn't look it.

Tapping three little numbers seemed to take eons. The dispatcher answered immediately, but that also seemed to take about a century or two. I told him we needed an ambulance.

Beside me, Clay whispered harshly, "Police, too."

"Police?" I responded.

The dispatcher must have thought I was making a request. "We'll send them both, ma'am. Fire department, too."

In my state of shock, I almost blurted, *Some of us are already here.*

I was only dimly aware of the sound of Clay's truck starting, and then the gears grinding against each other.

The siren on top of the fire station began its wailing, calling volunteer firefighters. If

Haylee was on her way here, she would run back to the fire station only to discover she needed to be in the carriage house.

"Help me up," Clay said.

"Lie still." I rubbed his back.

"Stop that." Was he laughing? "Or I'll never get up." He turned his face toward me. He wasn't laughing, but he was smiling.

With the dispatcher on the line, I couldn't tell Clay just what I thought of his ability to be a proper patient.

"Don't move," I reminded him. "Help is on its way."

"It is," the dispatcher said. "Keep the patient calm. You're doing a great job."

"Well, *he* isn't," I grumbled. "He's trying to sit up."

"Keep him still."

"I'm trying."

"Very trying," Clay contributed.

"Your leg is broken," I snarled at him. "And maybe your neck, too, not to mention your skull and your back. You know perfectly well that you need to lie still."

"I know perfectly well that you are adorable."

"Shh." What a time for him to try to woo me. Was he concussed?

"Willow, can you reach up underneath my

shirt and find the envelope I tucked there before I fell?"

I muttered, "What timing."

"What?" he asked.

"What?" the dispatcher repeated.

"Nothing," I said to both of them.

Clay told me, "The envelope is square, a bit bigger than a DVD, and I'm almost certain that there's a DVD inside it. And probably a sheet of paper, also."

To lift his shirt I had to step around him to the side where Loretta had been. I wormed my hand up into his shirt. His skin was warm.

"No tickling," he said.

Men. I knew better than to tickle an injured patient.

Unfortunately, I had to admit that the envelope wasn't there. I withdrew my hand. "It must have flown out of your shirt when you fell." I closed my eyes, trying to picture those horrible moments without focusing on Clay tumbling toward the ground. "I think I saw it bounce toward the double doors, but it's not there now. I wasn't watching Loretta when she stomped out of here. She must have picked it up and taken it with her."

"Did you see what was written on the envelope?"

"No."

"It said, *If anything happens to me, view this DVD.* It was signed by Antonio. Did you notice that Loretta appeared to be searching for something while I was measuring?"

"Yes."

"It must have been that envelope." He took a deep breath, but it sounded shaky. "And the night she first claimed she knew me and brought me out here, she seemed to be looking for something, also."

"Oh. I thought you were . . ." My face heated. "I figured you two were spending your time out here . . ."

"Getting to know each other as she said? Not the way she implied. She threw herself at me in the TADAM kitchen before we came out here, and again as we were leaving, probably to make certain she smeared her lipstick onto me, but most of the time we were in here, she actually was talking about how we might redesign the carriage house. But she was also peeking into corners and behind things, like she'd lost an earring or something. There must be something in that envelope or on the DVD that she doesn't want anyone to see." Again, he stopped to catch his breath, and when he spoke again, his voice was dark with anger, shot through with pain. "She pushed me,

Willow."

I stroked his hand. "From down here, I couldn't tell if the push was deliberate or accidental."

"I'm sure it was deliberate. She may not have known what was written on that envelope, but she must have figured that whatever it was, once I saw it, I had to be eliminated."

And he hadn't helped his cause by informing her point-blank that he had never met her before Saturday night.

I remembered Naomi telling us that when she and Ashley went backstage while Antonio was winding up his seven threadly sins stunt, they'd seen Loretta standing with her hand on the back of the chair where we'd all been hanging and re-hanging Antonio's jacket, and Loretta had appeared to have grabbed at the chair to catch her balance. A few minutes after that, I'd walked offstage and had kicked something that had rolled. Later, I'd wondered if that rolling object had been Antonio's vial of medicine.

Naomi and Ashley could have been only a second too late to see Loretta nudge that medicine underneath that chair where no one could see it. She hadn't been *catching* her balance. She'd been making certain that she wouldn't *lose* it while standing on one

411

foot and pushing the medicine vial farther underneath the chair with the other. "Loretta killed Antonio," I said.

"What?" the dispatcher asked. "Someone's been killed?"

"Not tonight, but please write down what I said. Loretta killed Antonio. Paula didn't kill her husband. And Loretta pushed Clay off the loft, too."

"This call is being recorded," he told me.

"Good." I looked down at Clay. "I guess Loretta realized that I hadn't read the envelope, or she might have pushed me off a loft, too."

"Good thing you weren't up there. After all those lies about knowing me before, I didn't trust her. I knew the loft was sturdy, but I didn't know what she might do to you."

I'd guessed, without really thinking about it, that Loretta had done as she'd said she would, and had driven Clay's truck away. I'd heard no more grinding of gears or the jackrabbiting of a vehicle when a novice depressed a clutch pedal. Now, listening carefully, I heard Clay's well-tuned engine purring beside the carriage house.

I glanced toward the door.

A trickle of smoke was coming in through a gap between boards.

I sniffed.

Smoke? No.

Despite the reek of skunk inside the carriage house, I recognized the additional odor.

Exhaust fumes.

36

Loretta was piping exhaust from Clay's truck into the carriage house.

But I didn't dare try to explain that to the emergency dispatcher. Clay would overhear, and he would again try to get up. It shouldn't be too long, though, before he smelled the exhaust and realized we were in danger.

I had to rescue both of us before he injured himself trying to do it.

The building was not tightly sealed. Oxygen would still get in. I wished we hadn't barricaded that skunk hole with concrete blocks, though. Both Clay and I had worked at that, and it might take me a dangerously long time to throw those blocks out of the way of that one rather large air-hole.

"Hang on," I said to Clay. "I'll be right back." I jumped up and ran to the big double doors that should swing outward.

I'd seen the two-by-ten fitted across the outside, and the way the doors had settled into the ground, but I pushed, anyway.

They didn't budge.

Exhaust was forming a cloud near the smaller door. I ran to it.

Locked. I rammed my shoulder against it. That achieved nothing besides pain and a likely bruise.

I peeked through a chink between panels in the old wooden door. Clay's truck was backed up tight against it. I couldn't see anyone inside the truck.

I turned around. The piece of stabilizer still hung from the lawn mower handle. I dashed to it. Handling it carefully so I couldn't accidentally mummify myself in it, I pulled it from the lawn mower.

In two seconds, I was pressing it over the gap in the door nearest the tailpipe. Exhaust wisped in above the top of it, but maybe most of the fumes would stay outside.

Clay was up on one knee and two hands, and was dragging himself, with his other leg still at a preposterous angle, toward the back of the carriage house. How could he stand the pain?

"Clay!" I shouted.

He kept going.

The dispatcher asked me, "What's going on?"

"Tell the firefighters to get here as quickly as possible, and to move the pickup truck away from the building we're in, or shut its engine off. We're in danger from the exhaust."

"Leave the premises immediately."

"The doors are locked."

"Stay on the line, ma'am, and stay calm. Fire, police, and ambulance are all on the way."

I wasn't going to lie down and wait for them.

I grabbed the pitchfork that Loretta had knocked down earlier. Like a knight bearing a lance, I lunged at one of the windows. It shattered with a satisfying crash.

"What's happening?" the emergency dispatcher demanded.

"I'm breaking windows." I ran across the carriage house and bashed the other window, too. There was nothing like a battering ram in an emergency.

The dispatcher warned, "Don't try crawling out over sharp points of glass, or you'll hurt yourself. Help will be there shortly."

"I won't." Even if I could climb out, would I be able to shut off Clay's engine? What if Loretta had locked the truck with the keys in the ignition?

Besides, with a broken leg, Clay could not possibly reach the windows and climb out. They were too far above the ground.

Thud.

What had fallen near the back of the carriage house? Clay had disappeared beyond the stall. I rounded the corner and found him sitting up, his legs more or less straight in front of him. He was tossing concrete blocks away from the hole we'd barricaded earlier.

Without pausing in his concrete-block-tossing, he ordered through clenched teeth, "Willow, get out."

"The doors are blocked," I told him as calmly as possible. "And I can't climb out windows without cutting myself." And probably tearing open an artery. I slipped the phone into a pocket and started flinging concrete blocks out of the way, also.

It was amazing how much we could accomplish when we were facing a life-threatening deadline.

"Okay," he said. "Put your face in that hole and breathe."

Sure, and keep the fresh air from getting to him? "You do it. I'm going to get my battering ram and enlarge the hole."

"Willow . . ."

"Clay . . ."

"I'm serious."

"So am I, Clay. Please get some of that fresh air into your lungs while I get the pitchfork."

He was in no position to stop me, and besides, I wasn't sure he was capable of much more than lying down again.

Smashing at the building's interior cladding and exterior siding with the pitchfork, I asked Clay, "Any chance that your truck will run out of gas soon?"

"The tank's full."

I pulled off a panel of cladding and loosened two of the outer boards.

"Crawl out," he ordered. "Go for help."

"It's on its way. Hear?"

Above the increasingly distressed-sounding voice issuing from the phone in my pocket, I heard the comforting siren of one of our fire trucks. It was coming closer.

This time I obeyed Clay. I threw the pitchfork out onto the bumpy, unkempt lawn and crawled out after it. Outside, I gained more leverage and pulled the boards farther from the wall. Nails screeched.

So did the dispatcher on the phone, but I didn't have time to reassure him. I flopped down on my stomach and reached for Clay. "Give me your hands."

"They're yours. They have been since the day I met you."

The poor guy was delirious with pain.

Still, he stretched his arms toward me, and we grasped each other's wrists. I somehow managed to get my feet underneath my hips. In a crouching position, I backed up, pulling Clay, who helped move himself with his one good leg.

Then we were both outside, lying on our sides, facing each other, and gulping in big breaths of air.

The dispatcher's voice in my pocket became frantic. "How are you?"

"We're outside!" My shout was jubilant. "In the fresh air!"

And what did the man who was delirious with pain do then?

He reached for me, grasped my head with both hands, pulled my face to his, and started kissing me. And it was more than a *start.*

37

Clay and I were doomed to have that particular type of conversation interrupted yet again.

From the sound of it, firefighters wearing big, heavy boots were thumping down that three-track concrete driveway toward the carriage house.

"Willow! Clay!" Haylee's voice was shrill with fear.

I tore myself away from Clay and his insistent hands and lips. "We're back here!" I scrambled to my feet.

In her firefighting gear, Haylee charged around the corner of the carriage house and stopped short. "What happened?"

"Clay's hurt," I said unnecessarily. "An ambulance is on its way."

She ran to him and knelt beside him. "Your leg . . ." Her voice dwindled.

"I'll be okay," he said.

Haylee turned to look over her shoulder

at me. Her eyes filled with compassion. She shook her head and raised her eyebrows.

Dressed to fight fires also, Ben yelled, "Hey Fraser, where are your truck keys? The engine's running and the doors are locked."

Clay said to Haylee and me, "I guess my keys are in the ignition."

Haylee patted his arm and rose to her feet. "Do you have another set?"

"At home."

She started toward Ben. "I'd better tell them. There's probably nothing they'd like better than smashing windows with their firemen's axes."

"Don't let them," Clay said between teeth clenched in obvious pain. "But don't let anyone go inside the carriage house, either."

"Don't worry." She disappeared around the corner.

Clay grasped my ankle in one strong hand. "Why are you way up there? Have a seat. Sorry I can't offer anything better than the ground."

The least I could do was distract him from the pain. I sat beside him and massaged his shoulder. Where was the ambulance?

"Yoo-hoo! Willow, Clay!" Edna's voice. "Why is there a fire truck here? Did you write a fire truck into your play, Mona?"

"No, but I will!" Mona's voice. "Has

anyone seen Kent? He should be here by now."

Maybe Kent had run off with Loretta.

Ben, Haylee, and the rest of the fire department were out of sight beyond the corner of the carriage house, probably contemplating breaking into Clay's truck.

Mona, Dora, and all three of Haylee's mothers surrounded Clay and me. When they found out that I was uninjured, they turned their attention to Clay.

Edna took one look at his leg and phoned Gord.

I looked up at Dora, standing beside me. "I thought you wanted to stay away from the smell of skunks."

"Sirens," she answered. "I like to follow the fire trucks so I can keep an eye on you and Haylee and your friends." She frowned down at Clay. "Looks like I was a little late to help *him*."

"You're a comfort, anyway, Dora."

She patted my head.

Running shoes thumped on concrete. Ashley and Macey jogged down the driveway to us. Macey demanded, "Do you folks need help?"

"We seem to have plenty," I answered.

Ashley pushed her hair out of her eyes. "You look terrible, Willow."

A few days before, she'd told me I was acting weird. "Thanks, Ashley," I said, "for yet another compliment."

She gasped. "I didn't mean —"

I gave her my best attempt at a smile. "I know."

Macey stared down at Clay. "Anyway, he looks much worse than you do, Willow."

"He is."

Clay responded by pretending to punch my knee. His knuckles were gentle. I grabbed his fist and held it tightly.

Mona did a little dance move with her hips. "There's Kent!"

Dressed in black jeans and a black muscle shirt, Kent strode past the fire truck to us. "What's up?" He looked beyond me and must have spotted Clay. "Can I call for help for you, sir?"

I said, "An ambulance is on its way."

Proudly, Edna added, "A doctor, too."

Mona looked from me to Clay and back again. "Did you two have a fight?"

I still didn't trust Kent. I stood up and positioned myself between him and Clay. "No."

Kent widened his stance and folded his arms across his chest. "My boss was killed. His wife was arrested. Now the man that Loretta was hanging around has been injured, by the look of things. I don't know about the rest of you, but I see one person, and only one, connecting those three people."

Only one? What about Kent himself?

Kent must have seen the distrust on my face. "Don't look at me like that," he said. "Yes, I was outside the conservatory on Saturday night after the fashion show and reception. I saw you. But do you know who else I saw? Someone who had just come out of the conservatory, but didn't see me?"

Paula, I thought, but I shook my head.

"Loretta. She had the key to the conservatory, and apparently, she used it to go back inside long after the fashion show was over, and long after Antonio collapsed, too. Why did she go in there at that time? I suspect she was searching for something, and I suspect I know what. I think Antonio took a video with his phone of at least one meeting between him, Loretta, and me. At first, the school was going to concentrate on fashion design only. At this particular meeting, Antonio suggested adding models to the school. Loretta liked the idea. She said we could tell the models that TADAM would help them break into modeling careers and land great contracts with national magazines and TV ads. I hadn't said a thing up to that point, but I had to ask how those two, him with no experience running a school of any kind, and her with only some experience in fashion design, were going to make these modeling contracts and TV ads become a reality. Antonio didn't answer, and Loretta just stared at me. I decided the meeting was over, and got up and left."

Yes, I could imagine Kent doing that.

He could certainly string lots of words together whenever he wanted to appear innocent. "But I'd barely gone out the door when I heard Loretta tell Antonio that the modeling contracts and TV ads wouldn't matter. They could just keep stringing the kids — that's what she called them, kids — along, telling them they needed to perfect their skills by taking more courses."

Macey broke in. "Antonio and Loretta did tell us that, which was strange so near the beginning of the term."

Kent flashed Macey a look that might have contained empathy. "Sorry, Macey. I should have warned you and the others."

Why hadn't he? As far as I was concerned, Kent was about as sleazy as Antonio and Loretta.

He didn't seem to notice the accusing expression I was undoubtedly unable to hide. He explained, "Loretta said that the important thing was to collect as much tuition from the students as possible. So I wonder if she was in the conservatory that night searching for the video he must have taken of that discussion."

Although Loretta was the one who had tried to kill Clay and me, I still didn't quite believe that Kent was totally innocent of everything else, including Antonio's murder. I asked Kent, "Why would she murder Antonio over that? Didn't he implicate himself in that same discussion?"

Kent's glance of dark derision made me glad that friends surrounded me. "There was more. Antonio kept promising that Loretta and I would be paid, but we weren't. We confronted him together and told him we would leave TADAM and get jobs teaching fashion design somewhere else, but he said he could reveal our secrets and keep other schools from hiring us. I didn't care."

Really?

Kent seemed to simmer with barely concealed rage, but he managed a shrug that looked almost casual. "Prospective employers might discover that I had a criminal record from when I was twenty-three. It wasn't that big a deal, and I'd been falsely accused. Besides, I wasn't all that keen on teaching. I'd rather design full-time, and that's probably what I'll do now. But Loretta claimed that she had a great offer from another school, and that she was going to leave TADAM to teach there. Antonio told her to go ahead and try, but she'd be sorry — he had proof that she'd said she was only interested in the modeling students for their tuition, and that she had no intention of helping them succeed. She told him that she didn't believe he had proof. He said he did. She claimed she'd only meant that learning to model wasn't easy and that the students would need to take lots of courses before they could hope to land major contracts. Antonio suggested that she could buy the video from him. She got a funny look on her face and said, 'Prove it. Show it to me.' But all he would say was that it was in a safe place." Kent socked one fist into his other palm. "So I'm guessing that, instead of giving in to his blackmail, she silenced Antonio and then set out to find the video."

That white envelope that Clay had found, the one that Loretta must have taken with her, had probably contained the DVD she'd been searching for, both this evening and Saturday night when she first took Clay to the carriage house with her. And now she was most likely on her way out of the area.

Sweat droplets stood out on Clay's forehead and his face had paled. Where was the ambulance? And where were the police?

Looking enormous in his firefighting gear, Ben ran to us. "We unlocked your truck without breaking anything, Clay, and we turned off your engine. We didn't touch the note on the driver's seat though. We don't think that Willow wrote a suicide note combined with a confession about murdering Antonio."

"I certainly did not!" I exclaimed.

Haylee had followed Ben. She grabbed my elbow. "The note was in Loretta's printing, curlicues and everything." She threw her arms, which were somewhere inside that bulky firefighter's coat, around me. "She tried to kill you two and make it look like you had committed suicide and murdered Clay!"

I pushed her away. "No need to get all mushy over it. She didn't succeed."

"Thanks to Willow," Clay muttered from the ground.

Suddenly, there was a screeching that would rival any long-lost ambulance or police car, and Paula came storming and flapping around the corner of the carriage house. "What are all you people doing here? Get out of here, all of you!"

Gord was close behind her. "Ma'am, sit

down. Don't get yourself worked up." He pointed to a rickety-looking wooden bench under a crab apple tree that had outgrown some former gardener's pruning. "Sit down and take a deep breath. Everyone will leave, eventually. I promise."

"Gord!" Edna called. "I'm glad you're here! Come see what you can do for poor Clay! His leg shouldn't look like that."

Gord strode to Clay and stared down at him for a second. "No, it certainly shouldn't." He knelt beside Clay.

Breathing heavily, Paula remained on the bench. Her face was more sallow than ever. I joined her on the bench. "Sorry, but Loretta and Kent wanted us to come over. Loretta wanted to renovate the carriage house into a cute little cottage. She thought TADAM could use the income."

Paula glared past me toward the carriage house. "It stinks. Skunks live there."

I didn't know how to tactfully word my next question, so I didn't bother with tact. "Loretta told us you'd been arrested for your husband's murder."

"Loretta lied."

Loretta is good at that . . .

Paula switched her glare toward me. "The police didn't believe me about who attacked me last night, so they charged me with doing it to myself. I thought it was you and Haylee. I was kind of faint, and heard your voices, so naturally, I thought it was you two, at first. Who do you think could have done it? Loretta?" She glanced toward Kent, who was pulling bits of glass out of the frame of one of the windows I'd broken. She whispered, "Or Kent?"

"Paula," I said gently, "you staged the scene to make it look like someone attacked you, but it was obvious that you did it to yourself."

She looked down at her hands clutched tightly in her lap. "Why do you say that?"

"Your hands were in front of you, not behind your back. You were sitting more or less comfortably."

"I wasn't comfortable. It took too long for anyone to find me, and then it was the wrong —" She clammed up.

I asked her, "Were you going to say the wrong people came to your rescue? Had you planned all along to blame Haylee and me?"

Her only denial was a slight shake of the head.

"You fooled us all at first. It was clever. But the police must have realized that you could have gotten out of your predicament by yourself."

She still avoided looking at me.

I added, "And you also told the police about Antonio's plans to destroy Threadville, which you assumed would make Haylee and me angry, then you hid copies of his business plan in our shops to make it look like we could have read them before he died. Why were you trying to frame Haylee and me?"

"I was afraid I'd go to jail, maybe even be sentenced to death, for something I didn't do." I'd never before seen her looking fierce. "They always suspect the spouse. And, besides, how could I know that you and Haylee didn't kill my husband? It made sense that you'd be angry about his plans for Threadville."

"If we'd known about them, we would have discounted them. His plans wouldn't have succeeded, and even if they could have, Haylee and I would never have killed him. Besides, the police don't always suspect the spouse. I think they're about to suspect Loretta, if they don't already."

Still without glancing my way, Paula rubbed the insides of her wrists across her eyes.

"You must miss him very much," I said.

"Anthony? Or *Antonio* as he'd begun calling himself?" There was no mistaking the sarcasm in her voice. "Being married to

431

a . . . an ambitious man like that isn't easy."

I wondered what she'd been about to say before she selected the word "ambitious." Woman-chasing? No wonder her grief in Vicki's cruiser early Sunday morning had seemed fake to Gord. It had been. And her demeanor and dishevelment at the TADAM mansion on Monday evening could have been due more to fears of being arrested than to grief. I asked her, "Why did you go into the conservatory after Chief Smallwood brought you home from Erie early Sunday morning?"

She picked at a hangnail. "I thought that walking around might help me sleep. A key to the conservatory was with Antonio's things. I wasn't sure if anyone had locked the conservatory, so for something to do, I walked over there and checked. It was a good thing I did. No one had locked it. So I locked it and left."

Actually, someone *had* locked it. I'd seen Loretta do it. But then she'd gone back. I asked, "Did you see Loretta nearby?"

She shook her head.

"Kent?"

"No."

"Anyone?" *Me? Or Macey, who had told Ashley she'd seen Paula leave the conservatory.*

"I wasn't seeing much. I wasn't looking, either. I was just . . ." Clutching at her sides, she bent forward. "Walking around. I must have been in shock." Slowly she straightened and focused on the group near the carriage house again. "Why is the fire department here? There's no fire."

I took a deep breath. Where to begin?

I took another deep breath.

Smoke.

"Actually, there is a fire," I said in, I thought, a remarkably calm voice. "It smells like someone's burning paper."

Something clanked behind the carriage house.

Yelling, "Fire!" I sprinted toward the trash cans in the narrow space between the carriage house and the chain-link fence separating it from the park around the conservatory.

In damp rubbish inside one of the trash cans, flames flared up.

Behind a neighboring house, pale knees between high boots and black short shorts flashed between trees.

Loretta must have been behind the carriage house the entire time, and now she was running away, toward her apartment building.

38

Loretta was escaping. She'd tried to kill me once that evening, and I wasn't about to try to capture her by myself. I also didn't dare scream for help. She would hear me, and the group talking to each other around Clay probably would not.

I could go back to the carriage house and enlist Ben, Haylee, and the other firefighters to charge after her, but Haylee's mothers and Dora Battersby would probably think they should join the chase.

The best thing I could think of was to follow Loretta. I would stay back, out of her hearing. Out of her sight, too, unless she turned around. I would watch where she went, and then tell the police.

Wishing I still had the emergency dispatcher on the line, I pulled my phone out of my pocket.

A twig snapped behind me.

I whipped around.

Kent put his finger to his lips with one hand and beckoned to me with the other.

I didn't want to go close to him, but I had my phone, and the far side of the carriage house was crawling with my friends. I took a hesitant step toward Kent, then peeked over my shoulder. Loretta was almost to the street where her apartment building was.

Kent closed the gap between us. "Don't go after her. Go back to your friends. I'll follow her. She won't get far. I've been trying to find evidence that she was the person who harmed Antonio, and although I hadn't found anything conclusive, I suspected that she might at some point decide she needed to make a quick getaway. After she left her apartment this evening, I blocked her car in with mine in the parking lot behind our building."

"Kent, where are you!" Mona was practically yodeling.

"Go back and keep Mona from following me," Kent demanded.

But I just stood there, stubbornly mute and unsure whether to trust him or not.

"Please?" he added.

Waylaying Mona would at least give me the excuse I needed to put distance between myself and Kent. I plunged through underbrush. Maybe Kent and Loretta would escape together, but if so, I would happily let Chief Smallwood and the state police carry out the investigation, with no interference from me.

Mona charged toward me. "Where's Kent?"

"Not back there." The lie was justified. Whatever Loretta was up to, and whether or not Kent had anything to do with it, I couldn't let Mona put herself in danger. "Let's go back to the others. He'll show up there again."

"He'd better. We have a rehearsal planned."

Tonight, after everything? "I think the police will want to close off the carriage house again. It's a crime scene."

"So where can we put on our *Seven Threadly Sins* play?"

Nowhere. "Maybe we can rent the conservatory."

"Good idea. That carriage house is probably too small." She peered behind her. "What were you doing back there?"

"Phone call." I dialed 911.

"What?"

I merely held up one hand for silence, and told the dispatcher, a woman, this time, that I'd just seen the woman who had attacked Clay and me, and where I thought she was heading. Staying on the line as requested, I shepherded Mona toward the carriage house.

At the rear of it, Haylee and Ben were next to the trash can where the one small flame seemed to have been extinguished. Haylee asked me, "Where have you been?"

"Looking for Kent," Mona answered. "Have you seen him?"

Haylee looked at me. I gave my head a slight shake. Haylee asked me, "Where were you, Willow?"

"Watching Loretta run away." I gestured to the phone at my ear. "I've told emergency where the police can find her."

Haylee said accusingly, "You chased after a murderer?"

"No. I only watched her. I'm pretty sure she's on her way back to her apartment."

Haylee pointed down into the trash can. "There's a wet DVD case in there, and what looks like a letter that must have been in the envelope with the DVD. The back of the envelope was torn off, but I know where that part of the envelope is. Loretta printed the fake confession and suicide note on it and left it on the seat of Clay's truck. She tried to burn the DVD in a trash can that had water standing in it from who knows when. The water drowned the fire before it did much more than singe the envelope. With luck, the heat didn't damage whatever might be on the DVD."

I pointed at trampled weeds behind the carriage house. "Loretta must have been back here the entire time Clay and I were trying to get out of the carriage house, and while the rest of you were arriving."

Mona twisted her hands together. "She could have killed us all! I'd better find Kent." She hurried toward the front of the carriage house.

"Ben and I will stay here with this evidence until the police come," Haylee told me. "Meanwhile, Clay's worried about you. Go show him that you're okay."

I didn't need urging.

I dashed around to the side of the carriage house, sat down beside him, and held his hand. His grip was tight.

Paula was still on the bench, her head down and her hands clasped between her knees.

A siren wailed, closer and closer, and then stopped. Shepherding Mona ahead of her, Vicki ran toward us. "Sorry it took me so long to get here. There was a pileup on the interstate when your first call came in, Willow, and when I was almost here, you called 911 again. State troopers were already on their way to talk to you. They went to Loretta's apartment building, instead, and I came here. Are you folks okay?"

The 911 dispatcher let me go, and I stood to greet Vicki. "Clay isn't, but the rest of us are. Loretta tried to kill him and me."

Vicki backed up and listened to her radio. After a minute, she returned to us and held both thumbs up in the air. "Loretta's already in the back of a state police cruiser. Her colleague, Kent, led us to her."

Mona crowed, "Kent's a hero! Where is he?"

Vicki pointed toward the street. "Probably outside his apartment building, giving a statement to a state police trooper."

"Mmmmm." Mona started toward the street.

Vicki called to her, "Don't interrupt them."

I couldn't tell if Mona heard her or not. She kept going.

Vicki turned to the rest of us. "Loretta damaged a few cars in her attempt to get away, but we'll likely be charging her with more than that."

I looked at Clay. "Two counts of attempted murder, perhaps?"

"That, too, plus I just asked the staties if they'd gotten matches for the fingerprints that were on Antonio's vial of medicine, the package of Jordan almonds, the brown shoes you wore in the fashion show, and the briefcase that was found in your cubicle. Antonio's prints were on his medicine. But there were also partials on that, the almonds, your shoes, and the briefcase the nuts were in. The lab used the latest computer technology and confirmed that Loretta handled all of those things."

"Did you already fingerprint her?" I supposed I should feel good that they hadn't fingerprinted Dora and me after Antonio's death.

"Yes, along with the rest of the TADAM staff."

I said, "My fingerprints would have been on all of those things, too, except I didn't touch the briefcase I saw in the cubicle Sunday morning and again Monday evening." I frowned, concentrating. "Actually, Loretta handled all of the briefcases." I don't know why I was saying things that might make Loretta appear to be innocent of harming Antonio. If nothing else, she had tried to kill Clay and me.

Vicki waved her notebook as if trying to dispel a noxious odor, which wasn't a bad idea considering that everything around us still smelled like a posse of skunks. "We have an envelope that he'd hidden in his apartment with instructions to open it in case anything happened to him. A DVD inside the envelope showed Loretta talking about ways of attracting students and keeping them. Her methods seemed underhanded, and didn't have a lot to do with teaching. We think Antonio may have been attempting to blackmail Loretta and get her to pay him to turn over the DVD. He'd also put letters in that envelope. I don't think we'll need a handwriting expert for this — who else would even want to print like that? But I'm sure we'll get one, anyway. In one letter, she told him that she didn't believe the DVD existed. In another, she said if it did, she would find it."

I pointed back toward the carriage house. "Antonio hid another DVD — probably a copy of the one you found — in an envelope in the carriage house, too, and Clay found it. You'll have to get the exact wording from Clay, but he told me the outside of it said something like if anything happened to Antonio, someone should watch the DVD. Loretta saw Clay pick up the envelope and try to hide it in his shirt. She . . ." I gulped. "She tried to take it from him and pushed him off the loft. He says she did it on purpose. I wonder how many copies of that

DVD Antonio squirreled away."

Vicki frowned and shook her head. "We'll keep searching."

"When did they find the envelope he'd hidden in his apartment?"

"Yesterday. Wednesday."

"What took them so long? Antonio died Saturday night."

Vicki heaved a huge sigh. "It wasn't until Tuesday evening that they knew for certain that Antonio had ingested an almond and reacted to it. Theorizing that someone had given him the almond and had hidden his medicine, we obtained a search warrant Wednesday morning."

"So why didn't they arrest Loretta then?"

"Not enough evidence. The partial fingerprints had to be double-checked by an expert, first. And at that point, we were mostly focusing on the widow." Vicki looked with consternation at Clay. "I'll get Clay's statement later. Meanwhile, they should be able to free up at least one ambulance from the pileup on the interstate." She stepped back and again spoke into her shoulder radio, then reported, "They'll be here soon. What happened to the envelope that Clay found?"

"Loretta took it with her when she went out and backed Clay's truck right up to the carriage house door." I waved toward the rear of the carriage house. "She lit a fire back there, and you'll find a damp DVD case, and maybe a DVD with the same file on it. And maybe copies of Loretta's threatening letters. The bottom of the trash can was filled with water, and the fire burned out after scorching the envelope. Haylee and Ben are guarding it, so come see what Loretta left on the seat of Clay's truck."

Vicki warned, "You're not to touch that truck."

She came with me, and we both looked in through the driver's window. I read the statement, printed with Loretta's swirls and flourishes, aloud, " 'I'm so sorry about putting a candy-covered almond into Antonio's pocket along with his mints and hiding his allergy medication that I decided to end it all. Clay wouldn't let me, so I pushed him off the loft in the carriage house. Then I backed his truck up to the door and left it running. Now I'm going to crawl into the building through a hole and block the hole from inside.' " It was signed W. "That's not my printing," I told Vicki.

She stared at the note for a long time. "That sounds like the theory about Antonio's death that you proposed to Detective Neffting."

"Yes, and it still seems reasonable to me."

"Did you tell Loretta or anyone else about that theory?"

"Not Loretta. Dora Battersby figured it out on her own, and I told Haylee and Edna about it."

"So any of them might have told Loretta."

"I doubt it. None of them is particularly fond of Loretta."

"Or told someone who told her?"

"I doubt it."

"Mona seems friendly with Kent."

"We don't tell Mona anything she doesn't need to know."

Vicki looked back at the group surrounding Clay. "We're going to have to borrow his truck, you know, and search it for evidence, but I guess he won't be driving for a while, anyway."

"I'll take him wherever he needs to go, and if I can't, someone else will."

"So you've decided to agree with me about him? He's a keeper?"

I smiled. "I knew that all along. Besides, it turned out that he didn't like Loretta, after all."

"I could tell that. Why couldn't you?"

"You're better at putting clues together."

Vicki pretended to write that in her notebook, then put her notebook back in her pocket and called Macey to come talk to her.

With obvious reluctance, Macey left Ashley's side and joined Vicki and me beside Clay's truck.

Vicki asked me, "Willow, you said that Macey told you that she'd slapped Antonio in her cubicle the night of the dress rehearsal. Is that what Macey told you?"

I nodded.

Vicki gave Macey a stern look. "Yet when Detective Neffting asked you about it, you said you'd slapped Kent. Are you sure about that?"

Flushing, Macey stammered, "No. It was . . . Antonio. But after he died, I got scared and —"

Vicki finished for her, "Nearly got yourself into a lot of trouble. Honesty really is the best policy." She stared at Macey's bowed head for a second, then led us back to the group around Clay, where she got everyone's attention and asked, "Who removed the yellow tape that the state trooper strung all around this carriage house?"

I answered, "Loretta told Clay and me that the police had taken it down because they'd gotten all the evidence they needed about Paula attacking herself."

"And you believed Loretta that the police

had taken down the tape?"

My attempt at a smile was lopsided. "I shouldn't have."

"I believed her, too," Clay said from the ground. "Though nearly everything else she said was a lie."

Vicki growled, "So you two went in there, with Loretta, the obvious liar?"

I nodded.

She asked, "Did anyone else go in, then or since?"

"Not that I know of," I said.

"So you three contaminated last night's crime scene."

I confessed, "We moved some concrete blocks and a pitchfork around. I also broke two windows and repurposed that super-sticky stabilizer that had been on the lawn mower handle. I used the stabilizer to block most of the area where the exhaust was coming into the carriage house."

Vicki's stern look was obviously fake. "Under the circumstances, I suppose I understand your motives and won't charge you for tampering with evidence."

"Thanks."

She reminded me, "Last night, you took pictures inside the carriage house, right? That you were going to print for me?"

"Yes. I'll do it tonight. Maybe late."

"It can wait until tomorrow." She glanced from the carriage house to the back fence to the driveway. "And now this entire area is a new crime scene, and you've contaminated it. Can you all please return to the front yard and sidewalk? Except Clay. We'll let you ride out in style when the ambulance gets here, Clay."

"Thank you," he said.

"And I suppose you want to stay with him, Willow."

"Yes, but Gord might be better for him."

"Nope," Gord said.

Clay only laughed, but the muscles of his face were strained.

I sat down on one side of him. Gord touched his shoulder, told him he'd be fine, and headed up the driveway with Vicki and everyone else.

"I'll come with you in the ambulance," I told Clay. "Unless Gord wants to go instead."

"You don't have to."

I stroked the side of his face. "Yes, I do. You came with me, once, remember?"

"Who will bring you home?"

I glanced up at the retreating backs of my friends. Haylee and Ben, walking close together, were at the end of the group. "Someone will. They're probably arguing right now about who should do it, and they'll probably all come."

A siren whooped and hooted, coming closer. Finally.

Clay brought his other hand up and pulled at my arm until the back of my neck was within his reach. His hand spread, warming my neck and drawing me closer. "That dress didn't make you look fat, Willow," he said. "You can commit all the threadly sins you want."

I would have thanked him if I could have spoken, but despite his injuries, he was still capable of a sudden, and very fierce, kiss. And knowing we were about to be interrupted yet again, we made the most of it.

WILLOW'S MACHINE EMBROIDERED FASHION FIGURES

When I was a girl, I loved playing with paper dolls, but not the kind you buy and cut out. I made my own. I drew a simple doll on cardboard, cut it out, then traced around it to create an enormous paper wardrobe for it. Sometimes I didn't bother cutting out the garments or trying them on the doll. For me, the fun was in the designing.

Now that I use machine embroidery to embellish nearly everything in sight, it's only natural that I would think of a way of making cloth "paper" dolls. If you don't know a child who would like to play with them, keep them for yourself and call them "fashion figures."

Materials:

Flannelette in skin tones
Scraps of fabric, lace, trims

Many colors of embroidery thread
Water-soluble stabilizer
Small paintbrush

Doll Construction:

(If you don't have an embroidery machine or software, lower your sewing machine's feed dogs and use a hand embroidery hoop to guide the fabric underneath your presser foot to stitch the designs you've drawn on the fabric.)

1. Open your embroidery software. Specifying a straight stitch, draw a simple outline of a doll.

2. Save a copy of this outline as an individual design to be used in making the doll's outfits (below).

3. In your first design, add facial features and lines between fingers and toes if desired.

4. Specifying a tight satin stitch in skin tones, trace over the original outline of the doll. Make certain that the satin stitching will be the final part of the design to be stitched. Those of you who have done appliqué work will recognize the technique.

5. Sandwich water-soluble stabilizer be-

tween two pieces of flannelette and tighten in your hoop.

6. Insert the hoop in your embroidery machine or attachment and stitch the doll. Stop the stitching before the satin-stitched outline.

7. Remove the hoop from your machine. Don't unhoop the fabric and stabilizer.

8. Being careful not to puncture the stabilizer, carefully clip the excess flannelette on both the top and the bottom of your "sandwich" away from the simple outline of the doll. Also, carefully clip the flannelette away from the hoop's edges, on both the top and the bottom of the hoop. Now you have hooped water-soluble stabilizer surrounding a flannelette doll.

9. Reinsert the hoop in your embroidery machine or attachment.

10. Stitch the remainder of design, the tight satin stitching outlining the doll.

11. Unhoop the stabilizer and doll. Cut away excess stabilizer. Using a paintbrush, dab warm water on remaining stabilizer

until it dissolves away.

Clothing Construction:

1. In your embroidery software, open the simple doll outline design you saved separately. Save it with a different name (e.g., ruffled cocktail dress). Specifying a straight stitch, draw an outline of the garment you wish to make, then erase the straight stitching (feet, hands, head?) that won't be part of the garment.

2. Still in your embroidery software, add additional fabric appliqués and other decorative touches as desired.

3. Sandwich water-soluble stabilizer between flannelette on the bottom and fabric for the garment on top.

4. Insert the hoop in your embroidery machine or attachment and stitch simple outline(s) plus your additional appliqués and decorations.

5. Remove the hoop from your machine. Don't unhoop the fabric and stabilizer.

6. Being careful not to puncture the stabilizer, carefully clip the excess fabric away on

the top and bottom of the garment and away from any appliqués. Also, carefully clip the fabric near the edges of the hoop on both the top and the bottom. Now you have hooped water-soluble stabilizer surrounding your doll's latest garment.

7. Reinsert the hoop in your embroidery machine or attachment.

8. Let your machine stitch the tight satin stitching outlining the garment and any appliquéd additions.

9. Unhoop the stabilizer and garment. Carefully clip the stabilizer close to the satin stitching. Using a paintbrush, dab warm water on the remaining stabilizer.

The flannelette on the backs of the outfits should adhere (lightly) to the doll's flannelette "skin."

Please send finished photos of your fashion figures and their clothes to Willow@ ThreadvilleMysteries.com.

WILLOW'S TIPS

1. Buy lots of different weights and kinds of embroidery thread and play with using them in your needle and (for heavier threads) in your bobbin. Test each one on fabric (I use unbleached muslin) and note on the fabric which tension works best for each one. When you're ready to use one of your new threads in a design, refer to your test fabric and your notes.

2. Test new embroidery motifs on scraps before stitching them on your large pattern pieces (or your new sheets or pillow-cases . . .). Keep those trial designs for use in crazy quilts or for appliqués on linens or clothing.

3. Chief Smallwood sometimes accuses me of having a wild imagination. Maybe that's not good in murder investigations (I tend to think that it is good, however . . .), but when

sewing and embroidering, let your imagination soar. If you don't like what you made, don't call it a mistake. It's a creation.

Most of all, have fun.

WILLOW

The employees of Thorndike Press hope you have enjoyed this Large Print book. All our Thorndike, Wheeler, and Kennebec Large Print titles are designed for easy reading, and all our books are made to last. Other Thorndike Press Large Print books are available at your library, through selected bookstores, or directly from us.

For information about titles, please call:
  (800) 223-1244

or visit our Web site at:
  http://gale.cengage.com/thorndike

To share your comments, please write:
  Publisher
  Thorndike Press
  10 Water St., Suite 310
  Waterville, ME 04901